ST. MARTIN'S

MINOTAUR
MYSTERIES

OUTSTANDING PRAISE FOR MARTHA C. LAWRENCE AND HER ELIZABETH CHASE MYSTERY SERIES

"A fine series." —*Library Journal*

ASHES OF ARIES

"In her fifth astrological adventure, psychic PI Elizabeth Chase faces an unusual and riveting mystery that will give pause to even the most ardent skeptics . . . . Lawrence effectively combines the earthly and the inexplicable in this fascinating page-turner, and its dramatic ending will delight committed fans as well as attract new ones." —*Publishers Weekly*

"To be honest, I had just about given up on American female PI novels—they all sound the same—but I picked this one up on a whim and found that I liked the characters enough in chapters 1 and 2 that I kept reading—and to my delight, discovered that the author can plot, that her characterizations are fair and accurate, and the psychic phenomena were downright interesting . . . . Lawrence hits the bulls-eye." —*The Drood Review of Mystery*

"Lawrence is an ingratiating storyteller who never fails to deliver a full measure of entertainment for all . . . ." —*The San Diego Union-Tribune*

"Lawrence has created a credible heroine with special gifts for crime solving and continues to place her in equally believable, hair-raising situations. What more could you ask for?" —*Alfred Hitchcock's Mystery Magazine*

"[Lawrence's] buildup to the ending is masterful—so suspenseful you cannot stop turning pages." —*San Diego Magazine*

MORE . . .

PISCES RISING

"As always, Lawrence delivers an insightful story with multi-dimensional characters and unrelenting suspense."   —*Booklist*

"Reviewers are supposed to remain objective but psychic sleuth Elizabeth Chase is already ensconced with my favorites . . . . a fascinating combination of the magical and the mundane we will want to see more of."   —*Washington Times*

"[Lawrence's] ability to weave a suspenseful tale, plus her uniquely gifted protagonist, add up to another hit."
    —*San Diego Union-Tribune*

"Unquestionably, Lawrence's most sophisticated effort to date and a pleasure to read."   —*Charlotte Austin Review*

"*Pisces Rising* moves at a fast clip as Lawrence keeps a tight grip on the story and an even tighter rein on her characters."
    —*Chicago Tribune*

AQUARIUS DESCENDING

"Lawrence is up there with the likes of Sue Grafton, Sara Paretsky and Marcia Muller . . . . Witty, quirky, nail-biting, and altogether wonderful."
    —Harlan Coben, Edgar Award–winning author of *One False Move*

"This solid new series is a natural . . . . and a supernatural as well."
    —Sue Grafton

"Refreshingly accessible . . . . immensely appealing and totally believable."
    —Diane Mott Davidson, author of *The Grilling Season* and *Prime Cut*

"Lawrence's humor is funny and happy-go-lucky, and in Chase, she's created a character who's a little bit sarcastic and down-to-earth, a little bit loopy and out there. It's an enjoyable combination leading to sharp dialogue and a fast read."   —*Boulder Planet*

ASHES OF
ARIES

MARTHA C.
LAWRENCE

St. Martin's Paperbacks

ASHES OF ARIES

Copyright © 2001 by Martha C. Lawrence.

Library of Congress Catalog Card Number: 2001034948

ISBN: 0-312-98041-8

Printed in the United States of America

St. Martin' s Press hardcover edition / September 2001
St. Martin's Paperbacks edition / November 2002

St. Martin's Paperbacks are published by St. Martin's Press, 175 Fifth Avenue, New York, NY 10010.

10 9 8 7 6 5 4 3 2 1

*In loving memory of Carroll H. Driggs
and to great moms everywhere*

Hurt not the earth, neither the sea, nor the trees.

—Revelation 7:3

ASHES OF
ARIES

CHAPTER 1

The hot Santa Ana swept across the open desert, hissing through the bone-dry cheatgrass and shaking the stiff sagebrush. I did my best to ignore it. There was a red and white bull's-eye target tacked to a hay bale ten yards away. I was trying to keep my attention focused there.

Willpower, girl. Mind over matter. You can do it.

I locked an unblinking stare onto the target, drew back the bow string, and let the arrow fly. The slim, feathered spear shot forward but caught the breeze and veered left, missing the hay bale entirely. I sighed in exasperation.

"Great. What am I now, zero for six?"

The wind whipped a shank of hair across my eyes and I called it the F word. As if to mock me, the gust grew in strength, sending up a flurry of straws around the hay bale.

Sequoia stood motionless beside me, his long, black ponytail dancing in the wind. The Luiseno Indian's name suits him well. Sequoia is broad and tall, with skin the deep color of redwood. Like the ancient tree, something about him inspires reverence.

"This isn't about keeping score, Elizabeth. This is about using the power around you."

Spoken like the twenty-first-century medicine man that

he is. A distant cousin of my best friend, Thomasina, Sequoia has lived most of his life on the Temecu Reservation east of San Diego. He claims to have learned his shamanic powers in Mexico from a mysterious woman he calls Aunt Christina. I believe he used those powers to save my life a few months ago. It's rare that I meet someone more versed in the unseen realm than I, which is why I'd signed on as his unofficial student. I still wasn't clear what archery had to do with shamanism, but had a feeling I was going to find out.

"What power would that be?" I asked.

"The wind. Don't fight it so much. Harness it." Sequoia pulled another arrow from the leather pouch strapped to his thigh and handed it to me.

I gave him a dubious look as I placed the notched end of the arrow onto the string and drew back the bow. The wind blew steadily, rustling the cheatgrass. I aimed at the target, corrected for the breeze, and concentrated. *Harness the power around you.*

The gust picked that moment to die and my arrow sailed right past the hay bale, missing by an embarrassing distance. Something inside of me snapped. I pulled my Glock out of my waistband, set my sights on the target, and blew three hollow-points into dead center. The gunshots reverberated in the open air and left my ears ringing. I confess the release felt wonderful.

"There," I said. "How's that for using the power around me?"

Sequoia lifted his Wayfarers off the bridge of his nose and squinted at the hay bale.

"Nice shooting, but you didn't harness the power of the wind." He dropped his shades back into place. "You got frustrated and pulled your gun. That"—he nodded toward the bullet-riddled target—"was the power of your anger."

"So?"

"So your anger used you, instead of the other way around."

Sometimes he sounded more like a psychologist than a

shaman. Having once worked as a psychologist myself this annoyed me, perhaps proving the point that doctors make the worst patients.

"Who cares? I nailed the target, didn't I?"

The heat was getting to me. As if reading my mind, Sequoia pulled a flask from a large pocket in his cargo pants, unscrewed the cap, and offered me a drink of water. Even lukewarm, it tasted sweet and wonderful. I controlled my urge to guzzle the whole thing and handed the flask back. Sequoia took a sip and screwed the cap back on, a thoughtful look on his face.

"When you act out of anger you might win the battle, but you're gonna lose the war. Anger makes you feel powerful, but it's the kind of power that doesn't last."

"But my anger got the job done," I argued. "I hit the damn target."

He walked toward the hay bale, collecting stray arrows along the way. "What are you mad about?" he called over his shoulder. "Let's deal with that first."

I went with the easy answer.

"Tom's death."

It had been just a few months since my fiancé had been killed in an investigation gone bad. The emotional fallout lingered, and probably would for some time.

"Besides that," Sequoia said.

I tuned into myself. First thing I noticed was the afore-mentioned heat. On an October day when much of the country would be putting logs on the fire, southern California was baking. It was only nine in the morning and the temperature was climbing toward ninety. Plus, the wind was making me miserable. Blowing down from the high desert, the scorching Santa Ana had sucked all the moisture from the air. I ran my tongue over my lower lip, which had become a ridge of flaky skin. It felt like a wound.

"What's really bugging me is this weather," I called, raising my voice to be heard over the wind. "This Santa Ana makes me nervous, like something bad's going to happen."

Sequoia returned to my side, the fistful of feathered arrows a bouquet in his hand. "Sounds like a premonition. Maybe you're afraid of what you know is going to happen, and your anger is covering up your fear."

A crow cawed in the distance. As I turned toward the sound, the Santa Ana blew another shank of hair across my face. The ends slapped my cheek so hard it stung.

"No," I said irritably, "it's just this damn wind. It's getting to me. Make it stop."

I brushed the flyaway strands out of my eyes and bent at the waist, gathering my hair into a ponytail. I twisted it into a knot at the top of my head and stood upright. Sequoia had turned away from me and was facing east, into the wind. He'd once told me that if I ever had a problem I had no answer for, I could face east and the answer would come to me. I looked at his stoic profile and wondered if he was seeking an answer now.

At that moment the wind simply died. It had been blowing hard, but suddenly it was gone, as if someone had pulled the plug on a giant fan beyond the foothills. A hush came over the land and I found myself standing in complete stillness. After a morning of nonstop gusting, the change was as dramatic as a full eclipse. At first I figured it was a temporary ebb, but the calm stretched for over a minute.

"Sequoia?"

He stood silently, still facing east, where the sun had risen halfway into the sky. I tried to read his face, but couldn't see his expression behind his sunglasses. Watching him, I had a sense he was communing with someone—or some*thing*—I couldn't see. Without the cooling effect of the wind, the heat from the blazing sun intensified. Despite the broil, I felt goose bumps rising along my neck.

"Sequoia, did you make the wind stop?"

He didn't move. My question sat on the breezeless air, unanswered. Even the crows were quiet.

A high-pitched electronic beeping erupted from the pager clipped to my waistband, killing the moment. Sequoia turned to me and nodded toward the pager on my hip.

"Better answer that one."

I pushed the button and glanced at the display. I didn't recognize the phone number but did recognize the three digits tacked on the end—911. Whoever was paging considered it an emergency.

I reached for the backpack that served as my combination purse, briefcase, and tool chest. I searched and came up empty.

"Shit. I think I left my cell phone in the car."

"You can use mine." Sequoia dug into another pocket of his cargo pants and handed over a phone. I dialed the number on my pager display and waited. After the first ring a somber male voice answered.

"Loebman."

"Hi. This is Elizabeth Chase, responding to your page."

"You the psychic PI?"

"That's correct."

A breeze had begun to riffle through the cheatgrass again. I got a funny feeling in my gut—whether it was from the wind or something else, I wasn't sure.

"Thanks for calling back. You know Detective McKenna?"

The name was fresh in my mind. McKenna worked SDPD homicide. We'd met on a case I'd worked recently and had stayed in casual touch.

"Yeah, I know Karl."

"He's the one who gave me your number. Said you were the real McCoy."

"And you are?"

"Oh—sorry. Bruce Loebman. I'm an area detective with the San Diego Sheriff, working the *Fielding* case." He emphasized the name, as if I should be impressed.

"Sorry, I'm not familiar with that one."

"The telecommunications mogul out in Rancho Santa Fe? His son's been missing for five days. It's all over TV. Crime Stoppers has been running public-service announcements on it every night. Surprised you haven't seen them."

Now I put it together. Frank Fielding was the CEO of a

wireless communications firm headquartered in north San Diego County. In the past few years the company's stock had rocketed in value. Fielding became a multimillionaire and moved to Rancho Santa Fe, the community my parents had settled into long before the place became synonymous with obscene wealth. I remembered seeing the story about the kidnapping on the news and thinking that a family like the Fieldings was the perfect target.

There was no need to ask how Loebman's case was going. If he had any solid leads, he wouldn't be calling me. I heard a sigh on the end of the line.

"Anyway, Karl said it might be worth my time to talk to you. so, uh, I'd like to do that." The hesitancy in his voice told me he wasn't sure about working with a psychic. I could have reassured him with my credentials—my double Ph.D. from Stanford, my state-certified PI license, my VIP commendations—but I hate self-promotion.

"Sure," I said. "Missing persons cases are my strong suit."

"Great." Hope was edging out his skepticism. "What do you pick up about the Fielding boy?"

I smiled to myself and forgave Loebman's naïveté.

"I don't know what McKenna told you, but this doesn't exactly work like a psychic hot line. I'll need to meet with you first and get briefed on the case. If I take it on, my standard retainer is five hundred dollars, plus expenses."

"Oh." Loebman took a minute to let that sink in. "Okay, that's doable. I'm at the Fielding place now. You got a pen? I'll give you directions."

"I'm not available right this minute. I'm way out in—" Sequoia's hand on my arm stopped me short. "Just a minute." I turned and looked into a face so solemn it took me aback.

"Go *now*," Sequoia said.

CHAPTER 2

I slowed and put on my right-turn signal as I neared the Fielding estate, wondering why my stomach was tightening. Perhaps it was a reaction to the intimidating design of the gate fronting the property. Constructed of sharply tapering iron bars, the gate spanned a wide asphalt driveway that snaked up into a forest of old eucalyptus. The loose limbs of the trees sailed like flags in the wind, showing just how much strength and velocity the Santa Ana had gained in the fifty minutes it had taken me to drive from the Temecu Reservation to Rancho Santa Fe.

I pulled up behind the unmarked silver Crown Victoria parked just outside the imposing gate. The passenger door opened and I hurried toward it, anxious to escape the wind. I dipped my head into the car.

"Detective Loebman?"

"Yeah, slide in."

A trim man in his mid-thirties gathered some papers from the passenger seat and held them over his lap as I got in the car. He wasn't dressed like any undercover cop I'd ever seen. His smooth face was freshly shaved, his crisp white shirt looked expensive and new, and the crease in his linen pants was as sharp as a paper fold. I eyeballed his outfit and smiled.

"Where we going—church?"

"Not if my rabbi has any say in the matter." He winked and cracked a lopsided grin. "Thanks for coming." In spite of his joke, Loebman impressed me as a solemn man. There was a sadness in his eyes that looked like it had been there for a long time.

It was hot in the car, hotter as soon as I shut the door. I could smell the citrus scent of Loebman's cologne in the close space. He studied me, a puzzled look on his face.

"Not what you were expecting, am I?" I was still clad in the jeans and tank top I'd worn to the reservation. A chalky dusting of desert sand covered my bare arms.

"Not really," he admitted.

"You gonna put that down?" I nodded toward the paper stack he was holding in his hands.

"Oh—I made an extra file for you. You want to see this stuff, or not? I'm not familiar with your, um . . . techniques."

Some psychics want absolutely no information from a case, fearing their imaginations will interfere with their extrasensory perception. I'm not the kind of psychic who can guarantee pulling information out of thin air, which is why I supplement my talent with a PI license. I reached for the papers.

"Yeah, let me see what you've got."

The top sheet told me that the Fieldings had filed a missing persons report late last Wednesday, the day their four-year-old son, Matthew, had disappeared. There's usually a forty-eight-hour waiting period before the cops will start the paperwork on an MP case, but underage kids are the exception. I skimmed the report but didn't go into it deeply, since there was a lot to cover. Documents from multiple agencies—Sheriff's Department, Search and Rescue Department, SDPD—bloated the stack. I continued flipping through the papers and came across a missing persons bulletin. Above the text was a color photocopy of a little boy gazing, enchanted, at a cake ablaze with four candles. The candlelight played up his big eyes, silky blond hair, button nose, and dimpled chin. Innocence bestows an otherworldly beauty on every kid this age—there's no such thing as an ugly four-year-old. But the Fielding child had the kind of angelic face that tugged on the heartstrings.

"There's been no ransom note, no demand printed in the newspaper, nothin'." Loebman nodded toward the opulent grounds behind the iron gate. "But Fielding's one of the richest men in one of the richest towns in the country. Dollars to donuts, this is about money."

"You sure this isn't a custody dispute?"

He shook his head.

"There's no dispute here. I was ready to resent Fielding for being so damn rich, but when I interviewed the guy I felt bad for him, man. He *is* in church right now, by the way. Praying. His wife, Roxanne, is in there glued to the phone."

"Where'd the kid disappear from? Day care? Shopping mall?"

"Right off the property. Roxanne says one minute he was in the backyard, the next minute . . . gone."

I glanced at the photo and, in an intuitive flash, *knew* the child was alive. Almost immediately, my left brain— that logical doubting Thomas in my head—shot the insight down as wishful thinking. I've learned to go with my first impression. Dollars to donuts, the kid was all right.

"We've tapped every available resource." Loebman pointed to the bulletin in my hands. "That's gone out to every law enforcement agency we can think of. Plus the hospitals and shelters. Volunteer search-and-rescue teams have been combing the surrounding area since we got the call, handing out flyers. We called in the ASTREA helicopter, tracker K-9s, you name it."

"I can see that." I sorted through the agency reports. "What'd the dogs find?"

"They headed out to Camino del Norte here"—he pointed to the main road—"then lost the scent."

"So you think someone abducted the kid in a car?"

"That's what we're assuming at this point."

"Any leads from the Crime Stopper ads?" A twenty-four-hour hot line, Crime Stoppers offered cash rewards to citizens who called in tips that led to arrests in felony crimes.

"Nothing but the usual dead ends and nutcase calls."

I was staring at the photo again. *Where are you, Matthew?* I waited for images or any impression whatsoever. Nothing. Outside, a hot gust of wind blew so forcefully that the car shuddered. In the outside rearview mirror I saw a white van pull over to the side of the road about ten yards behind us.

"Who's that?" I asked.

Loebman checked the rearview and scowled.

"Channel Three news van. They've been camped here off and on, doing live telecasts from the scene of the crime. Let's get outta here. You ready?"

I nodded as I slipped the paperwork into my backpack.

He picked up the phone from a car caddy between us and dialed.

"Yeah, this is Detective Loebman, calling from the gate. The other investigator just arrived. We're ready to come in now."

Seconds later the massive iron gate began to roll open, moving with slow, electronically controlled precision. Loebman fired up the engine and the car's AC rattled to life, blasting air that was still hot and stuffy through the vents. When the opening at the gate was wide enough, Loebman guided the car through the entry and up the winding driveway. As we entered the forest of wind-blown eucalyptus, I turned back to see the heavy row of iron bars closing behind us.

The Fielding house crowned the pinnacle of one of the highest hills in Rancho Santa Fe. Covered by eucalyptus on its east side, the hill dropped off sharply on the west. Loebman and I walked along an adobe brick path to the front door, enjoying an unobstructed view to the ocean. Even at this elevation there was no relief from the hellish weather. We stood at the front entrance, where a jasmine-covered overhang blocked the penetrating rays of the sun. In spite of the shade, the alcove held the heat like an oven.

Loebman rang the doorbell and we waited in silence. The Santa Ana pushed a few dried eucalyptus leaves up the steps, delivering them right to the door. After a couple of minutes I shifted my weight from one foot to the other.

"Think anyone heard us?" I was having doubts.

"She knows we're here. Give it another minute."

Made of old California adobe and hardwood, the house was a beautifully maintained early ranch—I guessed circa 1928. I was examining the thick wooden door, looking for signs of age, when it swung open. A pale woman with dark circles under her eyes stood before us.

"Sorry to keep you waiting. I was—" The woman waved a limp hand toward the rear of the house, ending the sentence with a sigh. She searched Loebman's face. "I'm sorry, Detective, I've forgotten your name again."

I didn't need to be introduced to know that this was Roxanne Fielding. To Frank Fielding's credit, this was no trophy wife. Roxanne was approaching forty and wasn't going out of her way to fight it. Her blond hair was streaked with gray and she carried a sensible amount of weight on her frame. She was wearing a roomy cotton sundress and comfortable shoes. If she'd put on makeup today, she'd long since cried it off. I saw dignity in her face and liked her immediately.

"Bruce," Loebman said gently. "And this is the investigator I was telling you about, Elizabeth Chase."

She looked at me and smiled sadly.

"The psychic."

"That's me." I looked her straight in the eye.

She nodded, reluctantly accepting the fact of my presence, and stepped back to let us inside.

We followed her into a spacious, high-ceilinged living room where high-end, high-tech furnishings clashed with the home's historic architecture. A sleek black leather seating system dominated the center of the room. Cubist bookcases framed a stone fireplace on the far wall. The adjoining wall was almost entirely covered by a chrome-framed abstract painting that resembled nothing so much as a gigantic computer motherboard. The only concession to the past was the richly colored Persian rug beneath our feet.

Roxanne found a spot at the corner of the leather sectional sofa and sank into it with a sigh.

"Make yourselves comfortable," she said.

Loebman sat beside her and I settled onto the sofa section that jutted out at a right angle. Roxanne folded her hands together and lowered her eyes toward the rug, as if saying a prayer to the divinity she saw in its intricate pattern. There was an awkward silence before Loebman looked to me.

"I'm not really sure how you want to proceed here," he said.

I stared at Roxanne's downturned eyes, wondering if she really was praying. Most people, particularly the relatives in a missing persons case, are at least a little curious about me and my work. But Roxanne had retreated from me completely. It almost looked as if she were dropping off to sleep.

Perhaps five consecutive days and nights of not knowing where her son was had beaten her into a shocked speechlessness. On the other hand, maybe she was hiding something. I stopped speculating and got to work.

"Give me minute." I closed my eyes, intent on quieting my thoughts, the necessary first step in opening up psychically. I relaxed my shoulders and took a deep breath through my nostrils.

I smelled smoke. Sharp and pungent, it hit the back of my throat, tickling the membrane. I coughed and opened my eyes. The nervousness I'd been feeling all morning turned to fear.

Loebman looked at me quizzically.

"You okay?"

"Something's burning," I warned.

CHAPTER 3

At the threat of fire, Roxanne Fielding sat up, her eyes wide. Loebman rose from the sofa and sniffed the air. He circled the room and looked at me, puzzled.

"I don't smell anything."

For a moment the big house was silent, save for the moaning of the hot wind outside. Roxanne got up and took a few tentative steps, her face rigid with worry.

"I don't, either."

I was about to argue when I noticed that the smoke aroma was gone. I pulled a deep breath though my nostrils and smelled nothing but the faint musk of the leather sofa.

"That's weird. I know I smelled smoke." I got up and joined Roxanne in the middle of the room. "Maybe we should check the kitchen."

Loebman headed for the back hallway.

"You two check the kitchen, I'll scope out the rest of the house."

I followed Roxanne into a bright, state-of-the-art kitchen. Sunshine poured through the windows, bouncing off the smooth granite countertops and gleaming stainless steel appliances. Roxanne looked in the oven and tested the stove burners with her fingers. The threat of fire had brought her to alertness, although the purplish rings under her eyes were even more pronounced under bright light.

"Whatever you smelled, I don't think it came from in here," she said.

I agreed with her. My fear of a fire was lessening with each passing minute.

"Have you ever had a fire here? Did your son ever play with matches?"

She shook her head.

"No, nothing like that. Why?"

"The smoke . . . I think I was picking it up psychically. I'm wondering now if there's some connection between your son and—"

"Fire?" Roxanne finished my sentence, an edge of panic in her voice. A vertical worry line appeared between her eyebrows. I didn't want to frighten her unnecessarily.

"Then again, it could be nothing."

The worry line didn't leave her forehead.

"My son never played with matches."

For a moment her eyes held mine, challenging me, until Loebman walked in and broke up our stare-down.

"I checked the whole house," he said. "Nothing burning, far as I can see. I'd like to take a look outside."

Roxanne walked over to the sliding glass door on the far side of the kitchen. The lock made a sharp clicking sound as she unlatched it.

"You can go out this way."

The door was off its tracks and she had a hard time pulling it open. I felt uneasy as I watched her struggle with it. I was about to assist when Loebman stepped forward and popped the door into place so that it slid open easily. As he stepped outside, a burst of hot air blew in. Roxanne shut the door and looked to me wearily.

"It's goddamn hot, isn't it? Let me get you a drink. What'll you have?"

"Water would be lovely."

While Roxanne busied herself in the refrigerator, I stood at the glass door and looked out. Bordered by a bed of orange lilies, a lawn circled the house like a wide green moat. Beyond the lawn, the eucalyptus forest stretched left to right, creating complete privacy. The Santa Ana was holding steady. Even inside, behind the heavy glass door, I could hear the wind shaking the leaves of the trees.

Roxanne returned with a Perrier. The cold bottle felt wonderful in my palm. I thanked her and took a drink. She nodded and collapsed into a chair at the kitchen table, as if the task had consumed her last bit of energy.

"You look exhausted," I said as I took a seat beside her.

She turned her pale face to me and shrugged. "If my son is . . . gone, I don't want to live anymore. I suppose that sounds like melodrama, but I mean it."

I understood. I'd felt that way the first few days after McGowan died.

"I've read the police reports, so I know you've gone over this dozens of times. But I need to hear in your own words what happened the day Matthew disappeared. I'm sorry. I know repeating this is painful."

She slumped her shoulders and nodded.

"He'd finished watching his morning cartoons and wanted to go outside to play. I thought I'd pick some flowers while we were outdoors. I got my pruning shears and a basket and followed him into the backyard." She had the gravelly voice of a smoker, though I didn't see any evidence of the cigarette habit lying around. "I was keeping an eye on him while I worked, I really was. I mean, he was right there." Her anguished tone was filled with regret.

"Did you see or hear anything unusual before he disappeared?"

She shook her head.

"No. I could hear him playing under the trees. He has this habit of talking to himself." She paused. "I could hear him chattering away, so I wasn't worried. I finished picking my flowers and when I called him, he didn't answer. I walked over to the trees where I'd just seen him and he was gone. Just . . . gone."

"What time was this?"

"About nine-thirty in the morning."

"Was anyone else home?"

"No. Frank was at work, as usual. Bonnie used to come on weekday mornings, but she quit a couple of weeks ago to focus full-time on her drama degree. It was just me and Matt."

"Bonnie who?"

"Oh. Bonnie McBride. She used to be our household assistant."

I'd probably find Bonnie's info in the case file, but I jotted down her name, just in case.

"You said you could hear Matthew chattering to himself. What makes you think he wasn't chattering to someone else? Maybe a stranger in the woods."

Again she shook her head, this time running her fingers through her fine, blond-gray hair.

"No. Matthew didn't—" She stopped abruptly, then started over. "It was kid talk. You know, just play talk."

I nodded to let her know I understood what play talk was.

"Could you hear what he was saying? I mean, how do you know for sure he wasn't talking to someone else?"

"I don't know. It just . . . sounded like his normal chatter, is all."

"Are you sure you didn't hear anything strange before he disappeared? Did his voice get louder, maybe?"

"Nothing like that. If I'd heard him raise his voice, I would've been there in a second." Again her eyes challenged me. I got the sense there was something she wasn't telling me.

"Was there anything out of the ordinary about that morning?"

"Nothing. That's just it. It was such a damn normal morning."

"The detective told me you haven't gotten any ransom notes or formal demands of any kind."

"That's right."

"Does your husband have any enemies?"

"No."

"Was anything weird going on in your lives that might have led to this?"

"I don't know what you mean by weird."

"Uncomfortable situations. Iffy people."

"Iffy?" The line reappeared between her brows, as if she were having a hard time getting the concept.

"People who left you with a bad feeling."

She thought about it for a minute.

"I guess there've been some of those. Doesn't everybody have a few of those people in their lives?"

"Probably, yeah."

I hadn't accused her of anything, but Roxanne was on the defensive. She clearly felt guilty. Of what, I wasn't sure.

"Could you do me a favor? Could you think about it and write me a list of the iffy people?"

"Yeah," she said slowly, not sounding too sure. "I suppose I can."

A gust of wind buffeted the sliding door and it shuddered with a low rattle. I got up and looked out the glass. My eyes were drawn to the center of the forest, where the wind-blown limbs seemed to beckon me.

"Do you mind if I go outside?"

She turned her weary eyes to the window.

"You won't find him out there. They've combed this property a million times. There were something like three hundred people in those search parties. Matthew's not out there—I know it."

I believed her.

"I'm sure the police have already asked you this, but do you have any sense of where he might be? Intuitively, I mean."

She rested her head on the back of her chair, directing her comments to the ceiling.

"Somebody took our son. I don't know who, I don't know why, I don't know where." She straightened up and looked at me accusingly. "You're the psychic. *You're* the one who's supposed to be telling *me* where he is."

"It doesn't work quite that easily." I gave this lecture every time I started a case. People expect miracles. In the years I've been investigating crime, I've discovered that miracles are pretty hard to come by. "When I work a case, I tend to pick up partial images. If I'm really lucky, I'll get a name or possibly some numbers. But it's not like the client hands me a file and I automatically crank out the suspect's location, birthday, and Social Security number. I wish I could."

Roxanne may or may not have been listening. She'd leaned forward and was resting her head on her hand, massaging her eyes with her fingers.

"I'm going to go outside," I said, "and see if I pick up on anything, okay?"

She didn't look up, but her head bobbed up and down. I took that as a yes.

The hot wind blasted me as soon as I was out the door. It blew through the trees on the other side of the lawn, hissing like a thousand snakes. I crossed the grass quickly, anticipating cooler temperatures once I entered the eucalyptus forest. Oddly, the heat was even more oppressive in among the trees. The menthol scent of the leaves was overpowering and the racket of the wind through them was deafening.

The ground beneath my feet was covered with dust and dried leaves. The wind had blown away most of the tracks, and the ones I could see looked as if they belonged to either search dogs or adults—not a four-year-old.

Something skittered through the dry leaves near my left foot. I caught a glimpse of a tail disappearing into the organic debris on the forest floor. Either a lizard or a mouse, I wasn't sure which. I'd learned from my shaman friend, Sequoia, to pay attention to the animals that cross my path. He taught me that animals often carry messages from the world of spirit. Or as I liked to think of it, the great unconscious—that ninety percent of the brain we don't use. I stepped in the direction where I'd seen the tail, my eyes and ears alert.

I walked a few yards and came across a gully. It wasn't wide or wet enough to be called a creek, but it probably became one during the rainy season. A huge eucalyptus abutted the creek's edge and the bone-dry earth was lumpy where its roots had gone searching for water. I stepped down into the shallow depression, thinking that missing bodies are often found in natural graves such as this. My eye caught a flash of red near the tree and my heart began to thump.

It was the red of a tiny Matchbox car, lodged in the tangle of roots. The hollow space at the base of the tree made a perfect hiding place for small toys. Behind the little red car I found a blue cat's-eye marble and a cheap plastic top, the kind you might get out of a box of cereal. The Matchbox car was made of metal, a good material for conducting psychic energy. I held it in my fist and closed my eyes.

The image of a large, friendly dog floated up into my consciousness. With the image came feelings akin to happiness and comfort. I was tempted to reject these first impressions. Presuming this was Matthew's toy, why would I be picking up on happiness and comfort? He'd been taken from his parents. Even if he'd gone willingly, after a five-day separation he'd be homesick.

I tried to see more. Again came a very general outline of a dog. It didn't seem real and I couldn't make sense of it.

"Hey, you okay over there?"

Loebman's voice was barely audible over the rushing sound of the leaves overhead. He approached gingerly, taking care where he stepped in his expensive leather shoes.

"Fine," I called. "Just checking something out."

He stopped at the edge of the gully. The hot wind blew through his hair, pushing it to one side of his head.

"Saw you crouched down like that, thought you might've twisted an ankle or something. What've you got?"

"I think I just found Matthew's toy stash." I held up the Matchbox car. "I'm going to keep this, if you don't mind."

Loebman shrugged nonchalantly and I slipped the toy car into my pocket. He stepped back to give me room as I climbed out of the gully.

"I've been walking around the entire house and haven't caught a whiff of smoke. You sure you smelled it?"

I dusted some dirt from the knees of my jeans.

"Like I was telling Roxanne, I might have been picking up on it psychically."

He looked at me dubiously.

"What does that mean?"

"I'm not sure yet. Maybe nothing."

The wind whipped even harder through the trees, blowing a bough of dried leaves into the gully. I had the sudden urge to leave.

"I've seen enough here," I said. "Think I'll take that file and start working the case on my own. What's your next move?"

"Finishing up background checks on the Fieldings' relatives and business associates. I don't know how much longer I'll be working this case. Department policy with missing persons is, I get to play with it for ten days. Day eleven, the case gets booted over to Homicide."

His last word hung in the air like a threat. I still sensed that Matthew was alive, but didn't see the point in saying anything until I had a concrete lead.

We headed back to the house, leaving the shade of the eucalyptus forest. My skin felt like tissue paper under a broiler as we walked across the lawn. When we got to the back porch, Loebman pulled open the sliding glass door and I stepped inside. Roxanne was no longer sitting at the kitchen table.

"Roxanne?"

My voice echoed in the large kitchen. Loebman walked around me and I followed him into the living room, which appeared to be empty. We were passing through when we spotted her stretched out on the leather sectional, eyes closed. I called to her gently.

"Roxanne, are you all right?"

She didn't respond. I shot Loebman a worried look and hurried to her side.

"Roxanne?"

I nudged her shoulder. No response. I leaned down and touched her forehead. Her skin was warm but she was completely limp. I could smell the sour odor of her unwashed hair.

Loebman stepped forward and shook her by the arm. He called out her name and questioned her in a loud voice.

"Have you taken any medication?"

He repeated the question several times before Roxanne finally opened her red-rimmed eyes. They quickly lost focus and fluttered shut again. Loebman motioned toward the phone.

"Call 911. I think we've got an overdose here."

CHAPTER 4

At the sound of the magic number—911—Roxanne opened her eyes a crack and made a feeble attempt to lift her head from the sofa.

"No, don't." She batted her hand at Loebman and me, objecting in mumbled half sentences. "I haven't . . . not on drugs. Just haven't slept for days. Tired." She closed her eyes again.

Loebman didn't look as if he believed her. I wasn't sure. I reached into my backpack and hunted for my cell phone.

"Better safe than sorry." I found the phone and turned it on.

"No. No press." Roxanne was as adamant as her weakened state would allow.

"I'm calling an ambulance, not the press," I assured her.

"She's worried about the news van camped at the gate," Loebman explained.

I got Roxanne's point. An ambulance rushing to the house would fan the flames of media interest. I came up with another idea.

"Let me call my dad. He's a doctor and he doesn't live more than half a mile from here. It'll be discreet and probably faster than an ambulance anyway."

Loebman looked doubtful.

"What if you can't reach him?"

"My dad would sooner go out without his pants than without his pager. He's a slave to his patients."

He considered it a moment.

"All right."

Roxanne, eyes still closed, lay completely still. If she objected to my plan, she wasn't saying so.

I dialed my dad's pager and punched in my number. Within a minute my phone rang back. This didn't surprise me. Dad always answers my pages in record time.

"Hey, kiddo." The lilt in his voice told me he was happy to hear from me. Again, not a surprise. I'm his baby, the apple of his eye. The only complaint I get from him is that I don't call often enough.

"This isn't a social call, Dad. We've got a medical emergency. You know where Frank Fielding lives, the place with the big iron gate?"

"Are you okay?" His voice was calm, but I could hear the worry in it.

"I'm fine. It's Mrs. Fielding we're concerned about."

"I'll be there in five minutes."

My father arrived seven minutes later, five if you didn't count the time it took him to call from the gate and come up the driveway. He went immediately to Roxanne Fielding and pressed his fingers against her wrist, checking her pulse. She seemed dimly aware that someone new was in the room, and lifted her heavy eyelids.

"I'm Dr. Chase, Mrs. Fielding. How are you today?"

Wearing a fresh white shirt and toting a black leather medical bag, Dad looked like some retro American hero from the cover of *The Saturday Evening Post*. I'd never actually witnessed him making a house call before.

Roxanne mumbled an incoherent reply. Dad pulled a stethoscope from his bag and fitted it over his ears.

"Pretty tired out by all this stress, aren't you?" He

probed her chest with the circular rubber stethoscope pad, listening for her heartbeat.

As I stood above him, I noticed that my father's gray hair was thinning on top. He was physically fit but well into his sixties, approaching retirement. The thought of Dad's advancing age filled me with tenderness and dread. He focused intently on Roxanne, gently pulling open her eyelids and rotating her head to examine each eye.

"What medications are you taking, Mrs. Fielding?" His voice was compassionate, nonjudgmental.

"I told them . . . no pills," she answered groggily.

"Just a little vodka, maybe?" He cast a knowing look my way.

"Mm . . . maybe."

"When was the last time you got some sleep?"

Dad seemed to be on to something here. I remembered how Roxanne had nodded off when I first arrived, just before the smoke scare.

"Haven't really been able to sleep. Love to sleep now."

The front door slammed shut and footsteps approached from the hallway. Loebman, Dad, and I turned to see a man—bald-headed and not a day over forty—enter the room. When he saw us gathered around Roxanne, he froze.

"What's going on here?"

I recognized Frank Fielding's distinctive pate from photos I'd seen in newspapers and magazines. A captain of San Diego's high-tech industry, he was revered for boosting the stock of his company, Starcom, to Nasdaq-record-breaking levels. Employees and shareholders had become overnight millionaires, sending stock prices even higher and spawning a phenomenon the press called "Starcomania." Like so many people in the public eye, Fielding appeared smaller and more vulnerable than the superimage projected by the media.

Dad removed the stethoscope from his ears and draped it around his neck as he got up and extended a hand.

"Mr. Fielding, I'm Albert Chase, your neighbor over on El Montevideo."

Fielding shook Dad's hand, a question in his face.

"Your wife was losing consciousness," Dad explained. "Rather than call in an ambulance for the benefit of the news reporters parked at your gate, my daughter paged me to have a look at her. Your wife will be fine once she gets some rest."

"You're a medical doctor?"

It wasn't a silly question. This was California, where a multitude of unqualified people called themselves doctors and healers. Dad smiled at the question.

"A neurosurgeon, actually, but I don't think she's going to require my expertise. Just some good old-fashioned bed rest. Her vitals are completely normal but she's severely sleep deprived. Not unusual under the circumstances. She's had a little alcohol recently, which is inducing some much-needed rest." Dad was speaking in the authoritative, easy tone that had always made me feel safe and secure. I could tell it was having a similar effect on Frank Fielding, who looked at me.

"This is your daughter?"

"Yes." I stepped forward and offered my hand. "I'm Elizabeth."

"Elizabeth Chase," he said, shaking my hand. "Aren't you the psychic detective they wanted to bring in?"

"Yes. That's why I'm here."

He nodded, making all the connections now.

"I'm not sure about the reality of ESP, but if you can help us get our son back, what the hell." He looked anxiously toward his wife lying on the sofa. "Excuse me a moment."

He brushed past us and knelt by Roxanne's side, speaking to her in a voice too low for me to understand. Her head bobbed weakly, but it was clear she was only half-conscious.

"I think it would be a good idea to get her moved into her own bed," Dad said.

Fielding nodded his agreement.

"Let's do that."

Fielding got his wife into a sitting position. I stepped forward to help and the two of us got her on her feet. Dad and Loebman offered their assistance but Fielding and I assured them we had it handled. Draping Roxanne's arms around our shoulders, we moved her into the master bedroom, half the time carrying her, half the time letting her take her own clumsy, sleepwalking steps. When we got her comfortably situated, I stepped out of the bedroom to give the couple some privacy.

Across the hall, a door stood open. I walked over and took a peek inside. It was bigger than my living room by half, but this was clearly a kid's room. The walls were painted with murals of distant galaxies, colorful planets, luminous moons, and sophisticated spaceships. A space shuttle model big enough for an adult to play in occupied one corner. The bed itself was designed like a rocket, resting on its side. It made me want to be a kid again.

"You can go in if you'd like."

I turned around to see Frank Fielding stepping out of the master bedroom. He quietly closed the door behind him and walked across the hall to join me.

"I mean, if you think looking at Matthew's room might be helpful." Slightly enlarged by the lenses of his glasses, his watery blue eyes gave him a deceptively gentle appearance. Behind his bald-guy-with-glasses geek façade, I sensed intense awareness and willpower.

"Thanks. It could be."

I stepped into the bedroom and right away got a strong sense of Matthew. Again came the feeling that he was alive. I went directly to his bed. Fielding stood at the door, watching.

"Do you need to be alone?"

"No, it's okay. This is going to sound like a strange request, but do you mind if I climb in here?" I pointed to the rocket bed.

"Go ahead." A wistful smile crossed his face. "It's fun. I've done it myself."

I tucked my body into the padded cavity of the rocket.

There wasn't enough head room for me to sit, so I had to lie on my side. For a moment I closed my eyes. Again I got the vague image of a dog, this time with a big, goofy tongue lolling outside its mouth. I opened my eyes and got up.

"Does Matthew have a dog?"

"No. We don't have pets. Roxanne is allergic to most animals, unfortunately."

"I keep seeing a dog, kind of a medium brown color, big, with a goofy mouth."

Fielding walked to a large wicker basket in the corner of the room and pulled out a stuffed toy.

"Something like this?"

He handed it to me. I recognized the stuffed replica of the Hanna Barbera creation.

"Scooby-Doo?"

"His favorite cartoon. He's almost fanatical about it, never misses the show. That's the only dog in his life I know of."

My heart made a little leap. If Matthew was alive and I was reading his energy, it could be that he was watching or thinking about the cartoon, taking comfort in it.

"May I borrow Scooby for a while?"

He hesitated, as if reluctant to let any part of Matthew go.

"It could help me find him," I added.

He turned the stuffed dog over in his hands, examining it.

"What does it mean, your seeing a dog?"

"I'm not sure yet, but I'm taking it as a good sign. Something for me to go on, anyway."

"The Sheriff's detective said you were a licensed private investigator as well as a psychic."

"Yes, that's right."

He brought the stuffed animal to his face and breathed. I guessed that he was taking in the scent of his son. He closed his eyes and his face twisted in agony. His fists clenched the toy until his knuckles turned white. The moment stretched and I began to feel uncomfortable. I was about to say something when he opened his eyes. They were harder now, resolute.

"Will you make me a promise, Elizabeth? Is it Elizabeth, or Liz?"

"Elizabeth, mostly."

"Will you promise me you'll do everything in your power to get my son back?"

"That goes without saying, Mr. Fielding."

"I don't mean that lightly. I'm asking for your personal commitment."

"I understand. I promise." Our eyes locked. It was one of those moments I knew I'd never forget.

"How do you plan to go about finding him?" he asked.

"The Sheriff's Department is doing background checks on your family and associates. I'll be doing similar kinds of things, and if I'm lucky I'll find a shortcut."

"A shortcut?"

"I've had some success locating missing people through something called remote viewing. Ever heard of it?"

"Sure." He nodded. "The government had a program, didn't they?"

"Yeah. My technique is a little different from the one they used in the CIA, but it's the same principle. That's why I want to borrow the stuffed animal." I pointed to the Scooby toy in his hands. "I can use it as a focusing tool."

He nodded and at last handed me the toy.

"Could we meet later this evening?" I asked.

"Of course, whatever I can do." He pulled a wallet from his pants pocket and gave me his private card. "Call me on my mobile when you need me."

It was past noon by the time Frank Fielding saw us to the door. The wind had calmed to a steady breeze but the heat had intensified. I guessed ninety-five, maybe hotter. I rode with Dad back to my truck, which was still parked outside the entry gate. The door handle on the passenger side of his Volvo had been sitting in the sun, and was so hot that

I had to cover it with the bottom of my shirt to open it. As we followed Loebman's Crown Victoria down the winding drive through the eucalyptus forest, Dad looked across the seat at me, one eyebrow raised.

"Well, what do you think?"

"The boy's alive. Where he is or who took him, I don't know yet."

"How do you know he's alive? What makes you say that?"

"Usually when I work with murder victims I'll get kind of a cold, disassociated feeling when I look at their pictures or hold their possessions. That's not what's going on here."

Dad nodded.

"That's good. If you find this kid, you're going to have some powerful friends in your corner."

Sequoia's face—those obsidian eyes that seemed to open into eternity—appeared in my mind.

"I already have powerful friends in my corner. And if the Fieldings have anything to do with their kid's disappearance, I won't be their friend, now will I?"

He looked surprised.

"Do you suspect the parents?"

"I'm an investigator, Dad. I suspect everybody."

We rode in silence for several moments, until I changed the subject.

"How's Mom?"

"The Santa Ana's ruining all her azaleas and she's not happy about it. If you get a break in your case here, you should stop over and cheer her up."

"I want to get to work on this right away, otherwise I'd stop by. Tell her I'll say a prayer for her azaleas."

We rounded the last curve and the front gate came into view. The iron bars rolled open and Loebman's car drove through. The news van, its antenna now towering into the air, was parked near the gate. A reporter stood against the backdrop of the gated forest, talking into a mike. A woman wearing a Padres baseball hat faced him from a few feet away, capturing his image on a television camera.

"Looks like they're doing a live feed," I said.

Dad scowled.

"Yeah, they're feeding, all right. Like vultures." He squinted at the crew. "That's Randy Twain from Channel Three. Must be a slow news day."

Ahead of us, Loebman gunned his car past the TV crew, turned onto the street and drove off. Dad pulled up behind my truck and stopped.

"Good to see you, honey. Go get 'em." He smiled and winked.

I was going to reach over and give him a daughterly hug but in light of the news crew, thought the better of it.

"Bye, Dad. Thanks for your help."

As soon as my feet hit the driveway, Randy Twain approached me, mike in hand. I gave him a backward glance. His looks were ready for prime time, no argument there. He was tall and athletic, with those nice, even features that the cameras loved. Even in the wind, his thick brown hair maintained its clean-cut shape. He smiled at me as if we were old friends, a pair of dimples appearing under his cheekbones.

"Excuse me. Could I have a word with you?"

I kept walking toward my truck, fumbling with my keys.

"I don't have anything to give you, man. Sorry."

I waved to Dad, indicating that I was okay and could handle the situation by myself. But Dad stayed put, his car idling.

"Are you working on this investigation in an official capacity? Is that man your partner?" Twain was following at my heels and talking fast now, sensing his time with me was limited.

I shook my head no and opened the door to my truck. As I slid behind the wheel and reached over to shut the door I caught a glimpse of his crestfallen face. I capitulated and threw him a scrap.

"Just neighbors," I said.

CHAPTER 5

"Get off of there, Whitman."

I gave my Himalayan a gentle shove, pushing him off the poster spread out on the dining room table in front of me. My cat automatically puts his butt on any papers I lay out to read. It's a given, as if he's been trained by cat professionals to do so. I'd taken the poster down from my office wall as soon as I got home. An aerial view of San Diego County, its amazing detail was authentic. Constructed from photographs taken via satellite, the poster showed not only streets and highways but the lay of the land, as well. I could see all the hills, valleys, reservoirs, rivers, and ponds of Rancho Santa Fe and the surrounding areas, as if I were looking down from an airplane.

The wind blew outside but in my dining room all was quiet, save for the rhythmic panting of my Rhodesian Ridgeback, Nero, who was stretched out on the tile floor, doing his best to stay cool. I studied the poster, hoping I might get a sense about what had happened to the Fielding boy by seeing a bird's-eye view of the spot from which he'd been abducted. When the tip of my index finger found the Fielding property, the map revealed a surprise. Although they were a half mile or so from my parents' house via automobile, the Fieldings were practically adjacent as the crow flies. The two properties were separated only by a hill.

"Amazing what you find out when you widen your perspective."

My cat blinked at me and I realized I'd spoken out loud. Nero's panting stopped for a moment as he too responded to my voice.

I sifted through the file and pulled out the search-and-rescue reports. For the next several minutes I read the narrative descriptions of where the teams had searched, following along on the aerial view of Rancho Santa Fe and the adjacent towns, Olivenhein and Encinitas. As Loebman had said, police and volunteer teams had covered every square foot within miles of the Fielding estate.

Outside, the Santa Ana was picking up strength. I worried what the wind might do to my house. Built in 1888, the place had weathered more than a few of these dry storms, I was sure. Comforted by that thought, I returned my attention to my work.

The United States Government caught on to the advantages of remote viewing years ago with the once-secret Stargate Program. Some people have a hard time believing that their tax dollars have been spent on psychic espionage. Things like that happen only on television or in B movies, right? Wrong. A few years ago the CIA launched a media disinformation blitz, admitting to the remote-viewing experiments but claiming that the program was a failure. I'm not big on government conspiracy theories, but I knew that this was a cover-up. A colleague of mine from Stanford Research Institute had participated in Stargate in the 1980s. He's still torn up about the way he used his psychic gift for the dubious ends of the government.

The standard remote-viewing technique is rather cold and clinical. The psychic is given a pair of numeric coordinates that represent the subject. When the numbers are given he allows his hand to scribble a mark—known as an ideogram—onto a piece of paper. The marks—squiggles, curves, and lines—constitute a sort of subconscious universal language with specific meanings: water, earth, building, man, woman, et cetera. From these images information is extrapolated about the subject in question.

I'd been trained in classic remote viewing while I was working on my Ph.D. in parapsychology, but I'd never warmed to the technique. What always works best for me is to hold a photograph of the subject, relax into a meditative state, go inside to a place beyond time and space, and wait for images or words to come forward.

Which is what I did there in my dining room. Placing my palm over Matthew Fielding's picture, I sat back in my chair, closed my eyes, and breathed deeply. Almost immediately, pinpoints of light appeared on my inner movie screen, swirling into shifting colors and shapes. I continued to breathe, relax, and observe.

I heard what sounded like the heaving of an angry god as a powerful gust of wind blew over the house. My eyes popped open. Meditating under these conditions was going to be a challenge. I made a decision to ignore the commotion outside and allow any sounds to become background noise. Again I closed my eyes and breathed.

The aerial view of Rancho Santa Fe appeared in my mind's eye. My perspective began to zoom in on the area where my parents and the Fieldings lived.

Two thumps sounded at the back of the house, so loudly that I jumped in my chair. The noises were too much to ignore. Wondering what on earth could have made such a racket, I walked to the back door and got my answer. The Santa Ana had picked up a lightweight lawn chair and an empty planter and had thrown them against the side of the house. The wind was in a foul mood; anything not bolted down was fair game. The atmosphere reminded me of the tornado scene at the opening of *The Wizard of Oz*.

I returned to my chair, closed my eyes, and tried again. As I tuned in I began to understand that it wasn't just the ruckus outside that was breaking my concentration. The

uneasy feeling I'd had off and on all morning, like the
Santa Ana, had gained in intensity. The more I'd tried to
ignore it the stronger it had become.

The wind groaned again. Whitman bolted from the table,
scattering my papers in his wake.

"Whitman!"

Something crashed behind me. I turned to see the jagged
end of a eucalyptus branch come pushing through the window. Pieces of glass fell to the floor and shattered. The
branch caught on the window frame and hung there like an
unwelcome guest. Hot wind rushed in through the broken
window, fluttering the long, aromatic leaves clinging to the
limb. I must have gasped because I realized I was holding
my breath. It took a couple of minutes before my heartbeat
returned to normal.

Nero followed me outside as I went to see what I could
do about the eucalyptus branch. There wasn't a cloud in
sight. The thermals had cleared away any smog and the sky
was so sharply blue that it hurt my eyes. I found some
plywood boards in the garage and carried them with a hammer and a box of nails to the ruined window. With gloved
hands, I yanked the branch out the way it had come in. As
it slid across the sill, shards of glass still clinging to the
window frame broke and tinkled onto the ground around
my pansies, whose tender leaves were wilting in the scorching heat.

I turned around to see where the branch had come from.
A stately eucalyptus stood a good twenty feet away, listing
sideways as the wind whipped through its branches. I didn't
like a wind with that kind of pitching power.

My hair blew into my face. As I gathered the tangled
mass into a ponytail and tucked it under my collar, I was
heartened by what looked like a fluffy white cloud bank
along the western horizon. Maybe a low-pressure system
would dampen the Santa Ana. My hopes died when I saw
a column of gray rising into the white. It wasn't a cloud
bank—it was smoke. And this was wildfire weather.

The nagging worry tugged again at my gut. I pushed it

down and focused on pounding a plywood board across the gaping window. I was putting up the second board when I heard a woman call out:

"My God!"

It was my mother's voice, no doubt about it. I froze, hammer in midair. I turned around to see if she'd made an unannounced visit. But other than a gray lizard skittering across my walk, there was no one in sight.

I had no doubt about the fact that I'd heard my mother call out. My heart began to beat faster. Not because I was hearing voices. I'm psychic; it happens. It was the tone of my mother's voice that troubled me. Panic, tinged with real fear. Something was wrong.

I dropped the hammer, went straight inside to the phone, and dialed a number I knew better than my own. My parents had lived in the same house, with the same phone number, for over thirty years. I punched the last digit and waited for the ring. It was a long wait. There wasn't even a tape-recorded message from the phone company telling me that my call didn't go through. I hung up and tried again. Again I got only frustrating silence.

I dialed my dad's pager number, the ominous feeling stronger now. Five minutes and no call-back later, the nagging worry had congealed into a painful knot in my stomach. I tried my parents' home phone again. By now the silence on the other end of the line made me want to scream.

I ran upstairs to get a better look at the fire. Standing at the railing of the widow's walk outside my second-story parlor, I could see that the smoke bank had plumed higher and darker. It looked as though the fire were directly behind the hills near Lake Hodges, in the northern end of Rancho Santa Fe. My parents' neighborhood. Abandoning the window repair job, I hopped into my truck and rushed through the yellow lights on Juniper as I headed in the direction of the smoke.

I took Del Dios west. With each mile closer, the cloud of smoke loomed larger. By the time I reached Lake

Hodges I caught the unmistakable odor of something burning. I kept hoping the perspective would shift as I drove closer, and I'd discover that the fire was coming from another part of the county. But as I neared Rancho Santa Fe I could see how accurate my first guess had been. My uneasiness turned to dread.

There were more cars now, most of them heading away from the fire, toward me. A fire engine screamed up behind me. I slowed and pulled to a stop at the side of the road. The engine roared past in a red-amber blur of flashing lights and hyperloud siren noise, turning onto Camino del Norte. I pulled out and followed the same route. The smoke began to darken the sky overhead.

I sped past the familiar orange groves and horse stables, my tires squealing on the sharp curves. Two miles from my parents' house, the blue sky completely disappeared, obscured by soot and smoke as dense as fog. The sun was a crimson ball through the murky gray atmosphere. More than anything, the sight of that blood-red sun horrified me. The heat was oppressive. I turned on the pickup's air conditioner full blast, but the fan pushed only hot, acrid air through the vents. My throat felt parched. I swallowed, as much from fear as from thirst, and wished I'd thought to bring a bottle of water.

Up ahead a white Bronco painted with the Fire Department logo and equipped with klieg lights was parked diagonally across the road, forming a barricade behind a row of orange traffic cones. Standing in the middle of the road, a firefighter in a yellow Nomex suit and a matching helmet was waving a red flag with one hand and making the stopping signal with the other. I braked, my heart racing. As I came to a stop I rolled down my window and a gust of smoky wind pushed into the cab.

"My family's house is back there," I blurted, hearing a tremor in my voice.

His thick, square hand rested on my open window. I noticed his fingernails were dirty. The face that leaned in looked sunburned.

"Sorry—there's no access to this area, ma'am. They've closed both ends of Camino del Norte. The fire's burned past El Montevideo."

Burned past El Montevideo. That was the street my parents lived on. I swallowed the lump in my throat.

"What about Via de Fortuna? Can I get through that way?"

"We're advising people not to go past this point."

He hadn't really answered my question. I must have looked stricken because his face softened and he spoke in a reassuring voice.

"The Montevideo area was evacuated a while ago. I think pretty much everyone got out."

I was trying to comfort myself with that when a beige Taurus pulled to a stop along the shoulder behind me. In my rearview I watched a man get out and walk toward us. As he approached I recognized Randy Twain, the television reporter I'd seen at the Fielding estate earlier this morning.

"Hey, buddy," I heard him say as he neared my open window. "I need some help here."

The firefighter turned to him attentively.

"Whatcha need, Randy?"

"My photographer's back there covering the fire." Twain pointed beyond the roadblock, into the thick of the smoke. "We've been keeping in contact by cell phone." He held up his cellular, as if to prove this last statement. "But it's spreading fast and she needs to get out of there. Can you give me a lift to pick her up? She's off road and that piece of shit"—he pointed to his Taurus with disgust—"isn't going to cut it."

The firefighter shook his head.

"Sorry. I can call a unit from the field but I can't leave my post. I've got to stay here and keep traffic from getting past."

Twain frowned.

"Damn, Zev, I need some wheels. How long will it take a field unit to get here?"

The firefighter shrugged apologetically. "I don't know. They're pretty busy right now."

Twain had called the firefighter Zev, so I assumed they were acquainted. I saw an opportunity and jumped at it.

"I'll drive you back there," I said.

Twain looked into my truck, noticing me for the first time.

"Really?" he asked hopefully.

"Yeah. Hop in."

The firefighter crossed his arms over his chest and stared at me, but didn't object. I met his gaze, hoping I looked worthy of the task. Twain circled around to my passenger side and climbed in.

I put the truck in gear and Twain gave the firefighter a nod.

"We'll be right back, don't worry."

Zev's sun-bleached brows pulled into a scowl. Friend of the newscaster or not, he clearly was uncomfortable letting a couple of civilians drive into the fire zone.

"Careful in there, and make it quick."

I gave him a thumbs-up and hit the gas before he could change his mind.

Twain mumbled gratefully to me as he twisted around in search of his seat belt.

"Thanks for helping out. Jane's young and gung-ho. Which is great, of course, but I'd feel sick if anything happened to her. So thanks, really." He looked at me more carefully now. "Hey, aren't you the woman who was at the Fielding place this morning?"

"Yeah."

I answered in a grim monosyllable, not feeling capable of small talk. Outside, the smoke was thickening. With each passing yard the crummy visibility was getting worse. My survival instincts were on red alert. I wanted to know that my parents were okay, that my childhood home hadn't burned to the ground. More than anything I wanted to wake up from this nightmare.

"I have my own reasons for wanting to drive back here,"

I said. "My parents live at the end of El Montevideo."

"Oh, God." His voice was genuinely concerned. "I'm so sorry."

Headlights beamed our way through the smoke up ahead. As the car loomed toward us the driver leaned out his window. I opened my own window to hear what he had to say. Barely slowing as he passed, the driver yelled:

"Don't go back there!"

My throat tickled and I let out an unladylike hack. I shut the window again and Twain's cellular rang. He answered with a worried hello. After a brief pause he said:

"I understand. I'm on my way." He was using his modulated newscaster voice but it didn't quite hide his rising panic. "Look for a white truck. We'll pick you up roadside." He clicked off his phone with a beep, a troubled look on his face.

"What's she doing back here without a car?" I asked.

Twain leaned forward, as if putting his nose to the windshield would help him see through the thickening haze.

"She did have a car, one of the station's Explorers. She parked it and got out to videotape the fire. Then the wind switched directions and the flames made it unsafe to get back to the Explorer. She says she's heading up the road on foot. I can barely understand her, she's breathing so hard. Can't this truck go any faster?"

The smoke was now a dense gray, swirling outside the windows.

"I'm not going to speed when I can't see where I'm going." My voice was sharp and bitchy—a sure sign that I was afraid.

It was early afternoon but dim as evening outside. I could make out no more than fifty feet ahead of me, and barely recognized my old neighborhood. Without warning, a glowing hunk of wood thumped against the windshield, sending a shower of red sparks up and over the cab.

"Shit!" I gripped the steering wheel harder. "This is officially dangerous."

Even as I said it, the truck began to rock unsteadily,

pushed by the hot, angry winds. I looked over at Twain. He was gripping the dashboard, eyes wide, the color drained from his face.

"I don't know about this," he said uneasily.

Another voice, this one from the inside, spoke to me. *It'll be okay. Keep going.*

Now the air was filled with a storm of flying embers, swarming like giant red fireflies in the gray smoke. Through the haze I could barely see the eucalyptus trees lining the road. Their branches waved in the hot wind as if pleading for help. I pushed harder on the gas pedal, sensing that time was running out.

The wind shifted and the smoke cleared enough to see that up ahead one of the towering trees had burst into bright orange flames. Twain jerked in his seat.

"Jesus! Let's get out of here!"

He reached toward the wheel to turn us around. I pushed his arm back and kept my foot on the gas. The conflagration in the eucalyptus had started a chain reaction. The two adjacent trees were now beginning to burn, their flaming branches sending thick black smoke into the wind.

"Hang on," I said. "She's just over this rise." I hoped to God I was right.

CHAPTER 6

I kept a wary eye on the problem area up the road. A burning eucalyptus branch dropped to the ground, its flaming leaves setting a small blaze in the dry grass below. The blustering wind spread the fire like napalm. Within seconds flames covered the embankment and were racing our way. That was it for me. For Twain, too.

"We have to turn around *now*," he said firmly.

But I was already slowing for my U-turn. As we crested the rise, I took one last glance up the road—and hit the brakes.

A woman was taking shape through the swirling smoke. A bulky Sony Betacam perched on her shoulder, she was running toward us on faltering legs.

"Hey, wait—" Twain began.

"I see her," I said.

I sped forward to close the space between us. Twain opened his door and pressed up against me to make room for her. She piled into the truck cab before I'd even come to a stop, the sharp smell of the fire coming in with her. It was the same camerawoman who'd been working with Twain this morning, sans her Padres cap. Her short red hair stuck out in all directions and the T-shirt she wore was smudged with gray ash. Beneath the soot, her skin was an alarming shade of red. Bright beads of sweat stood out on her forehead. All of twenty-two or twenty-three, she looked more determined than frightened.

Twain took the television camera from her and put it down on the floor of the truck.

"All right, Jane!" he said jokingly. "For a minute there I thought I was going to have to hassle with some workers' comp claims."

His banter didn't even register with her. I caught a glance of the young woman's face as I accelerated out of my U-turn. Panting noticeably, she was staring out the windshield with an unfocused gaze. If not in shock, she was close to it.

"We'll be out of here in no time," I promised. "You okay?"

"I—" Her voice caught and she coughed fitfully. Again I regretted not having a water bottle. Twain patted her thigh reassuringly.

"Don't talk. Just relax."

I tried to keep my attention on the road. As I drove away from the fire, the storm of red embers thinned out but smoke still swirled in front of the windshield like a gray veil. It occurred to me that the Fieldings' little boy had disappeared not far from here. I hoped to God he wasn't anywhere near the inferno behind us. The next time I looked over, Jane had slumped forward, her head resting on her knees.

"You sure you're okay?" I remembered reading that it was toxins from smoke inhalation, not flames, which killed most fire victims. Jane didn't seem to hear me.

Twain grasped her by the shoulders, sat her upright, and called her name in a loud voice. Her head wobbled and she let out a moan.

"Little dizzy," she managed.

Visibility was improving the farther I drove away from the fire. I was nearing the spot where the roadblock had been. Twain's Taurus still sat on the shoulder, but the orange traffic cones that had been lined up across the pavement were gone, along with the Fire Department Bronco. The firefighter was nowhere to be seen.

"What happened to the roadblock?" I asked.

"Zevnik must have moved the perimeter back," Twain said. "That means he knows the fire's spreading."

I slowed as we approached Twain's car.

"What about your Taurus?"

He dismissed it with a wave. "Screw it. I'll deal with it later. We need to get some help for Jane."

I agreed. She'd leaned forward again, head in her lap.

"I'm fine," she mumbled, "just dizzy."

I looked over at Twain. From his worried expression, he didn't believe her, either.

Another mile showed me that Twain was right. The roadblock had been moved south, to the corner of Del Dios Highway. The white Bronco was parked roadside and the familiar orange cones were lined up across the pavement. Zevnik stood behind the barrier, redirecting traffic. When I pulled to a stop and rolled down my window, he looked over from his post.

"Am I glad to see you!" he called. "The strike team radioed just after you left. Burn-back's taking over that whole area."

"We need first aid," I said abruptly.

Frowning, he walked briskly to my pickup, leaned through my open window, and zeroed in on the woman slumped on the far side of the passenger seat.

"Can you hear me?" Zevnik's voice was clear and commanding.

Keeping her head down in her lap, Jane nodded. She didn't speak.

Zevnik jogged back to his Bronco. Seconds later he returned carrying an oxygen mask, its clear, ribbed tube hanging from the mouthpiece. He passed it to me through the open window.

"What's her name?" he asked Twain.

"Jane."

"Put that over her face."

Twain pulled Jane upright. I handed him the oxygen mask and he slipped it over her nose and mouth. Leaning into the cab, Zevnik coached her in a firm voice.

"Okay, Jane. I want you to take some deep breaths for me."

The camerawoman's chest rose and fell as she inhaled the oxygen. After several moments the alertness returned to her gaze. Her eyes were shockingly bloodshot above the mask. She took a few more breaths and removed the apparatus, shaking her head.

"Whoa, that was weird. Everything got fuzzy, like snow on a TV set. I could hear you guys, but it sounded like you were really far away."

"That'll teach you," Zevnik said sternly. "Never underestimate the power of a burn-back."

"Burn-back?" I asked.

Zevnik looked toward the growing cloud of smoke. "Yeah, this is a classic burn-back. The main fire started in that heavily wooded area along Camino del Norte, so it was generating a lot of flying brand. Some of these winds are reaching forty, fifty miles per hour. They carried the embers out past the main fire. Ignited some brush here in this area and it's burning back to the advancing fire. I was beginning to think you guys might have got trapped."

I could hear the screaming sirens of more fire engines. Zevnik turned at the sound. A moment later he poked his head in for another look at Jane.

"How you feeling now?"

"Feel fine," she said. "Really."

Zevnik turned to me with a frown.

"Get her over to the evacuation center at San Dieguito Academy. There's an emergency medical unit there. Someone should take another look at her, no matter what she says."

"We'll do it," Twain said, shifting in his seat between Jane and me. My truck's air conditioner was no match for the hot air pouring through my open window. I felt sweat where our bodies were touching.

Jane's crisis was ending, but mine wasn't. The fire near my parents' house was worse than I'd dared to imagine. I flashed back to that moment I'd been fixing my window and heard the haunting echo of my mother's disembodied voice:

My God!

I stared at Zevnik, almost too afraid to ask the question that burned in my mind. I was clinging to the firefighter's statement that the area had been evacuated in advance of the fire. When I found my voice, my heart was pounding.

"Do you know if there've been any casualties?"

"I don't know for sure." He took off his helmet and used a red bandana to wipe the sweat from his brow. The thick, honey-colored hair on his head was packed down and damp. "When you get over to the evacuation center at San Dieguito you'll be able to get more information."

"I don't need medical care," Jane said firmly. "I need to get my tape to the live truck and onto the air ASAP. Trust me, there've been casualties. You're not going to believe what I just saw."

Fear sent ripples through my gut and a cold weight clamped down on my chest.

"Were there houses on fire?" My voice, high and trembling, didn't sound like my own.

"Houses are the least of it," Jane said. "I think I saw someone burning to death."

CHAPTER 7

Someone burning to death.

The camerawoman's words conjured up images so fearful that for a moment I couldn't breathe. Outside my driver's-side window, Zevnik was putting his helmet back on. The look on his sunburned face was neutral, almost resigned. Suddenly his decision to stand around at this roadblock struck me as idle and irresponsible.

"Can't you *help*?" Fear made my voice sharp.

"They've called in every available strike team, ma'am. I'd be all over that fire if I wasn't under orders to stay here, believe me." His voice carried a tone of regret, maybe even resentment.

Seconds later two fire trucks, emergency lights flashing, turned up the street and headed for the fire. Their huge wheels blazed right over the orange traffic cones lined up across the road, sending three of them flying. I had an irrational sense of being invaded, as if hostile forces had taken over the quiet road to my parents' house.

Twain had pulled out his cell phone and was making a call. I leaned past the middle seat to fire questions directly at the camerawoman.

"Where did you see someone burning? Tell me what you saw."

"There were a couple of houses on fire." She reached for the television camera at her feet. "You can see for yourself when we get to the news truck. We've got to get this on the air." She bobbed her head toward the road, signaling me to get a move on.

Not budging, I spoke to her in a slow, deliberate voice. "I need to know because my parents live back there. A house next to an orange grove. Oleanders lining the driveway. Please tell me it wasn't them."

For a brief moment, a fraction of my horror was shared. Jane's mouth made an O and she gave me a look of unmistakable pity.

"I'm sorry. I don't know what to tell you. I'm not familiar with the area . . . there was so much smoke it was hard to see. But no, I don't remember any oleander-lined driveway."

"How about an orange grove?"

She pursed her lips, thinking. I was about to press for the answer when Twain, still talking on his phone, motioned us to keep it down. From the sound of his side of the conversation, he was getting directions. I kept quiet as he finished up the tail end of his call.

". . . in five or ten minutes, depending on traffic. We're about five miles away." He hung up and pointed west.

"The crew is at the top of Linea del Cielo. We're supposed to meet them there."

I drove through the overturned traffic cones and headed right on Del Dios. Much as I wanted to rush to the evacuation center, seeing what Jane had captured on her Betacam would be the quickest way to witness what had happened in the fire. If my parents were all right, hurrying to greet them wouldn't change anything now. If they weren't all right . . . I turned off my thoughts and drove the next few miles filled with a numbing dread.

"That's it," Jane said, pointing to a vehicle at the crest of the hill.

The news truck wasn't a truck at all, but an oversized white van. It was the same vehicle I'd seen at the Fieldings' that morning, which seemed like days ago now. "Live News—KFEC—Channel Three" had been painted in loud colors along its sides.

I pulled to a stop behind the van. I heard Jane's door pop open. Before she hopped out, she leaned past Twain to look at me.

"Hey. Thanks for getting me the hell out of there." Before I could respond, she'd jumped out and was jogging to the news van. Twain started to slide out after her.

"Thanks doesn't even begin to say it. We're really indebted. I owe you one. Come on, let's have a look at this."

I set the parking brake and followed Twain to the news van. Walking along the shoulder of Linea del Cielo—which roughly translates to Skyline Drive—I took in the panoramic view. The plume of smoke I'd seen from Escondido had grown into what now looked like a storm front. Streaked with ruddy black, the enormous smoke cloud stretched for miles toward the ocean. As a California native, I'd lived through decades of fire seasons and seen plenty of fires. But those fires always happened on television, in other communities, to other people's families. Not here. Not to mine.

In and around the news van, activity was frenetic and my presence was completely ignored. The driver—a guy in a South Park T-shirt—rushed to the back, opened the doors, and reached in to pull down a red lever. A massive white antenna began to rise from the top of the truck, climbing high into the air. He caught me staring up at it.

"Beams the video over to the receiver on Mount Woodson," he explained. "Goes up sixty feet."

I looked through the open side doors into the belly of the van. Jane was flipping a series of switches along a control panel. I heard the grinding hum of a generator kicking in.

Twain was on his cell phone again and I listened in.

"Unit twenty-two to Transmissions." There was a pause

while Twain waited to be connected. "Hey, Cliff. We're about twenty seconds away from some live feed from the Rancho Santa Fe fire. Yeah. Just waiting for a tone."

I looked at the three small television monitors inside the van. A pattern of colored bars popped up on the middle screen. Jane pushed her tape into the recording equipment.

"I'll do voice-over in a minute," Twain said into the phone, "but we're going to feed raw video to you first. Here goes." Twain nodded to Jane, who pushed a button on the recorder. The images she'd captured began to play.

The camera was panning on a row of cars driving one-way along a smoke-shrouded road. The vehicles were loaded down with furniture and boxes, their occupants grim-faced. As the camera panned left, I recognized the familiar round-post fencing that ran along the side of the road. I knew exactly where the fence would end and the orange grove would begin. I was looking at the street I'd grown up on.

"Tell me what's happening here, Jane," Twain said.

She pointed to the screen.

"This was the road I came in on, where I pulled over and got out of the Explorer. At this point the fire was at least half a mile away."

I searched vainly for my dad's Volvo in the lineup of cars evacuating the area. No such luck.

The video cut to bright orange flames rising beyond a forest of eucalyptus trees. My heart began to pound. I knew the spot well; I'd been there just this morning.

"The main fire was on this hill," Jane continued. "I walked off-road to get a sight line to the flames."

The video cut again, this time to a much closer view of the fire. The density of the smoke made it appear as if the scene had been shot at night. We were looking up a hill at a bright red-orange ball. As the camera zoomed in, the red-orange ball came into focus and details emerged. The black silhouette of a large house stood out against the churning red-orange fire that was consuming it.

"My God," I said softly.

The camera zoomed out again, revealing the extent of the fire. The entire hillside was in flames, save for the asphalt driveway. The eucalyptus trees lining the drive created a tunnel of fire that ended at a gate made from sharply tapering iron bars. Trapped behind the gate, nose pressed to the bars, was the shell of a late-model Jaguar. Flames poured from every window.

My knees felt like wet sponges.

"That's what distracted me," Jane was saying. "I should've gotten out sooner, but you have to admit, it's incredible video."

Powerful feelings hit me like a one-two punch. The first was relief. This was not my parents' house, nor my parents' car, nor my parents' death. The second feeling was horror, brought on by a terrible *knowing* I had at that moment: Frank and Roxanne Fielding had perished in that Jaguar.

CHAPTER 8

I didn't bother saying good-bye to the members of the Channel Three team, who were too busy putting the hellish image of the burning Jaguar on the air to notice me slipping away from the news van. The video hadn't revealed whether or not the flames had reached my parents' house. What I'd seen on the map this morning—that a mere hill separated my family's property from the Fieldings— haunted me. I hurried to my truck and fired it up, more anxious than ever to get to the evacuation center.

The road to the coast was glutted with traffic, I assumed from the overflow created by streets blocked off from the fire. Stuck in the hot cab under smoky skies, for the next eight miles I fought a losing battle to stay calm. I was grinding my teeth by the time I reached the crest of Santa Fe Drive. As I drove down the hill, the cool blue Pacific stretched before me like an unbroken promise.

RED CROSS DISASTER SHELTER—NEXT RIGHT. An arrowed sign with the Red Cross logo directed me into the parking lot of my alma mater, San Dieguito High School. The name had been changed to San Dieguito Academy and the place no longer held a reputation as the most laid-back school on the mainland. In my day, students earned PE credits for surfing and worked on their tans in the central courtyard. Today there was tension in the air as I searched for a parking place in the jam-packed lot. Most of the cars were recent models beyond the budget of high school kids. Cars belonging to fire refugees, no doubt.

I headed for the gymnasium at a jog. The entry was the same old scuffed double doors that I remembered from years ago, but I hardly recognized the place inside. The entire floor was covered with rows of aluminum cots. A baby blue blanket topped each makeshift bed, giving the gym the cheerful look of a nursery. Cheer was noticeably lacking. People sat on the cots, gazing into space, or wandered about looking displaced and confused. Some had found their way to the back wall, where two guys in Red Cross caps and badges were filling a row of portable tables with bag lunches, Styrofoam cups of coffee, and cans of Coke and 7-Up. Waiting in line for coffee was a trim woman with gray hair piled into a loose bun on her head.

"Mom!"

She turned at the sound of my voice. When she spotted me, her shoulders sagged with relief.

"Am I ever glad to see you." She pulled me in for a one-armed hug, balancing a cup of coffee in her other hand. More than a few stray hairs had escaped from her bun and her face looked sunburned. "We've been trying to call you since we got here."

We. "Dad's okay, then."

"He's in the first aid unit they set up in the back room." Mom nodded toward the rear of the auditorium. I must have looked dismayed, because she was quick to elaborate. "He's treating fire victims."

Which is exactly where he would be. I'd forgotten that Dad was a volunteer physician for the local Red Cross. It had been a while since he'd been called into duty. If memory served, his last stint was after the big quake in 1994.

"Did you get our page?" Mom asked.

I checked my waistband. Empty. I'd taken my pager off when I'd gotten home and, in my panic-fueled haste, had forgotten to bring it along. I thought back to that moment earlier today when I'd been boarding up my window and had heard Mom's disembodied voice.

"I got your message, let's put it that way."

She nodded, accepting that at face value. Telepathy between the two of us didn't happen every day, or even every year. But the few instances when it had happened were notable events in our family history.

"I saw the smoke all the way from Escondido. I rushed over but couldn't get past the roadblock on Camino del Norte. Mom, is the house—?"

"I don't know, honey." She said it matter-of-factly, no drama. "What's important is that the three of us are fine." The pragmatic attitude was typical of my mom. She's either very brave or very good at hiding her feelings, I've never really been sure which.

"Let's go have a seat in my boudoir," she said with a wry smile as she led me across the gym. "There's a detective here who was asking for you. Dark hair, fastidious dresser."

"Loebman."

She nodded and looked around.

"I don't see him now. He was here not too long ago. Dad told me you're working with him to find the Fieldings' son."

"Do you know the Fieldings?" I asked.

"Not personally. Those poor people. I know that's an ironic thing to say, given how wealthy they are. But first their son disappears, and now this fire."

I couldn't bring myself to tell her that I'd seen videotape of the Fieldings' Jaguar going up in flames. She'd had enough of a scare without me putting those images in her head. I scanned the room, looking for Frank or Roxanne. It was possible they'd abandoned their burning car and someone had given them a lift out of the fire zone, the way I'd picked up Jane.

"You haven't seen them here by any chance, have you?"

She shook her head.

"I'm not sure I'd recognize them if I did."

We'd arrived at the end of a row of cots. Mom sat down on the blue blanket and took a slug of her coffee. I recognized some of the belongings stashed under the cot—her laptop, a familiar piece of luggage, a leather-bound album that I knew contained our family photos. Taking up the remaining space was a white cardboard box with a red lid.

"What's in there?" I asked, pointing.

She pulled the box out from under the cot. The lid had been punctured with holes.

"Is that—"

"Mr. Poe," she said. "His cage wouldn't fit in the car. Can you take him home and baby-sit until things blow over? No animals allowed in the shelter. If anyone catches on, I'm going to get a lecture that I have to board him."

"But, Mom, Mr. Poe's a bird. You forgetting I have a cat?"

"He's a Moluccan cockatoo," she corrected. "He'll intimidate the living daylights out of Whitman."

"All right, I'll take him when I go. If you see Loebman, let him know I'm here. I'm going to go find Dad."

Following the hand-lettered signs on the wall, I found the first aid unit at the rear of the gym. The door stood open. From the athletic posters on the wall I gathered that in less eventful times, this served as a coach's office. Today it had been converted into an ER of sorts. A hefty, middle-aged man sat on a padded bench in the center of the room. My father was holding the man's foot, wrapping his ankle in an Ace bandage. Somebody must have said something funny, because the two of them were chuckling.

I stood in the doorway and stared at my father. I don't know when just looking at a person had filled me with such intense happiness. I leaned on the doorjamb, drinking in the sweet reality that my parents had made it out of the fire alive. Dad finished up the ankle wrap and went to a portable basin to wash his hands. His patient thanked him and slid off the bench. Favoring his right foot, the man walked past me out the door.

"You're the best, Dad."

I'd surprised him. He looked up sharply and, when he saw me, smiled.

"Well, look who's here."

"The best," I repeated.

He waved away the compliment, water droplets flying.

"Volunteering here keeps my mind off the fire. This isn't cutting-edge medicine, you know. I'm mostly just handing out aspirin, eye drops, and Valium."

"I don't mean you're the best doctor in the world. I mean you're the best dad in the world."

He reached for a paper towel to dry his hands.

"You buttering me up again?" His smile was big enough that I could see a little glint of gold on his right molar. As he dabbed at his right hand with the towel, I noticed that his forearm was bright red and shiny with ointment.

"What happened to your arm?"

He glanced at it and shrugged. "Don't worry, it doesn't hurt all that much. No hair left, but it's barely a first-degree burn." His face darkened. "What amazes me is, the fire didn't even touch me. That's just from radiant heat. That's how much power that thing had."

I felt my mouth hanging open. He'd been *that close* to the fire.

"Jesus, Dad."

He looked beyond my shoulder to the door.

"Come on in, we're open for business," he said.

"Is this your father?"

I recognized the voice and turned to see Randy Twain. Jane was right behind him, her camera bag in hand.

Now I was the one caught off guard. "Randy . . . hi. Dad, this is—"

"Randy Twain." Dad gave Randy a tight nod. "I recognize you from TV. What can I do for you?"

Dad distrusted the media, and his voice was curt, bordering on cold. I felt mildly embarrassed. Randy didn't seem to notice the slight. He walked in and patted Dad's back with enthusiasm.

"Hey, man, I'm glad you're okay. I met your daughter here at the roadblock by the Rancho Santa Fe fire. She was scared for you. I know exactly how she felt, too, because I was scared for Jane here."

Twain summarized the story about our trip into the fire zone to rescue Jane. He was laying it on thick, making me sound as if I'd braved the hottest pits of Hades.

"Honest to God, if it weren't for your daughter, Jane might not have made it out of there. And you know what?" He looked into my eyes, holding the gaze a little longer than necessary. "I didn't even get her name."

"That's Elizabeth," Dad said proudly. There was one sure way to my father's heart, and Randy had just found it. I'd never seen Dad defrost so quickly.

"Well, Mr. Chase—"

"Dr. Chase," Dad corrected.

"Oh—you're the doctor on call?"

Dad nodded.

"Then you're the person we've come to see. Jane took in a little smoke back there and I promised the fire department we'd get her checked out."

Jane stood impatiently, one hand on her hip and one carrying the camera bag. Dad directed her to the padded bench.

"Why don't you put your bag down there and have a seat."

She hedged before doing as he asked.

"It was nothing, really. I never even got that close to the flames." Her voice sounded hoarse.

"Did the fire make you cough?" Dad asked.

"A little bit. Just for a few minutes, when the wind changed and the smoke and stuff got thick."

Dad put a hand on her shoulder and a stethoscope to her chest.

"Deep breath, please." As he listened, his brow furrowed. "That 'smoke and stuff' carries particulates that can do serious damage to your lungs. It sometimes takes a day or two for symptoms to show. How long have you had that scratchy voice?"

Jane cleared her throat.

"It's always that way. Comes from yelling at Randy." She smiled at her coworker.

Dad went to the supply table where several oxygen kits had been laid out. They were a little different from the apparatus that Zevnik had let us use. Sleek and portable, these tanks had skinny clear plastic tubes that fit around the face and delivered oxygen directly into the nostrils. Dad picked up a kit and handed it to Jane.

"No work for the next two days. Wear the oxygen tube at least six hours a day and sleep with it for the next couple of nights. Chances are better than good you've got some pulmonary cell damage. Your lungs are going to be susceptible to infection for the next few days. Oxygen's the best way to help those cells recover. I'm sure you don't want to be coming down with a case of pneumonia."

"No, not really." Jane strapped the tank over her shoulder and slid the tube into place. "Thanks." Her cavalier attitude had come down several notches.

"I've been using a little oxygen myself," Dad confided. "That's a hell of a fire out there, isn't it?" He held up his forearm to show her, the red skin glistening under the fluorescent light. "Had no idea a fire could spread that fast."

"You were there." Jane's voice was hushed. An instant intimacy sprang up between them.

"I was out in the garden with the hose, trying to save my wife's azaleas from drying up in the wind. Didn't even see smoke. Just heard this incredible roar. The flames came up over the hill in a matter of seconds. Never seen anything like it."

Jane nodded humbly.

"It was surreal."

"That's a good word. The sky was literally filled with it. My wife came out of the house and I remember yelling to her, 'That's not air, that's fire! That's not the sky, that's fire!'" Dad was telling it like an amusing story, half laughing at himself. Abruptly, the smile left his face. "It was the most terrifying thing I've ever seen and at the same time, the most beautiful thing I've ever seen."

Randy had been listening in silence, intently watching my father.

"What an incredible story. Would you mind repeating that for the camera?"

His enthusiasm was so natural that I almost didn't notice how Twain was trying to use my dad. Jane reached for her camera bag, but Dad put up his hand to stop her.

"I'm working here."

"Of course." Randy nodded. "Maybe later?"

"Plenty of evacuees out there. I'm sure you can find another victim to interview."

I had no doubt the double-entendre was deliberate.

"Find another photographer for the next day or two, while you're at it. This one needs to go home and rest." Dad kept his hand on Jane's shoulder until she looked at him. "That's an order."

Where was Matthew Fielding? Now that I knew my parents were all right, my concern turned to the four-year-old I'd been hired to find. By now, Matthew was most likely an orphan. If he was anything at all. I walked back through the gym, hoping to find some answers.

The big room was getting noisy. At least a dozen more evacuees had arrived during the time I'd been in the first aid station. I studied the crowd, searching for Loebman. The Fielding property fell into the Sheriff Department's jurisdiction. It was possible Loebman would have some news about Frank and Roxanne, if not the boy. Walking beside me, Twain seemed to read my thoughts.

"What were you doing at the Fielding place this morning?" he asked.

I pretended not to hear him, having spotted the detective standing in a tight cluster of people. As I approached, I could see they were watching a TV that had been rolled into the gym on a cart and plugged into a wall outlet.

"Loebman!" I called.

He saw me and waved. I walked around the crowd to join him. Twain stayed right on my heels.

"Your dad was at the Fielding place, too, wasn't he? He was driving the Volvo that dropped you off at your truck at the bottom of the driveway. What was that all about?"

"I told you. We're just concerned neighbors." There was perhaps too much snap in my reply. Twain held up his hands.

"And I'm just a concerned news reporter."

I came up behind Loebman at the edge of the crowd and spoke to the back of his head.

"Hey."

Loebman turned and, when he registered who I was, a suspicious look crossed his face.

"You knew this morning the fire was going to happen. How'd you know?"

"I didn't *know*. I smelled smoke. That's all." He looked vexed and I didn't blame him. "My gift is frustrating that way. More often than not I get pieces when I want the whole enchilada. What's the news on the Fieldings?"

The dark look in his eyes answered my question.

"The deaths aren't official until we process the scene. Right now that scene belongs to the fire department. We're going to need a statement from you and your father. You were two of the last people to see them alive."

I had more questions but would wait to ask them, since Twain was still standing within earshot. New pal or not, Twain represented the media, a group that had an annoying habit of tipping off perpetrators by reporting confidential investigation facts. This case was challenging enough without Channel Three mucking it up.

Whoever had the remote was flipping through the channels. Scenes of the fire were playing on every major network and we got a moving slide show of the inferno. The most popular image was the footage of the Fieldings' Jaguar burning behind the gate. It played over and over, like a trailer to a tasteless horror flick.

The shot cut to an aerial view. A logo in the corner of the screen let us know that this was live coverage from the news helicopter.

"Keep it on this channel," I called out.

From high above, the camera revealed the fire burning beyond the intersection of Del Dios Highway and Camino del Norte. Zevnik's Bronco looked like a tiny white toy at the roadblock. Del Dios was jammed for miles with cars. Loebman made a disgusted hissing noise under his breath.

"Some of those are just looky-loos that don't even live in the area. These fires bring out a lot of nutcases. Makes it dangerous for everyone else because they block the roads to and from the fire. Harder for the firefighters to do their jobs."

Someone turned up the volume and the droning voice of a newscaster filled us in:

"Power to the area has been lost and already eleven hundred acres have been burned. At least eight structures have been destroyed and officials have reported seven injuries. More than two hundred firefighters are engaged in battling the fire. Fire department officials have stated that it's too early to estimate when this fire will be contained."

The helicopter was sweeping along the edge of the fire line. In the dying light, the fire looked like a glowing red scar running between the blackened territory already claimed and the golden-green land being threatened. On the charred side I recognized the hill where the Fielding house had burned. The helicopter continued northwest, revealing the patchwork of devastation that the landscape had become. The fire was capricious. Some houses had burned to the ground, others had been spared. The helicopter was moving over the hill now, in the direction of my parents' place. I put my fingers to my mouth and bit my knuckle. My parents' orange grove came into view. At least half of the trees had burned, but their house was still standing.

"Yes!" I pumped a fist in the air.

It was not a logical response to the travesty being shown on the television. Loebman looked at me as if I were crazy. I pointed at the set.

"Look in the right corner. See that house still standing? That's my parents' place."

CHAPTER 9

"Pretty boy."

The voice—sophisticated, if a bit muffled—came through the holes in the box on the passenger seat. The words completely surprised me.

"Mr. Poe," I said. "I didn't realize you actually *spoke*."

"Pretty boy. How cliché. Pretty boy. How cliché." Repetitive, but delightfully droll.

"And you editorialize, too. Cool."

I waited at the light on Juniper, five minutes from home. Above the signal, the ruddy, smoke-scourged sky was fading into darkness. The winds had finally calmed down. So had my heart rate. The fire department had issued a cautious statement that the fire "most likely" would be under control by morning. I'd invited my parents to stay with me until they could go home, but they'd declined. Dad was determined to continue his volunteer medical services and Mom didn't want to leave Dad. Both insisted that sleeping on cots would be fun for a day or two. In the meantime, Mr. Poe would be my companion.

"Carpe diem!" The cockatoo's high, thin voice made me laugh. Crazy bird was full of opinions and suggestions.

When I reached my block I recognized Sequoia's vintage, canvas-topped Jeep parked along the street. He traveled extensively in his work as a shamanic teacher, but rarely came down from his mountain home to make social calls. I was honored that he'd come to see me but it worried me a little, too. Turning into my driveway, I noticed the Jeep was empty and figured he must be waiting for me at the front door.

I pulled my truck into the garage and walked into the house through the side entry. As I put Mr. Poe's box on the kitchen table, I wondered where Nero was. Enduring the dog's slobbering greetings was a homecoming ritual, and I missed it.

"Nero?"

I heard tapping at the rear of the house, remembered my broken window, and figured it out. I walked through the kitchen and into the dining room. In the last light of dusk I saw Sequoia standing outside, putting the finishing touches on a new window. I turned on the overhead light and waved to him through the crystal-clear glass.

He motioned for me to join him outside. I went out through the porch door, noticing that he'd straightened up the lawn chairs and planters overturned by the Santa Ana. By the time I rounded the side of the house, he was putting his putty knife into a toolbox. Nero, who'd been supervising his work, bounded forward to greet me.

"Long day," Sequoia said.

An understatement. We'd met at seven this morning to practice archery on the res. That seemed like weeks ago now. It was past six o'clock in the evening.

"I can't believe you replaced my window. Thank you so much."

Sequoia shrugged as if it were no big deal.

"Tried to page you."

"I guess everybody and their dog tried to page me today. I was in a hurry when I flew out of here."

Using the heel of his sheepskin boot, Sequoia pushed aside a few remaining shards of broken glass.

"Could've at least used the door." There was a tiny smile at the corner of his mouth.

Nero had discovered my smoke-saturated clothes and was sniffing me as though I'd turned into the bitch of his canine dreams.

"Blame Mother Nature for that broken window," I said, "not me."

Sequoia ran a rag along the edge of the new window-pane, cleaning off the last smudges of putty.

"Mother Nature's not done yet. But you know that already, don't you?"

Much as I wanted to deny it, I knew what he was talking about. The tremor in my gut hadn't disappeared, and I had a strong sense that whatever had started today was far from over.

"The animals know it, too," he said.

"What do you mean?"

"Just stand here a minute. Listen."

For the next several seconds we stood without speaking. Nero continued to sniff my clothes. The faint sounds of traffic along Juniper Street drifted over the fence. The wind was calmer now, a mere breeze rustling through the leaves.

"I don't hear anything," I said.

"Just notice the sounds."

I listened more attentively this time. Somewhere in the distance a dog was sending up a mournful howl.

"The dog sounds worried," I said.

Sequoia nodded.

"A wise person can hear a lot in the silence. How'd the window get broken?"

"Wind pushed a eucalyptus branch right through the glass. I was boarding it up when I saw smoke over Lake Hodges. Hell of a fire."

"I know. I saw the smoke all the way from the reservation."

"My parents nearly got burned out of a house they've lived in for more than thirty years. What's worrying me is that there's a four-year-old kid missing. That's what the emergency page was about this morning. Kid's parents live in a house that was destroyed in the fire today."

"Lived," he corrected.

"Right, lived." Past tense, whether he was talking about the house or Matthew's parents. From the look I'd seen on Detective Loebman's face, I was fairly certain that both were history.

"I think you're ready for the fifty-pound bow," Sequoia said. The comment seemed apropos of nothing, but I welcomed the change of subject.

"If you say so." Nero, apparently satisfied that he'd smelled every scent on my person, sat on his haunches, staring at me with his patented I-want-dinner gaze. "Come on," I said, "let's go inside. I'll write you a check for the window."

"Save it for when I get back. I'm on my way to catch a plane."

"Where to?"

"Connecticut. Yale invited me to do a guest lecture series on the psychology of shamanism."

"And you do windows, too. What a guy. Come on in and at least have a cup of tea before you go."

Sequoia looked at his watch and shook his head.

"I'm pushing it as it is. Plane leaves at seven-thirty."

I walked Sequoia to his Jeep. As the engine was warming up, he rolled down his window.

"Remember what I said this morning about not fighting the wind, but going with it, and using the energy around you?"

"Yeah, I remember."

"Keep that in mind this week, okay?"

"Okay." I still wasn't sure what he meant by that, but didn't ask him to elaborate for fear of making him late for his flight.

"See you for our next session. Wednesday afternoon, right?"

Inside the house, my phone began to ring. "Right," I said. "Excuse me, I think that's my office line."

"Go ahead and get it. I'm on my way. See you later."

I ran into the house, heading for the study. *Business call,* I thought. Maybe it was Loebman. I grabbed the receiver on the last ring before the machine kicked in, and said a breathless hello.

"Howdy, concerned neighbor."

At first I didn't recognize the friendly voice on the other end of the line.

"Didn't tell me you were a concerned neighbor with a PI license. Let alone the part about your being psychic. Wowser."

Randy Twain, Channel Three. I could just see the charming dimples at the edges of his smile. I wasn't in the mood.

"I've been doing some research on this fascinating career of yours," he went on. "Kind of sneaky, aren't you?"

"Just have a healthy respect for people's privacy."

"Your own, too, apparently. Makes you a chip off the old block, doesn't it? Your father strikes me as exactly the same type."

"I suppose he is. Look—"

"This is wild. We've got a psychic detective at the home of one of San Diego's most notable businessmen the morning before a fire wipes his place out. Were you trying to warn the Fieldings? Or did your psychic powers fail you?"

There was a pause while I counted to ten.

"This is the thanks I get for risking my neck to rescue your photographer today."

"Oh, hey, I'm sorry." His apology sounded sincere. "I didn't mean to offend. It's just that, man, this kind of story doesn't come along every day."

"What's the point here, Randy?"

"Nothing, really. Just, you know . . ." He didn't finish the sentence, so I finished it for him.

"Fishing for news bites."

"No, actually. I was calling to help you out. I'm going to take a wild stab here and guess that you were hired to help find Matthew Fielding."

"No comment."

"And I'm not asking for a comment. But I thought you'd like to know that there was some serious bad blood between Frank Fielding and the general counsel at Starcom."

"Why would I care?"

"Because you're on the case, whether you'll admit it or not. And it doesn't take a genius to figure out that the missing kid and the fire might be related, right?"

"Possibly."

"Take it or leave it—the guy's name is Larry Gandle. I've been covering Starcomania for two years, so I know beaucoup about the company. Most of it I can't put on the air. But it's info that might help you find the kid. Another thing: there's a rumor Fielding was having an affair with one of his VPs, a woman named Pam Jaffer." He spelled the name for me and I found myself jotting it down. "I can't substantiate that, but it's worth mentioning."

It all sounded very noble, but I suspected ulterior motives.

"What's your agenda here, Mr. Twain?"

"Honestly? You impressed me today. I figured if you were courageous enough to drive into a five-alarm fire, you might be brave enough to go out with me."

I felt my shoulders droop as a wearying sadness came over me. The reminder of Tom's death sent my heart into a downward spiral. *Maybe I should continue to wear his ring,* I thought, *to ward off uncomfortable situations like these.*

"Not available," I said. "Sorry."

"Figured as much." He got right back on track without missing a beat. "But I've been covering the Starcom story since the company went public and, like I say, I've got a lot that I'm sure would be helpful to you."

"Leave me your number and I'll keep that offer in mind."

He gave me three phone numbers, home, office, and cell.

"Call me for the kid's sake, if nothing else. I'd look for him myself if I had the time. I got to meet the little guy earlier this year when I did a profile on the Fieldings for *Hello, San Diego*."

I'd seen the show a few times, our local television version of *People* magazine.

"Really? What was he like?"

"Real shy. Quiet. But a great little dude. He's a *Scooby-Doo* freak, so we had some common ground."

The comment startled me. Twice I'd seen the big brown dog in my mind's eye; first when holding Matthew's toy car in the eucalyptus forest, and again when I'd lain down in Matthew's rocket bed. I tried to keep the surprise out of my voice.

"You're a Scooby fan?"

"He's The Dog, man. Besides Uncle Lou, I mean."

"Uncle Lou."

"My dear, departed hound. Named after crazy Uncle Lou on my father's side, because they both drank out of the toilet."

I couldn't suppress a laugh.

CHAPTER 10

Sometime before sunrise, a tow truck had driven into the burn area and hauled away the Jaguar that had contained the bodies presumed to be Frank and Roxanne Fielding. Dr. Samuel Whitestone, the San Diego medical examiner, had supervised the removal and the bodies had been delivered straight to his office for processing. Loebman and I returned to the scene a few hours later, at first light.

As before, I met Loebman at the entrance to the estate. Nearing the driveway I saw the gate standing open, its bars misshapen as if they'd been pried apart. The eucalyptus forest was gone, reduced to smoldering stumps on either side of the winding driveway. *Like a war zone,* I thought. I had a cruel sense of déjà vu as I opened the Crown Victoria's passenger door.

"What a difference a day can make, huh?" Loebman smiled wearily at his own joke and the dark circles under his sad eyes deepened.

"Man, no kidding." I slid in and buckled my seat belt before I remembered that we were only traveling to the top of the driveway. This morning Loebman wore a Van Gogh–inspired tie over a sky-blue shirt and a new pair of Levi's.

Not a wrinkle in sight. He started the engine and put the car in gear.

"Time can make or break an investigation like this. We're going on the assumption that this was arson. If we're wrong about that, fine. Better safe than screwed. Loss of life in an arson fire is first-degree murder, which is why Wong's here this morning."

"Wong?"

"Yeah, Rick Wong. Our best homicide detective. He's up there with Carolyn Arnold from the Rancho Santa Fe Fire Department. They're chomping at the bit."

"High-profile case."

"A real career opportunity," he agreed.

"They know my specialty?"

"Yep."

"Either of them have a problem with it?"

"If they did, they didn't show it."

I stared in disbelief as we approached the top of the hill. The massive stone fireplace and towering chimney came into view, rising forlornly from the fire-devastated landscape. Rubble and rebar lay in heaps on the large cement foundation, all that was left of the house. I remembered the jasmine-covered trellis above the old oak door and felt the pang of loss.

Loebman pulled up behind a Rancho Santa Fe Fire Department Suburban and an Explorer painted with the Sheriff's Department star logo. He cut the engine and gave me an apologetic look.

"I told Wong about the smoke you smelled yesterday before the fire broke out. He's going to hammer you with questions. Don't get defensive. Fact is, you were one of the last people to see the Fieldings alive. As it appears now, you had some kind of previous knowledge about the fire. You're going to have to explain that."

It takes a certain amount of bravery to come clean with premonitions. I'd heard from a lot of people over the years who had clear foreknowledge of disasters but refused to

speak up for fear they'd be accused of instigating the ca-
lamity.

"I'll stick to the truth. That usually seems to suffice." I
stared out the windshield at a man and a woman standing
in the ruins.

"Who's the woman again?"

"That's Carolyn Arnold from the Rancho Santa Fe Fire
Department. She fought fires for years. Now she's mostly
an arson investigator. Don't know her personally. Just the
rumors."

"What rumors?"

"I don't like to repeat things I can't substantiate."

I studied the woman. Tall and sturdy, she stood with one
hand on her hip, the other holding a camcorder, her legs
slightly spread. She wore a dark blue uniform and work
boots with soles thicker than radial tires. Any woman who
looked that openly powerful probably got stereotyped.

"Let me guess the rumors. Lesbian ball-buster, right?"

Loebman took too long to come up with an answer.

"You didn't hear it from me," he finally said. "Rick
Wong there's your typical homicide dick, but once you get
past the macho posturing he's a pretty good guy. Any questions before we join them?"

"Nope."

I got out of the car and began to walk. The smell of the
fire was everywhere and tickled the back of my throat.
Again, déjà vu. I felt disoriented, because apart from the
towering chimney, all the familiar land markers had burned
to the ground. Loebman stepped carefully into the rubble,
fighting a losing battle to keep the ashes off his shoes. I
followed behind him, searching for anything familiar in the
remains. It felt like a hollow victory when I recognized a
piece of the adobe tile flooring. I stopped and stared, trying
to fathom what had happened here.

"Morning."

I looked up into the lens of a camcorder. The arson
investigator held it there for several seconds, then lowered
the camera and extended her hand.

"Carolyn Arnold. Elizabeth, right? Thanks for coming out here so early."

I nodded but the casual banter I took for granted wouldn't come.

"Sorry," I said when I regained my voice. "I think I'm in a bit of shock here."

"I can see that." She walked a few steps to a large black tote, lowered her six-foot frame onto her haunches, and placed her camcorder inside. "Want a cup of coffee?"

"Coffee would be good."

She pulled a silver thermos out of the tote, poured black coffee into a plastic mug, and held up it for me. She pivoted toward Loebman and Wong, who were carrying on a conversation at the periphery of the crumbled foundation.

"Hey, guys," she called, "want coffee?"

They looked over, said "Yeah" in unison, and started walking our way. Whatever they'd been discussing had left their expressions grim.

"Elizabeth," Loebman said as he approached. "Like you to meet Rick Wong from our homicide unit."

An inch or two shorter than Carolyn, Wong had broad shoulders and a thickly packed frame. He didn't look middle-aged, but his straight black hair was shot through with gray.

"Any news on the missing boy?" I saw concern in his narrow, intelligent eyes.

"Not yet," I answered.

"Loebman tells me you smelled smoke here yesterday before the fire broke out."

I nodded yes.

"Carolyn says it's possible the fire was hidden in the house, doing a slow burn inside the walls before it flared up. Where were you when you first smelled the smoke?"

I scanned the lot and started moving carefully through the piles of rubble. When I got to the stone fireplace, I stopped.

"We were sitting in the living room, which I think was about here."

The others followed me, Carolyn bringing up the rear. She'd pulled out a pen and pad and was jotting notes.

"I smelled smoke for only a few seconds. Then the smell completely disappeared. Does it make sense that it would go away completely like that?"

Carolyn shrugged.

"Maybe. Fire is strange stuff. What happened next?"

"Loebman checked the back of the house and Roxanne and I went into the kitchen." Again I looked around the rubble. Several feet over I saw a blackened box which resembled the charred remains of a dishwasher. "Kitchen used to be over there, I think."

I headed in that direction and again the others followed. I heard twittering and looked up as a pair of birds flew over our heads in the clear blue sky. Just yesterday this space had been a cook's dream, with gleaming countertops and new appliances. Today the countertops were gone and the appliances were scorched virtually beyond recognition. Not a trace was left of the kitchen table or the chairs in which Roxanne and I had sat. I looked where the sliding glass door used to be. Beyond the scorched lawn, the view stretched for miles. Without the eucalyptus forest, the property felt completely exposed. I looked down again and touched the blackened box. It felt warm.

"Is this the dishwasher?" I asked.

"Let's see." Carolyn circled it, found the latch, and pulled the door open. "Based on the melted glasses inside, yeah, I'd say this was a dishwasher."

I walked around to take a look. Inside were two lumps: on the left, a blob of mottled glass; on the right, a hunk of metal that I guessed to be the remains of silverware. I tried to comprehend the heat that had produced these things, and couldn't.

"Man. How hot did this thing get?"

Carolyn pushed the black-crusted door shut again.

"At least a thousand degrees."

"I remember we came in here so Roxanne could check the oven and stove burners. Everything was okay. The only place I smelled smoke was in the living room. You think maybe the fire started in the chimney and somehow spread to the rest of the house?"

I looked up at Carolyn. Something in the way her mouth was set and the knowing look in her clear blue eyes told me that she knew more than she was saying. I was about to ask her what she was thinking when an image appeared in my mind: a tremendous yellow-orange blast that flared and burned like the *Hindenburg*.

"There was an explosion," I said.

The muscles in Carolyn's face tensed. In my peripheral vision I saw Rick Wong turn his head to look at her. She played it cool, keeping her eyes on me instead of returning Wong's glance.

"What do you mean?" she asked.

"I just got a visual of a huge explosion, like a bomb dropping. I think that's what caused the fire."

Loebman screwed up his face.

"You think someone bombed this place?" His voice was skeptical.

"Where was the explosion?" Carolyn prodded.

"I don't know. I'm just seeing this huge ball of fire."

Wong crossed his arms over his bulky chest.

"What part of the house burned first? Can you see that?"

Holding the picture of the explosion in mind, I tried to place it into context. I recognized the thoughts that came next as my own feeble guesses. The three of them looked to me expectantly and I turned up my hands in a defeated gesture.

"I don't know."

Carolyn took a cardboard tube from her black tote, pulled out a roll of paper and unraveled it. It looked like an architectural drawing.

"I pulled the blueprints on this property this morning." She studied the drawing carefully. "These come in handy when we have structural fires." She looked up to get her bearings and checked the drawing one more time before rolling it up and putting it back into her tote. She slung the tote over her shoulder and headed for the north end of the lot. The rest of us followed.

"What are you thinking?" Wong asked.

"We won't know until the lab tests come back, but from the looks of the burn pattern, I think the propane tank's a damn good bet. Most of these houses out here use propane. Could've been a piping problem or other defect. The gas company will send their own investigator, which'll help. They always cover their asses with paper for the inevitable court case. Sometimes we get good information from those gas company reports."

My head was shaking back and forth. I realized the gesture was unconscious on my part.

"No," I said. "Someone set this fire. And the person who did has something to do with Matthew's disappearance."

Carolyn stared at me, looking open to the idea. Wong shrugged.

"Maybe, maybe not. That's the tough part about fire investigation. Not finding out where and how it started, but who or what started it. You can't interview property."

"Not true." Carolyn looked out across the rubble. "This property will talk to me. I just need to spend a little time getting acquainted with it."

"Think it might have been a car bomb?" I asked.

She shook her head.

"I'm ninety-five percent sure that the fire started up here, at the house."

"I don't understand," I replied. "How could the Fieldings have gotten all the way to the bottom of their driveway and not gotten out? Fire doesn't travel that fast, does it?"

"With a dry eucalyptus forest and thirty-mile-an-hour winds, it *books*." Carolyn sighed, sounding tired. "What worked against the Fieldings is that the power went out. The electric gate wouldn't open. They were trapped."

The gate had always struck me as creepy. For a moment I got a sense of Frank and Roxanne's nightmarish last minutes in the Jaguar, with the fire raging behind them and their escape blocked by the iron bars.

"Wasn't there some kind of manual override button?" I asked.

Carolyn looked to Wong and shrugged.

"Don't know. Even if there were, they might've forgotten about it in their panic. Again, I'm just speculating at this point. For all we know, they were dead when the car caught fire. We'll have to wait for the autopsy results."

I directed my next question to Wong. "You find any witnesses? Neighbors, passersby?"

"The Channel Three news photographer was the first and only witness to the actual fire that we know of."

"Jane Sharpe," I said.

Wong nodded.

I looked again at the tons of rubble and groaned as a wave of hopelessness washed over me.

"Roxanne was going to write me a list of the iffy people in their lives. If she did, it's history." I shook my head. "This is so discouraging. Yesterday a houseful of physical evidence could have helped us find Matthew. Today it's nothing but worthless ashes."

Carolyn opened her tote bag.

"Not worthless." She pulled out a pair of surgical tweezers and some clear Ziploc bags. "You can find answers in the ashes if you know how to look for them." She squatted down and began collecting pieces of debris.

I walked to where I imagined the bedrooms had been and leaned down to poke through the ruins. For several minutes I sifted through the fine, white ash. Most of what I found depressed me. A doorknob. A charred file cabinet, its contents vaporized. The twisted base of a metal lamp. I was covered from head to toe in soot when I found what seemed like a miracle: an unburned page from Dostoevsky's *Crime and Punishment*. Some italicized words near the bottom of the page jumped out at me:

> *This* must be ended today, once for all, imme-
> diately . . . he *would not go on living like that.*

The page glowed in the early morning sun, the words vibrating like a living prophecy.

"Carolyn," I called. I walked over to the far side of the lot, where she was still packing up Ziploc evidence bags and placing them in her tote. "Look at this." I held the page out for her to see. She leaned closer and squinted at it.

"That'll happen, things being spared like that. Like I always say, fire is strange stuff."

"Remember what you were saying about the way property can talk? I feel as if this page just whispered in my ear." I looked into her face. Her eyes were bright and an intense feeling of kinship passed between us.

"What did it tell you?"

"That this fire wasn't an accident. That it's no coincidence Matthew's parents were killed the week he disappeared. That there's one very pissed-off mind at work here."

"And our two fine minds working to catch him." She winked. "He doesn't stand a chance."

"I hope you're right."

CHAPTER 11

The wind was getting stronger. An eddy twirled at the edge of the rubble that had once been the Fieldings' home, picking up some ashes and spinning them into a small funnel. The panicky fear I'd felt yesterday came flooding back, moving through my chest like an adrenaline rush. Sequoia's words from last night came back, too:

Mother Nature's not done yet. But you know that already, don't you?

He'd admonished me to listen, to notice the sounds around me. I tuned in on the breeze blowing past. The rushing air seemed like an urgent whisper:

Hurry.

"You okay?"

Rick Wong was watching me stare at the fluttering ashes. I nodded to let him know I was fine. Loebman had gone to his car to make phone calls. Carolyn was at the other end of the ruined lot, still collecting charred bits of evidence. Wong stood behind me with a clipboard in his hands, flipping through some papers.

"I need to ask you some questions about your visit here yesterday."

After Loebman's warning, I'd been waiting for Wong's questions.

"Of course," I said.

We took a seat on a slab of cracked cement foundation. Wong squinted at the sun coming up and reached into his breast pocket for a pair of wraparound sunglasses. He filled in the top section of a report form with our names, the date, the time, and our location. He had small hands and the letters he formed were neat and compact.

"Just give me an account of yesterday's events, beginning with your arrival at the Fieldings'," he said.

I recited from memory as thoroughly as I could, walking through each moment in my mind. Wong frequently interrupted me to ask for clarification and then jotted down notes.

"What struck me," I said at one point, "was that Roxanne said she didn't hear anything unusual when Matthew disappeared. She said she didn't even hear him raise his voice. That makes me think whoever abducted the child knew him."

Wong nodded as he jotted a note.

"You read people pretty well?"

"Well as anyone, I guess."

"This is the address and phone number of Frank Fielding's sister, Debbie Fielding-Cross. We'd like you to pay her a visit. She and her husband are childless. Rumor has it they've been trying to conceive for years. Could be a motive for nabbing the kid." He tore the note off his pad and it fluttered in the wind as he passed it to me. "She's also named in the Fieldings' will to be Matthew's guardian should they die before he reaches eighteen."

"Really," I said.

Wong nodded. "We've got the relatives and household help under a microscope. Other than the sister here, no obvious red flags yet."

"Sounds like you're pretty familiar with the kidnap case."

"From day one."

"Loebman said Homicide didn't get involved in missing persons cases until they were ten days old."

"One of the first things we do in a kidnap case is look at sex offenders who've worked in this area. That's my bag, so I got brought in early. I've been looking over Loebman's shoulder from the minute this case came in. So has the media. Nothing against Loebman. Just a big case, a lot at stake."

"Got it." I looked across the lot, where Carolyn was finishing up her photographs and continuing her search for evidence.

"So what else did Roxanne Fielding say?" Wong asked.

"Just that it was a normal morning. She and Matthew were alone, she said, because the household help had left a couple of weeks before." I raked my memory for the name. "Bonnie somebody."

"Elsa," Wong said. At least that's what I thought I heard him say.

"What?"

"Elsa," Wong repeated. "Maid's name is Elsa Poulson. She was at the doctor's office the morning the kid disappeared. We've already confirmed that with her doctor and verified her signature on the doctor's office sign-in sheet. She has diabetes; she'll be sixty this year. Worked for the Fieldings for eleven years."

I felt confused.

"That's odd. I remember Roxanne specifically saying the woman's name was Bonnie, not Elsa. Bonnie McSomebody." It hit me a second later. "Bonnie McBride. I wrote it down."

Wong didn't say anything but I saw him jotting "Bonnie McBride" into his notes.

"Maybe she was their personal assistant, not their house-keeper," I ventured.

He clicked his pen a few times, thinking.

"If this Bonnie does exist, the timing of her departure from the Fieldings is curious, to say the least."

"Hey!"

Our heads turned in the direction of Carolyn's voice.

"Eureka, guys. Come over here."

Wong and I looked at each other and rose quickly. When we reached the other side of the burned lot, Carolyn was looking up with a self-satisfied grin.

"Look at this."

She held up her long surgical tweezers. Pinched between the tines was an unrecognizable piece of debris.

"What is it?" Wong asked.

"Evidence that the fire was set," Carolyn stated flatly.

I struggled to identify the debris.

"What was it before the fire?" I asked.

"The butt end of a cigarette tucked into a book of matches. Look closer." Wong and I bent down for a closer look. "The matches have burned away," she explained, "but see how the tube of the cigarette is stuck here, under these match stems?"

Now that she'd explained it, the matchbook and cigarette remnants were easy to see. Carolyn carefully placed them into a Ziploc bag.

"Particularly if you're trying to set off a propane tank, you have to be careful not to kill yourself. This is a time-delay device. The smoldering cigarette gives the arsonist about ten to twelve minutes to get away before the matches light. He must have used some kind of accelerant—I'm guessing gasoline-soaked rags or towels. We'll see when the lab tests come back."

I looked at the charred bits in the clear plastic bag, wondering what kind of person would willfully unleash the random, uncontrollable destruction of a fire during a Santa Ana. Carolyn caught my eye and smiled grimly.

"Told you property talks to me."

CHAPTER 12

The waitress slid three hot plates onto the table in one smooth move. Eggs over easy for Loebman. Huevos rancheros for Carolyn. A vegetable omelet for me. Coffee and orange juice all around. Wong had a nine o'clock meeting with Dr. Whitestone, the medical examiner, and hadn't been able to join us.

"I've got to eat fast," Loebman said. "I'm sitting in on the autopsy this morning. Come to think of it, this could be the last meal I feel like eating for a while."

The waitress came around with the coffeepot and took care of our refills. Loebman poured a packet of sugar into his cup and stirred it with his spoon, looking half the time at his coffee, half the time up at me.

"McKenna told me you'd found a couple of kids with this psychic talent you have. Tell us about it."

"The first time it was almost an instantaneous thing. Kevin Woods was his name. That was the case where I found my calling, really. I was reading a newspaper article about a missing boy and an address flashed in front of me. Turns out that's where the kid was. He was badly injured, so it was a really satisfying find. His mom still sends me Christmas cards."

Carolyn stared at me and made a *hunh* sound.

"How'd you do it?" she asked.

"I wish I knew. Things like that have been happening to me my whole life. That's why I got my Ph.D. in parapsychology. I still can't explain it. These days I just try to put it to good use."

"I wish you could do it again now." Loebman tapped his spoon against the side of his cup. "And find the fuckin' asshole who took Matthew Fielding."

Carolyn furrowed her brows at him.

"Hey, easy. You're not taking this one personally, are you?"

"Probably. It hits close to home."

"Why's that?" I asked.

Loebman picked up his cup and stared into his coffee as he told his story.

"My biological father took me from my mom when I was the same age as Matthew, four years old. I didn't see my mom again until I was twelve. Most of that time I was holed away in a trailer park in Canada. The guy was usually off getting wasted. Finally got busted in a drunk driving accident and I was returned to my mom." He took a slug of coffee and swallowed hard. The sadness in his eyes made sense to me now.

Carolyn shook her head. "That sucks, Loebman."

"Robbed me of my childhood." His mood had turned dark and for the next several minutes he just picked at his food.

Carolyn ate with gusto, demolishing her eggs and mopping up the ranchero sauce with a warm flour tortilla.

"So how will you be approaching this case, Elizabeth?" she asked.

"Same way any detective approaches a case. Interviewing relatives, for starters. Wong wants me to look at Frank Fielding's sister, which seems like a logical place to begin."

Loebman looked at his watch, pushed back his half-eaten breakfast, and got up from the table.

"Gotta go. See you guys later." He got up and threw a

ten-dollar bill next to his plate. Carolyn and I wished him a fun morning at the coroner's and watched him walk out. I turned back to Carolyn.

"Loebman told me there are rumors going around about you," I said.

"Is that right."

"Yeah, but he was too decent to repeat them. Anything I should know?"

Carolyn laughed.

"I tend to open my mouth and say unpopular things. What's said about me is anyone's guess but I'm sure it's not flattering."

"Give me an example of something unpopular you said."

"Let's see. How about my first big blunder in the department? This was years ago, when I was a new firefighter. An eager beaver"—she paused to roll her eyes at the stupid pun—"as they liked to call me then."

"What was your big blunder?"

"One night I was sent to check up on a brushfire that had been put out by the day-shift guys. A canyon fire that had burned a lot of mesquite and some big trees. I don't know if you know this or not, but roots can burn underground for up to two weeks after a fire's put out. That's what had happened here, because the fire was starting up again."

The waitress came by and refilled Carolyn's cup. Carolyn kept right on with her story.

"I didn't have any equipment with me, let alone manpower. Being an eager beaver and all, I got on the two-way and reported a rekindle over the air." She chuckled and shook her head. "Just didn't know any better at that point."

"Know any better than what? What'd you do wrong?"

"Honey, everybody in Scannerland heard my report about that rekindle. It made the guys on the day crew look bad, don't you see?"

"No, I don't see."

"Things are changing—a little—but back then you sure

didn't criticize the work of an all-male crew, not if you wanted them to speak to you again."

"You weren't criticizing, you were reporting a fire."

"No, my naïve friend. I was establishing my rep as a callous bull dyke."

When she'd finished pouring our refills and clearing a few plates, the waitress smiled and dropped our check on the table. Carolyn grabbed it, refusing my money.

"If you're going to live up to your rep as a callous bull dyke, you're going to have to stop picking up the tab," I said. "You're being far too gracious."

"Maybe I'm just being controlling."

Somehow I didn't peg Carolyn as a control freak. Maybe I'd change my mind when I got to know her better.

"So what callous thing have you done recently?" I asked as we left the restaurant.

"In the department's eyes? Let's see. I didn't get emotional when one of my crew died in a structure fire. I was sad but I didn't cry. A lot of the guys were sobbing like little kids. They didn't like it that I wasn't crying. They said I was heartless."

"Are you heartless?"

She pulled her keys from her pocket.

"We're born and we die, and I accept that." She pushed the auto unlock button on her key chain. A few feet away, the locks of her Suburban popped up. "I don't think I'm heartless. I think I'm spiritual."

CHAPTER 13

An hour later I waited on the front porch of the Fielding-Cross residence. The property wasn't as opulent as the Fielding estate had been, but what a great location. Built on the hill above San Diego's Old Town, their place looked down on the historic Whaley House, now a museum and reportedly haunted, although I'd never sensed a thing inside. Also in sight were the tourist-filled shops of the Bazaar del Mundo and the La Casa de Estudillo, an Early American mansion, Mexican style. It must have been like living in a postcard.

The door swung open and I saw Debbie Fielding-Cross's resemblance to her brother the moment her face appeared. She had the same watery blue eyes and probably the same poor vision. It was easy to see the transparent outline of contact lenses on her irises in the bright mid-morning light.

"You're the one from the sheriff's?" she asked.

I'd called before coming. It's something I don't ordinarily do, since the element of surprise can often work in my favor. Today I'd erred on the side of courtesy. If this woman was innocent, she'd had enough unwelcome surprises this week.

"I'm so sorry about the loss of your brother," I began.

She slumped her shoulders and lowered her eyes. "Thank you."

"Thank you for agreeing to talk with me this morning. I know it's a horrible time, but time's something we can't waste in an investigation like this."

"I understand. Please come in."

Moving slowly, with the rounded shoulders of someone who's feeling defeated, she led me into a modest living room. She took an overstuffed armchair, leaving me to sit on the sofa.

"Someone else from the sheriff's came here a few days ago. Did I tell you that already?"

"Yes, you mentioned it on the phone."

Wong had given me the highlights of his interview with Debbie Fielding-Cross, so I already knew that she worked as a paralegal for a mid-sized firm downtown, that she'd lived in this house for nine years, and that her husband used to be a firefighter for the San Diego Fire Department. He'd taken early retirement after a work-related injury and now sold insurance to supplement his pension.

The armchair had been designed to swallow its occupant, but she sat forward, with her hands on her knees. I pulled my notebook and pen out of my backpack.

"What a great place to live," I began.

"Everybody says that, but the truth is, there's too much traffic from Old Town and it's too noisy. Plus, this house is too cramped, and the roof leaks."

My eye was drawn to a candle burning on a table in the corner of the room. As I looked closer, I saw there was a framed photograph propped up near the candle. I walked over to have a look.

It was a picture of Matthew, a different shot from the one in the missing persons bulletin. This photo showed him looking not at a birthday cake, but directly into the camera. His face was filled with childlike enthusiasm and seemed to be saying, "Get ready, world, here I come."

"He's a darling little boy," I said. "Were you close to him?"

"I'm very close to him," she answered. "He's like a son to me." She answered in the present tense, as if she knew Matthew was alive. Wishful thinking—or Freudian slip?

"I understand you don't have kids of your own."

"Not yet. We're on a waiting list for an adoption." She spoke slowly, as if she reviewed every word before letting it out. "It's hard for Larry and me because we're sort of a mixed couple. My husband is Mexican-American."

"That makes adopting more difficult?"

"It shouldn't, but it does."

I knew from Wong's notes that Debbie Fielding-Cross was her brother's senior by only three years but she looked older. I tried to figure out why. She wasn't overweight, nor were there any severe wrinkles on her face. But she carried herself like an old woman whose muscles had lost their spark and whose joints had lost their spring. I guessed that grief had something to do with it.

"I'm hopeful about getting Matthew back," I said. "I have a pretty good record of finding lost kids."

"Oh, I know we'll find him. I know in my heart. That's just the way it's going to be." She gave me a look that made me believe her.

"Tell me about his parents. Was Roxanne a good mother?"

"Absolutely. The best. And my brother was a great dad. They were wonderful parents. You'd know that right away if you'd met them."

"I did get to meet them, briefly."

"Then you know"—her voice caught and she paused to contain herself—"what wonderful people they were." Her eyes began to fill with tears.

"Tell me about Matthew."

She snuffed back her tears and put on a brave smile.

"He loves Jell-O pudding. He loves *Scooby-Doo*. You know, the cartoon? And he's into anything about space exploration, planets, the solar system. Four years old and he's completely aware of the cosmos out there. He's a remarkable child. Very bright. He would *never* talk to a stranger.

Whoever took him had to have done it by force."

"When I spoke with Roxanne she said something about her and Frank looking for new household help. There seems to be some confusion about this. The sheriff's detective I'm working with said that the housekeeper is named Elsa Poulson, but I remember Roxanne telling me her name was Bonnie. She said something about her leaving to get a degree or something."

"Bonnie McBride," she said, nodding. "She used to work for Frank's company and then went to help Roxanne, who wanted to spend more time with Matthew and less time managing things at the house. Bonnie was an aspiring actress and went off to become a star. I think she's supposed to be in a production in San Diego somewhere pretty soon." She stopped there, a smirk on her face.

"Do you not like her?"

"I just think she's full of herself, is all."

I watched Frank Fielding's sister carefully as I launched the next question.

"Are you aware that your brother's will names you as the person who gets custody of Matthew in the event of his and Roxanne's death?"

She hung her head, nodding.

"We talked about it when Matthew was born but it was one of those just-in-case things. You never think . . ."

She covered her mouth and started to cry. Deep, heart-wrenching sobs that didn't feel faked. Several times she mumbled "sorry" and tried to stop. I found some tissues and after she'd gone through several the tears let up. I stood to go, leaving one of my cards on the coffee table.

"Will you call me if you think of anything that might be helpful in finding Matthew?"

She looked up at me, her nose red and her eyes swollen.

"Something you think of later could help me find him."

She nodded but didn't speak.

"I'll let myself out."

CHAPTER 14

The wailing riff of an electric guitar reverberated in the hot, dry air as I approached the La Jolla Playhouse. The ticket booth was unmanned and I didn't see anyone as I walked into the narrow lobby. The guitar was louder in here, coming from behind the door to the stage area. I cracked it open and peeked inside. The seats were empty and a group of actors and musicians crowded the stage. As quietly as possible, I slipped into a seat at the rear of the darkened theater.

For acting students with aspirations, the University of California's La Jolla Playhouse was the place to be. Several successful Broadway shows had their beginnings in this theater by the sea. I'd called the UCSD graduate drama program to confirm that Bonnie McBride was a student there, but the dutiful woman on the phone refused to divulge her phone number. After a few dead-end calls, I'd finally thought to contact the playhouse. Bingo. Bonnie was in rehearsal this afternoon.

Several loud claps echoed in the near empty theater.

"Okay, places," the director called. "Come on, people." Tall and thin, he had a dark goatee, close-cropped gray hair, and moved like a cat. A former dancer, I guessed.

A young actor with a mop of curly blond hair strode gracefully to center stage and stood gazing into the empty seats, an imploring look on his face. The director called out a beat.

"And one, two—"

I recognized the composition as soon as the music began. In a clear tenor the mop-topped man made a musical plea for people to see him, hear him, touch him, and feel him. I sat back and enjoyed the theme song from *Tommy*. It had been years since I'd seen the Who rock opera performed live.

As the last verse came to a close, my eyes were drawn to the side of the stage, where a woman in a wild Medusa wig and a rainbow-colored satin negligee waited to come on. Even standing in the wings, her charisma attracted the eye. On the final downbeat she strode into the spotlight and descended on the hapless Tommy, belting out an electrifying solo that proclaimed her to be the Acid Queen.

Tommy cowered as the Acid Queen lifted her silk-stockinged leg, cancan style, and draped it over his shoulder. She dominated with her body as well as her vocal cords, creating a character as powerful as she was hateful. The woman's gift was world-class, and I couldn't imagine that she'd be in San Diego long. When the Acid Queen's number ended, there was a reverent stillness among the cast. The director stepped forward.

"Okay, let's break on a high note. Not bad, Bonnie."

She lingered onstage, talking with the director. I walked down the center aisle, applauding as I approached.

"Amazing performance," I called up to her. "I think you just channeled the original Acid Queen. Pete Townshend would be pleased."

The director said a humble thanks, but Bonnie's smug look told me she knew all about the glory of her talent. Up close her face was beautiful, with oversized cheekbones, big doe eyes, and a sweet, full mouth.

"Thanks," she said without warmth. "Are you from *The Guardian*?"

"No, I'm an investigator for the Sheriff's Department. Working on the Fielding case. Could I ask you a few questions?"

She froze for a moment and looked furtively at the director.

"Sounds important," he said to her. "Take five."

Bonnie motioned me to the side of the stage.

"In my dressing room," she said with a sigh. "This way."

I followed her down a dim hallway. I guessed her height at a full six feet, her weight not a pound over one-forty. Head high, she held her shoulders back above her narrow waist. With her firm hips pumping beneath the shimmering satin costume, she transformed the simple act of walking into an event.

At the end of the hallway she turned into a small, cramped dressing room. Garment racks hung with elaborate costumes took up most of the floor space. Bonnie took a seat on a padded stool. There was no place for me to sit.

"Close the door," she said.

She frowned at the mirror in front of her and pulled off her wig. Beneath the Medusa locks, her real hair was pale blond and cropped short. Without the big hair, her doe eyes looked even bigger. They assessed me coolly, without an iota of Bambi innocence.

"You're a cop?"

"An investigator hired by the cops. I'm looking for Matthew."

"I figured someone would want to talk to me eventually." She studied herself in the mirror. "It was like I just left there and then . . ." She gazed into the mirror with a faraway look on her face. "You know what this keeps reminding me of?"

Her eyes found mine in the reflective glass and I shrugged.

"It's like that night I was on the freeway in a rainstorm. Traffic was really intense. I just wanted to get to my off-ramp in one piece, you know? This idiot got on the freeway and started speeding into the fast lane. Missed my rear bumper by a hair. I heard screaming brakes and looked in my rearview. He'd smashed into another car and both of them were spinning toward the center divider. My hands shook all the way home."

I had no idea where she was going with this. "And this reminds you of what again?" I asked.

She turned from the mirror to look at me directly.

"This whole thing with the Fieldings. It's like that accident all over again. Like I just missed a total fucking catastrophe. Do you mind if I smoke?"

I was surprised that she'd asked. It seemed out of character somehow.

"Go ahead," I said.

She took a cigarette from an open pack on the dressing table, found a lighter and snapped it on.

"It's freaking me out," she said, lighting up.

"How was your relationship with the Fieldings?"

She blew out smoke and made a halting sign with her hand, the lighted cigarette squeezed between her fingers.

"First, let's get something straight. This production goes on in three weeks. I've got a lot riding on this show. I can*not* afford to let anything distract me. I *must* get through this without falling apart. When the glowing reviews come in, then I can fall apart. But not before."

"Right," I said, nodding. I was intrigued by the way she talked about falling apart, as if her very being would disintegrate at the onset of strong emotions. In fact it was her put-together act that would fall apart. Her personality, soul, identity—whatever you wanted to call it—would be solid as ever. Perhaps more so. An actress of all people should know that.

"What?" she asked, sensing that my thoughts had strayed.

"Just thinking." I studied Bonnie's face in the mirror. It was as blank as it was beautiful. "I spoke with Roxanne the day before the fire. She talked about you. Sounded like she was proud of you."

"Really?" Her eyes lit up, hungry for recognition.

"I got the impression she was supportive of your goals."

"She was, she really was."

"And that you left on pretty good terms." Roxanne had said no such thing. I was winging it at this point.

"Good as could be expected under the circumstances."

"You mean the circumstances of her having to find a replacement for you?"

"Yeah."

"So as I understand it, you were their personal assistant, right?"

She nodded yes.

"And how long had you been working for them?"

"Nine, ten months. Something like that. Starcom was getting hot right about the time I graduated from college. I got a job there two summers ago as an administrative assistant. Not really my field, but I needed to pay some debts and the money was too good to pass up. Where else could I make thirty-five grand to be a glorified secretary? Plus, it was a pretty hip place if you had to work nine to five."

"But after nine or ten months you left the company to work for the Fieldings at their home?"

She nodded again.

"Roxanne was needing more help at the house. Frank asked me if I'd be interested in being the family's personal assistant."

"Were you happy working for them at their home?"

"Oh, yeah. It was a supercushy job. I basically got the same salary and benefits, but only worked part-time, running errands, grocery shopping, coordinating with the hired help."

"Which hired help, in particular?"

"There was Elsa, the housekeeper and cook. She and I would coordinate meals and stuff."

"Did Elsa live with the Fieldings?"

"No, they didn't want a live-in. They had a thing about privacy and living a normal life. As if that's possible when you have a jillion dollars. I thought it was pretty ridiculous, myself."

"Where did Elsa live?"

"In Encinitas. Her husband would drop her off and pick her up every day."

"Any other employees at the house?"

"Manny and Joe would come work on the landscaping a few times each week. That was one of my jobs, to keep an eye on the grounds."

"Manny and Joe who?"

"Ramirez. They ran a gardening service called Green Acres."

"How close were you to Matthew?" I watched her carefully now. She shut her large eyes, as if shutting out unwelcome emotions.

"Close." When she opened her eyes, they were moist with tears. "A big part of my job was to watch Matthew when Roxanne had to be somewhere she couldn't take him."

"Do you have any idea who might have taken him?"

"If I did, I would have called the police." She pursed her lips and shook her head. "It could have been anyone, you know? The Fieldings were so well known. Perfect targets for weirdos."

"Maybe the kidnapper was someone close to them."

"Like who?" She screwed up her face. "I don't think so. No one I can think of, anyway."

"Did Matthew ever talk to you about being afraid or wanting to run away?"

A surprised smile crossed her face and she swiveled in her chair to look at me.

"Oh, my God. You don't know, do you?"

"Know what?"

"Matthew didn't talk."

The news stunned me and my mind rushed backward, trying to figure out how I'd missed this vital piece of information.

"Was he deaf?" I asked.

"No, he just didn't speak."

I thought back to my conversation with Roxanne Fielding.

"Wait a minute," I said. "His mom told me she could hear him talking to himself in the woods the morning he disappeared."

Bonnie pointed with the long, deep red nail of her index finger.

"Talking to *himself*. He was what they called a selective mute. He'd speak in a real quiet voice to his mom, sometimes to his dad. But he never talked to anyone else, ever."

"I don't think the Fieldings told the police about this."

"That doesn't surprise me a bit. They were in total denial about it. 'He'll grow out of it,' and all that."

Through the closed door I could hear the muffled sound of music starting up in the stage area.

"Talk about irony," I said.

"What?"

"Matthew Fielding was a selective mute and here you are, starring in a rock opera about a deaf, dumb, and blind kid."

"Matthew was none of those things," she said, bristling. "He just didn't talk. Frank was great but he worked too hard. When he was stressed out, there was a lot of tension in the house. I used to think maybe Matthew was reacting to that."

A voice called from the hallway.

"Break's over, Bonnie. Everybody's waiting."

She picked up the Medusa wig and stuffed her blond wisps back inside.

"I'd like to keep chatting, but—" She rose to go.

"You gotta go." I stepped aside for her to pass. "I'm going to leave my card on your dresser here."

She gave me a backward glance.

"Fine."

"Call me if you think of anything else. And by all means, break a leg."

CHAPTER 15

Hang Up and Drive.

I'd only seen the bumper sticker once, but its common sense had shamed me into pulling over when I needed to make a call. I took the next off-ramp and found a shady spot in a strip-mall parking lot. Shade or no shade, the heat was stifling as soon as the air conditioner was shut off. I reached Loebman on his cell phone.

"Bruce, it's Elizabeth. Got a hot tip for you."

"What's that?" Never really a lighthearted guy, Loebman sounded positively morose this afternoon.

"The kid doesn't talk."

"What?"

"I tracked down Bonnie McBride, the Fieldings' former personal assistant. She's pretty much living at the La Jolla Playhouse, rehearsing for a show. Get this—she told me that Matthew was a mute."

"If he was, that's the first time I've heard it." He paused. "I kind of doubt it. The parents would've told us."

"They were in denial. I guess he was what they call a selective mute. He did talk to his parents. Just nobody else."

There was silence as Loebman gave it some thought.

"Not sure what this means," he said at last.

"If Matthew wandered off by himself, it means he can't ask for help. Even three-year-olds have been known to pick up the phone and dial 911. But if the kid can't talk, that's not an option. What are you up to? You sound like you've just been to a funeral."

"Close. I'm at the ME's office. Couriered some dental records down here. The autopsy went almost six hours. Forensic dentist confirmed that the bodies in the car were Frank and Roxanne Fielding."

I shuddered. I had a high threshold for gore, but drew the line at burned bodies.

"No way you could tell otherwise. They were completely black. No fingers, no faces. Eyes melted shut, noses gone. Their mouths were just holes. It was awful."

"Did the autopsy reveal anything that might be useful to us?"

"Maybe. We know they were alive when the car caught fire. Both bodies were in pugilistic attitude. You know what that is?"

"Something about the body being drawn into a boxing pose."

"Yeah. When the large muscles fry, they contract. If they'd been dead, there would've been more rigor, less contraction." He didn't sound well.

"You okay?"

"I've seen a lot of autopsies but this is as close as I've come to losing my lunch. How about you? Any ESP revelations? We could use some leads here."

I was pursuing a lead as we spoke—Pam Jaffer, a name Randy Twain had given me, the Starcom VP with whom Frank Fielding had allegedly had an affair. But I wasn't going to throw her to the cops without checking it out first.

"I just gave you Bonnie McBride," I said.

"I was thinking more like places we can look for the kid."

"I'm working on that. I can't dial it up, Bruce. Sorry."

"We got a hall pass from the judge about an hour ago to search Fielding's office at Starcom. Wong and another detective are there now, interviewing employees."

Great criminologists think alike. I had just pulled off the I-5 in the heart of Sorrento Valley and wasn't more than three hundred yards from Starcom. The corporate compound overlooked the edge of a deep, sage-covered canyon, its familiar logo in full view of eight busy lanes of freeway traffic.

"Maybe I'll stop in and say hello to Wong. I'm in the neighborhood."

"Okay. Thanks for the McBride tip. Talk to you later."

Starcom cut an impressive sight. More like a corporate village than a corporation, its buildings covered several rolling acres. As I pulled into the visitor parking area, I saw the Channel Three news van stationed near the entrance. Official word of Fielding's death had gone out, so the news team was probably getting the company's reaction. The last thing I wanted to do was run into Randy Twain or Jane Sharpe and her intrusive camera. I began scheming ways to get into the building via the back route.

I found the employee parking lot and parked as far back as possible. Passing by a loading dock, I walked to the rear of the main building. I peered between the rear bumpers of countless employee vehicles in my search for a back entrance and cursed when my quest ended in a retaining wall. I stood on tiptoes and peeked over the top. Just beyond the wall was a back door into the building. I was scheming how to scale the wall when I felt eyes on me. Trying my best to look nonchalant, I turned around.

Several yards away someone had stepped onto the loading dock. The person had short, unisex-cropped hair and the build was too androgynous for me to determine the gender. I could make out jeans, an earth-color T-shirt, and one of those black back supports wrapped around the person's waist. Whoever it was leaned against the iron railing, smoking a cigarette.

"You gonna make a break for it?" The laughter was deep and distinctly female.

"I was trying to find my way back into the building," I called back.

"Why? That way lies madness." Again the laugh.

I walked toward the loading dock and looked up into a face deeply, though not unpleasantly, lined from sun exposure.

"Where am I?" I asked.

"Hell," she replied flatly. "This"—she gestured with her cigarette toward a half-open aluminum roll-up door—"is the shipping and receiving department. You'd be surprised how many packages we get here in hell." She didn't smile when she said it, giving the impression that on some level, she believed the place to be damned.

"Can I find Pam Jaffer in hell?" I asked.

"The Vice Demon of Misinformation? You can't miss her. Her insidious influence reaches everywhere." She cackled, dropping her half-smoked cigarette and grinding it out. "Pam Jaffer's in the administration building. Receptionist will give you directions."

"I was hoping to avoid the receptionist."

"I see." She smiled conspiratorially, as if the idea of breaching protocol pleased her. "Follow me."

She pushed against the bottom of the aluminum door and it rolled all the way up with a banging noise. I followed her through a receiving bay stacked high with boxes and mailing machines. When we reached the far side of the bay, she opened a door that led into the Starcom complex.

"Thanks so much. I'm Elizabeth, by the way. To whom do I owe my gratitude?"

"I'm Abby."

The name conjured up a monastery filled with monks or nuns. Ironic that she considered her workplace hell. Then again, didn't everybody?

"This place will make you feel like a rat in a maze. Come on, this way."

I saw what she meant. Several cement paths fanned out from the inner courtyard. She walked me along the one on the far left, which led to a building at the canyon's edge.

This was the edifice people saw from the I-5, with its Starcom logo and huge plate-glass windows facing west toward the ocean. The woman pointed to the southwest corner of the building. "Go through the double doors, take the elevator to the top floor, and look for Suite 111."

The door to Suite 111 was standing open when I arrived.

"Pam Jaffer?"

The room was so bright from the sun pouring through the large plate-glass window that I had to squint my eyes. When they adjusted for contrast I made out a handsome woman sitting behind a terribly clean desk. Fair-complected and strong-boned, she bore a striking resemblance to the late Roxanne Fielding.

"Yes." In one melodious syllable, her voice communicated intelligence and good breeding. "And you are . . . ?"

I did something I rarely do. I flashed my badge. It's a cheesy little silver-toned shield I ordered for $37.50 out of a Gall's catalog, but it looks impressive in its black leather case.

"Investigator for the Sheriff's Department." I stretched the truth, hoping it wouldn't snap. People can get testy about that impersonating-an-officer taboo. "My name is Elizabeth Chase."

"I'm sorry," she said pleasantly. "You've been misdirected. The other detectives are in the conference room." She stood up. "I'm on my way to a board meeting in that part of the building. I'll walk you over."

I was about to tell her that I wanted to talk with her, not the sheriff's detectives, when I realized this was perfect. I could do a stealth interview as we walked.

"Thank you," I said.

There was something regal in her manner and I understood why the shipping clerk might mock her. I stepped aside as she passed by to lead me down the hallway. From close up I could see the exhaustion behind her perfectly painted face. I walked slightly to the rear of her, just at the edge of her peripheral vision.

"I can only imagine what a tragedy like this does to a company," I said.

"Not just the company. It's a very personal loss for a lot of us."

"Were you a close friend of the Fieldings?" I tried to keep the question casual sounding.

"For many years."

"Did you know the little boy?"

She nodded.

"Maybe you could clarify something for me. I've heard that Matthew was a mute. Do you know if he spoke at all?"

"What a peculiar question."

"I have a good reason for asking."

She stopped to think about it. She looked stunning in her pale blue suit; a woman to the House of Chanel born.

"I . . . don't know. I only saw him a few times. I don't recall ever hearing him say anything, now that you mention it."

"Did his mother ever talk to you about it?" Pam Jaffer was rumored to have been Frank Fielding's mistress, so I watched closely for her reaction.

"No. I didn't know Roxanne very well."

"But you socialized with the family?" I tried to keep my tone light but her guard went up.

"Socialized in the way that business associates do. We weren't close in a personal sense."

"Who'll be heading up the company now that Frank Fielding is gone?"

"That's what this meeting is about. Our corporate attorney is handling things for the time being."

"That's Larry Gandle, right?"

She nodded yes.

"We'll be holding a press conference soon."

"You think it's likely Gandle will stay on as president?"

"I really can't say." We had walked halfway to the end of the hall and were passing a pair of wooden double doors. As we walked by, a man carrying a sheaf of papers came through the doors and zeroed in on Pamela.

"I need five minutes with you to go over these before we start." His voice was urgent.

She looked to me apologetically. "The executive suite is at the end of the hall. You'll find the other detectives in there. I'm sorry, you'll have to excuse me."

As soon as she was out of sight I turned back and headed for the exit. I wasn't ready to talk to Wong yet. Something was urging me to look around on my own. I went down the elevator and walked out of the lobby.

Outside, sunglasses were a must. I donned my shades and followed an urge to take the cement sidewalk that circled around to the back of the building. A three-foot hedge lined the sidewalk like a guard rail. Beyond the crop-topped hedge, a half-acre of open space filled with sagebrush and native grasses stretched to the edge of the canyon. Starcom dominated the acreage along the canyon, commanding a sweeping view of Sorrento Valley. Its nearest neighbor was a multistory apartment building to the east.

I looked back at the glass-walled building. Hoping I wasn't being watched, I hopped over the hedge and walked to the edge of the canyon. I found a smooth patch of ground and had a seat. The freeway below was pure noise, a muffled jet perennially taking off. I remembered a time when traffic was intermittent on this stretch of Interstate-5. Relatively speaking, not so long ago. The noise of the cars joined with the rushing of the hot wind blowing up the canyon.

"Pay attention to the energy around you."

It was Sequoia's voice, clear as a bell. I turned around, half-expecting to see my shaman friend. There was no one nearby, but in the distance I saw a man walking alongside the Starcom building. He spotted me and started to walk in my direction. It wasn't until he reached the hedge that I realized who it was.

"Hey," he called, "it's you!"

CHAPTER 16

Wearing pressed beige chinos, pricey leather loafers, and a navy blue blazer, Randy Twain stepped over the hedge and picked his way through the scrubby open space to the edge of the canyon, where I sat with my arms wrapped around my knees. He stumbled slightly on some uneven ground but never lost his live-at-five smile.

"What are you doing out here all alone?" He beamed down at me, hands on hips.

In truth I'd been trying to decide whether I'd imagined Sequoia's "pay attention" or if I'd heard his voice telepathically. I was pretty sure it was the latter.

"At the moment I'm listening to the delightful roar of the freeway." I frowned at his tailored attire. "You're all dressed up."

"You know what they say. Clothes make the man. Naked people have little or no influence on society." When he saw my frown he added, "My famous namesake said that."

"Don't you have a news show to broadcast?"

"I've done my taping for the day. It's all up to the news editor from here." He looked over the canyon's edge, as if expecting to see something exceptional down below. "Seriously, what are you doing out here?"

"Listening, like I said."

"Listening," he scoffed. "I can barely hear myself think this close to the freeway. What a racket." He squinted up at the sky. "This sun's hot as hell. Come on, let's go get a drink. I'll give you the inside scoop on how Starcom's dealing with the loss of Frank Fielding."

I'd been on the verge of an insight before Twain had interrupted me.

"Thanks, but not now. Maybe another time. I'm thinking." I turned back toward the freeway and rested my chin on my knees. Twain didn't move a muscle. I could feel his eyes on the back of my head.

"Thinking about the Fieldings?" he asked. "Or are you still pretending you're not on the case?"

I turned around and our eyes locked. He knew damn well I didn't want to talk, but he stood his ground, smiling away.

"I don't know," I replied. "Are you still pretending it's your business?"

I'd said it with a smile to soften the blow, but still he grabbed at an imaginary wound in his chest.

"Ooo, ouch. Next time give me a prestrike warning, will ya? You're hurting me."

Twain had been on the air in San Diego long enough that I knew he had to be pushing forty, but I would never have guessed it from his firm, glowing skin and thick hair. His dimples were adorable, no argument there. It was the way he knew that his dimples were adorable, and exploited them, that made me suspicious.

"Sorry," I said.

He waved it off.

"I was kidding. No harm done. I have one of those Teflon egos. You have to, in this business."

From below us, the freeway noise seemed to surge, though it didn't seem possible that any more cars could cram onto the lanes.

"Come on," he said. "There's a Jamba Juice right up the street. Best smoothies in the world. My treat. Business aside. Friend to friend."

I lifted my sunglasses off my nose and gave him a dubious look.

"If you're such a friend, how come you didn't tell me that the Fielding child was a mute?"

"What?"

"Matthew Fielding didn't talk. Last night on the phone you said you did a profile on the Fieldings. How come you didn't mention Matthew's muteness when I asked you what he was like?"

I waited for his reply but he didn't have an instant answer. The sky was the kind of bright that screams retina damage. I slid my sunglasses back into place.

"I didn't mention it because I didn't know about it," he said. "I'll have to think back." A sly smile crossed his face. " 'Course, I'll remember better over a blueberry smoothie."

I felt a tingle on my shoulders and noticed that my arms were getting red in spite of a heavy layer of sunscreen. A signal to go. As I started to rise, Twain took my arm and gave me a hand up. He smelled as fresh as he looked.

"Thanks." I smiled at him sweetly. "Has anybody ever told you you're a relentless pest?"

"All the time. It's right there in my job description. 'Shall make himself a relentless pest, and other duties as assigned.' "

"In that case, you deserve a raise."

Twain leaned his elbows on the pale wood bar and studied the blackboard on the wall, where a boggling array of power drinks and smoothies were described in colored chalk. Behind the juice bar, a woman was pouring a pastel orange liquid from a blender into two tall glasses. A noisy air conditioner was putting up a full-time defense against the heat, so our arrival had gone unnoticed. When she turned around and saw us, her eyes lit up.

"Hey!" she said. "Aren't you Randy Twain?"

Randy allowed that he was and when she told him she'd been his loyal viewer for many years, he mumbled his humble thanks. We placed an order for a pair of blueberry smoothies—mine with extra protein powder—and found a table within blowing distance of the air conditioner.

"Ever get tired of being recognized?" I asked.

He hiked his shoulders.

"Comes with the job. I've been working in television in this town for over fifteen years now." He shook his head, as if he didn't quite believe the figure. "Jesus," he mumbled under his breath.

"So everybody knows you."

"And vice versa. Rick Wong, for example. I've known Rick since the day he started in the Sheriff's Department. We met covering a plane-crash story."

I felt whatever cover I had slipping away.

"We had a long talk about the fire yesterday. He confirmed that you're an investigator on the Fielding case."

"You could have said something."

"Yeah, but then I wouldn't have the pleasure of watching you guard your secret employment so ferociously."

The woman behind the counter called out that our order was ready. Randy jumped up and brought our smoothies back to the table. He watched me take my first sip and smiled.

"This place was a good idea, wasn't it?"

"Yeah. I guess."

He studied me closely, suppressing a smile, as if I'd suddenly broken out in purple polka dots.

"What?" I asked.

"So you're a psychic detective, huh? I gotta tell you, Elizabeth, I don't believe in the whole psychic thing. Not one tiny bit. No offense."

"None taken." I smiled. It was the first genuine thing I'd heard him say. "I wouldn't believe in this stuff either if I didn't keep having these experiences."

"Like what? Give me an example. A recent one."

"Recent. Okay, here you go. I was outside fixing a win-

dow when I heard my mom's voice calling, 'My God.' She
lives fifteen miles away, but at that minute I knew she was
in trouble. I tried to call my parents' house and didn't get
an answer. That's what got me over to the fire yesterday."

He finishing sipping from his straw and waved a dis-
missive hand.

"That one's easy to explain. Your mom was on your
mind. You probably call her all the time but this one time
she happened to be in trouble. You're just choosing to forget all the other times you call her and nothing's going on."

I'd heard my mother's voice out loud, not in my head,
but I had no desire to argue. Clairaudience—hearing things
you couldn't possibly hear—sounds crazy until it happens
to you. I understood Twain's point of view, which was
entirely logical. Incorrect, but logical.

"So how'd you get into the business of being a psychic
detective?"

I repeated the story I'd told to Bruce Loebman and Carolyn Arnold at breakfast this morning, the one about reading an article in the paper about a missing boy and seeing
the address flash in front of my eyes.

Twain's dimples reappeared.

"How convenient. Why don't you just find the Fielding
kid that way?"

"Wish I could, but I can't call up that kind of thing on
command. The insights happen when they happen."

"Maybe you're not a very good psychic."

"Maybe. But most people who claim to be able to control their psychic ability are full of shit. You're better off
being a skeptic, really, with so many charlatans out there."

Some new customers walked into the bar, bringing a
wave of hot air in with them. Twain slid his sunglasses
back on.

"Why are you so secretive?" he asked. "You're not embarrassed about being a psychic, are you?"

"No. It's just that I want to stay undercover. I can be
more effective if people don't recognize me. So can I ask
you a favor?"

"Name it, psychic girl."

"Please don't divulge my involvement. On or off the air. It'll put me at a serious disadvantage."

"Hey, the public has a right to know what crimes have been committed and what's being done about them. Are you asking me to suppress information?" There was playful innuendo in his tone.

"No, I'm just asking you to leave out a nonessential part of your story."

"All right. For now, anyway."

There was an outbreak of enthusiastic shouting as the new customers, a man and two kids, debated which flavor of yogurt cones to order. One of the kids was a little boy about Matthew's age.

"How much time did you spend with the Fieldings when you were taping that profile?" I asked.

"Couple of hours, at least."

"And Matthew Fielding never said a word during that time?"

"Not that I remember."

"Can I get a copy of that show?"

"Yeah, sure." He looked at his watch. "Why don't you come down to the station with me? I'll dig out the videotape for you."

"How very helpful of you." I wondered why he was being so accommodating. He picked right up on my suspiciousness.

"You rescued our star photographer from the flames of hell yesterday, remember? The station owes you one. Really."

CHAPTER 17

Twain drove a forest-green Jaguar. It was an older model than the Fieldings' Jag, but as I buckled my seat belt and studied the elegant dashboard, I couldn't help thinking that this was similar to the setting in which they'd died.

"What happened to your Taurus? Did you lose it in the fire?"

"I wish. That piece of crap is like the cockroach species. Ugly, annoying, and impossible to get rid of. The Taurus is back at the station. This is my personal car."

"Nice ride," I said.

Twain shifted into reverse and swiveled in his seat to back out.

"Thanks to my rich uncle."

"The one you named your dog after because he drinks out of the toilet?"

"No," he said with a smile, "that's Uncle Lou, on my mom's side of the family." He looked pleased that I'd remembered. "I got the Jag from Uncle Albert, on Dad's side. Albert believes it's bad luck to keep a car more than three years. Sold this to me for an embarrassing price."

"Lucky you."

By now it was heading toward five o'clock. The wind

had been building all day and seemed to be gaining in strength as the sun went down. A tumbleweed blew across the street as we made our way to the interstate. I hadn't seen one of the round, bleached-out plants for years, certainly not inside the city limits. I wondered how far it had tumbled. When we reached the freeway, traffic was backed up like a slow-moving drain.

We joined the surge of cars and crept south, the hot wind blowing bits of trash and debris across the lanes. With radiators taxed beyond capacity, cars fell like wounded soldiers along the emergency lane.

"Mind if we just chill and listen to music?" Twain turned the air conditioner up to high and pushed a CD into the console.

"Not at all."

He turned on the stereo and we were serenaded by Sting, bemoaning his fate as the King of Pain. Classic album but what I liked most about it was the title: *Synchronicity.*

We got off the freeway in Kearny Mesa and wound through an industrial area to the Channel Three station. Twain turned the Jaguar into an unmarked driveway. We passed through an electronic gate—this one opened without a hitch—and drove to the very end of the employee parking lot, which was mostly empty. He looked across the seat and smiled.

"I know we're out in the Timbuktu of the parking lot here, but I wanted to show you something."

He pulled into a space at the far end of the lot next to the only other car in sight, a dirty Ford Explorer.

"This is the SUV Jane had to abandon at the Rancho Santa Fe fire," he said as he cut the engine. "Check it out."

As soon as I got out of the car, I had to tuck my hair under my collar to keep it from tangling in the wind. Ordinarily the wind died down as evening approached, but not today. I walked around the Explorer. The right-side bumper drooped like melted wax. The paint on the entire right side was bubbled and black.

I muttered an *oh-my-God* and gawked at the car.

"Don't worry," he said cheerfully. "Jane gets a new one. Just thought you might want to see why she needed a ride yesterday."

The car seemed to carry the essence of that fire, and for a moment I was back in the smoke, hot wind, and flying embers. I shuddered at the memory. When I looked up, Twain was motioning me to follow him into the station through a rear door.

We entered a long hallway, passing several friendly staffers who said hi to me and greeted Twain by name. We walked across the wide-open newsroom, an area buzzing with last-minute prebroadcast activity. Twain turned into a dark, closetlike room against the far wall. I followed and stepped into what felt like a cave.

"Welcome to the edit bay. Have a seat."

We were standing in a darkened eight-foot-square cube, its slate-gray walls making it appear even smaller. Two television monitors were mounted above a desk with two chairs. Dozens of tapes were lined up vertically along the wall shelves. A strip of mini halogen track lights gave the room a dim glow.

"I was watching the archive copy of the Fielding profile yesterday, so I know it's in here somewhere. We can watch the newscast while I look for it. See how badly they butchered my story today. Have a seat."

Twain plopped into one of the chairs and rolled aside to make room for me. I took the remaining chair. Two half-full coffee mugs sat on a desktop littered with empty candy wrappers. Coffee rings stained the desk and several of the wrappers had fallen to the floor. A sign on the wall read: Please, No Food or Drink.

Twain switched on the right monitor. Connie Jorgensen and Bill Bainsley, the five-o'clock anchors, were delivering the news.

"I'm going to keep the volume down until my story comes on. That way I don't have to listen to Butthead." He muted the set and began skimming the spines of the videotapes along the shelves.

"Butthead?"

"Bainsley," he clarified. "Our overpaid anchor."

"Is that any way to address your esteemed colleague?"

Twain paused in his search and turned to watch Bainsley on the monitor.

"I was being literal. That really is his butt, cosmetically enhanced to look like a head. But it's a butt, trust me." He turned back to the videotapes. "I *know* that Fielding profile is in here somewhere because I was just looking at it last night."

Keeping an eye on the muted newscast, I saw the Starcom logo appear in the graphic box above Connie Jorgensen's head.

"I think this is your story."

Twain was on television, standing in front of the Starcom headquarters. The Starcom logo was prominent on the building visible behind his right shoulder. Twain unmuted the set.

". . . have beleaguered this high-flying technology company. Over the past several months, the company's stock value has fluctuated dramatically in response to overseas markets. Starcom was dealt yet another blow when its founder and president, Frank Fielding, perished with his wife in a fire at their Rancho Santa Fe home yesterday. The mood today at Starcom headquarters in Sorrento Valley is somber."

The camera cut to an interview with a female employee who described in a roundabout way that the company was in a state of shock. The camera cut again, this time to a man wearing a black shirt under a black jacket.

"This is Gandle, the guy I was telling you about," Twain said, making me miss the first half of the man's statement.

". . . so while we're deeply saddened by this tragic loss, there won't be any disruption in day-to-day operations."

The camera cut back to the anchor desk. The newscaster I would forevermore think of as Butthead was on to the next story. Twain muted the set again.

"Damn."

"What?"

"They cut the most pertinent part of Gandle's interview. He's the acting president, you know. He was practically glowing when he described his bold plan for the future. You could see the glee in his eyes. But what does my editor do? Fluffs the story with throwaway remarks by supposedly grieving employees. Christ." He frowned at me. "What was your impression of Larry Gandle?"

Before I could answer, a redheaded man popped his head into the edit bay.

"Hey, Randy. Great soap opera. Nice work."

"Fuck you, Cliff," Twain replied good-naturedly. The man ducked out, his laughter trailing behind.

"There wasn't enough on Gandle for me to get an impression," I said when we were alone again.

"That sucks. I had that bastard, right on camera. My producer's as bad as my editor. She wouldn't know a hot issue if it ripped off her shirt and breathed fire on her chest. My job today? Get emotional reactions to Fielding's death. The weepier the better."

"You sound frustrated."

"I'm not frustrated. I just feel like a pimp, is all."

"You're not long for this place, are you?"

He looked at me with surprise.

"Maybe you're psychic after all. Or is it that obvious?"

"It's pretty obvious." I said it to the back of Twain's head. He was combing the shelves again, looking for the videotape.

"Nah, I'll never leave. But I'm tempted. I got an offer to do a goofy guest show thing on the East Coast. I'd actually get to be funny on camera. Do you know how sick and tired I am of making that serious news reporter face? I'm a wild and crazy guy, man. It's like I committed some horrible crime in a past life and now I'm condemned to deliver unfunny news."

"I thought you didn't believe in stuff like past lives."

"I don't. I was being ironical."

"So why not take the job back East?"

"Short answer? Fear of failure. Hey—here's something you might want a copy of." He passed me a videotape. The label said, "RSF Fire, 13:22:10:5."

"This is the video Jane shot yesterday?"

He nodded.

"It's a dupe. Keep it. I gave a copy to Rick Wong, too. Evidence in a criminal case."

"I take it this is the date," I said, pointing to the label. "But what do these other numbers mean?"

"Those are the numbers that appear on the master tape's window burn, which you'll see on your screen. They correspond to the time. Supposed to, anyway."

The tape began at 1:22 P.M. Just a little over an hour after my father and I had left the Fieldings'.

"How long were you guys taping at the bottom of the Fieldings' driveway?

"You mean after you gave me the brush-off?"

"Yeah."

"I don't know. Twenty minutes, maybe."

"Did you notice anyone in the area?"

"Rick Wong grilled me on this already. No, I don't remember anyone. Just cars passing on the road once in a while." He continued to rummage on the shelves. "Hey, finally." He held up a tape. "The Fielding profile." He popped it into the tape player. "Let me just make sure it's all here."

Twain fast-forwarded through the first several minutes and I got a sense of the piece as the frames sped by. Frank Fielding's childhood and education. The creation of Starcom. The building of the Sorrento Valley headquarters. The manufacturing of computer parts and cell phones. The assembling of the corporate team. I caught a glimpse of a familiar face.

"Stop the tape. Back up a little."

He rewound the tape. When Pamela Jaffer came on the screen, I told him to pause it.

"Is that the woman Frank Fielding was supposedly sleeping with?" I asked.

"One of them, yeah. Pam Jaffer. If you believe the rumors, he was sleeping with several employees. Don't even remember where I heard the one about Pam."

I studied Pam Jaffer's face, frozen on the monitor.

"I interviewed Pam today and tried to see her with Frank. It didn't feel right. There may be some envy about her position with the company. Jealous tongues wag. But what other employees was he linked to romantically?"

He punched fast-forward again.

"Didn't pay attention. I thought Fielding seemed pretty devoted to his wife. Then again, he was a man, and men can be dogs."

On the screen I recognized the Fieldings' Rancho Santa Fe estate before it had been burned down.

"Slow it down. I want to see this."

Twain slowed the tape to regular speed. Frank and Roxanne Fielding were playing crochet on the lawn as Matthew looked on. The day was bright and windless; the drooping branches of the eucalyptus trees in the background were motionless. Looking happy and proud, Frank and Roxanne called to Matthew. The camera panned to the child. He turned toward the lens, clutching something against his chest. It was his beloved stuffed animal, Scooby-Doo.

CHAPTER 18

I felt as if I were driving on the moon. On all sides, the terrain was an appalling ash gray. Gone were the hundred-year-old trees and thick hedges that had given Rancho Santa Fe its character. Decades of imported Colorado River water had created a false Eden here that Nature never intended. Now the original desert was laid bare. Most of the sprawling estates had been saved by firefighters, but the lush landscaping had been vaporized in a matter of hours. The houses stood exposed, banished from Eden.

"You're awfully quiet, Mr. Poe."

The bird hadn't said a word since I'd packed him into the car. Late this afternoon my parents had returned to their house. Mom had called to say that it wouldn't feel like home until I could return her beloved cockatoo. I'd jumped at the chance. Not because I didn't enjoy the bird. Seeing my folks living like castaways and sleeping on cots at a high school gym had unsettled me. I had a childish desire to see that my world was in order and things were back to normal.

Things weren't normal, and wouldn't be for a while. I stared at the fire-ravaged land whizzing by. If I'd harbored any wishful thinking that Matthew Fielding was hiding out here somewhere, that notion was gone. In the smoldering aftermath of the fire, there was no place left to hide.

Muscles tense, I accelerated up the last hill toward my parents' house. I said a silent prayer of gratitude when their hilltop home came into view. The orange grove down below looked as if it had taken the blast of a giant blowtorch, but the fire-resistant ice plant covering the hillside had protected the house. The oleanders lining the driveway were still intact, but as I tunneled through them I saw that their dark green leaves were blanched with ash.

I got out of the truck and heard somebody splashing in the swimming pool out back. Carrying Mr. Poe in his box, I walked around to the backyard. My father was standing at the side of the pool holding the long-handled net used to skim bugs and leaves from the surface of the water.

"Hey, Dad."

He looked up with a vexed expression.

"You do the craziest things in a panic. For some cockamamie reason I tossed my golf clubs into the pool before we evacuated yesterday. I couldn't bear the idea of them melting." He shook his head. "Now they're probably going to rust."

I looked into the pool and saw a green golf bag sitting on the bottom near the shallow end. "Golf clubs can be replaced. How's that burn on your arm?"

"Today it hurts like hell, to be perfectly frank."

I put Mr. Poe's box on the patio table and walked to the edge of the terrace, taking in the condition of the valley.

"Oh, man."

The view had been ruined. The valley was charred black and the trees that had once softened the horizon had burned to jagged skeletons. The people on the neighboring hillside had lost their horse barn; only part of the corral fencing was still standing. The sun had gone down, and in the dusky light the moonscape effect was even more pronounced.

Dad gave up on his golf clubs and joined me in looking over the scorched terrain.

"I talked to Detective Wong for quite a while today. That poor woman was burned alive, did you know that?" There was a bitterness in his voice I'd never heard before.

"Yeah, Dad, I knew that. Her husband was, too."

"The detective said that fire was set deliberately."

"I know. I was there this morning when the arson investigator found the ignition device."

"Son of a bitch." My father rarely expressed emotions this raw. "I've lost patients before. A couple of them during surgery. But I've never had a patient murdered." He looked at me with a piercing gaze.

I didn't know what to say. He was leaning on me, I realized, wanting me to make some kind of sense of it for him. The role reversal made me feel awkward.

"The detective said something about you smelling smoke when you were at the Fieldings' yesterday. Did you see this coming?"

"No, not this. If I had, I would have done something to prevent it."

"Of course you would have." He put his hands in his pockets and glared at the ash-covered land. The Santa Ana blew locks of his fine gray hair up off his head, revealing his suntanned scalp.

"What else did Wong talk to you about?"

"He asked me about Mrs. Fielding's medical condition when I examined her at the house yesterday. I told him she was exhausted and probably under the influence of alcohol."

"Anything else?"

"He also asked if I'd seen anyone on my way in, which I hadn't. Just your truck, that cop's car, and the news van." He walked back to the pool and scowled again at the submerged golf clubs.

"Do you want me to get those out of there, Dad?"

"But you're not wearing a bathing suit."

"I'll fish them out. Just a sec."

I walked to the side of the yard and down the hill to what Mom liked to call the garden depot. It was a wooden shelter—too well designed to be called a mere toolshed, although it did house tools—that was painted to blend with its surroundings. The garden depot also housed a large green tank. The tank was one of those monuments from my childhood that had always been there. I'd never had reason to question what it was, so I'd never thought about it before. For the first time I realized it must be propane.

I grabbed a long-handled hoe and hurried back up to the terrace.

"You're going to fish the clubs out with that thing?" Dad looked dubious.

"Why not? At least you had the good sense to dump them in the shallow end."

"Good sense had nothing to do with it." He laughed at himself while I maneuvered the hoe. I finally managed to hook the hoe blade under the handle of the golf bag. I dragged the golf clubs along the bottom of the pool and up the steps, feeling as if I were pulling in an eighty-pound albacore.

"There you are." I hauled the soaking golf bag over the lip of the pool and dumped it at his feet.

"You got them out." We turned at the sound of Mom's voice.

"Hey, Mom. I brought Mr. Poe home. He's sitting on the table there."

"Thanks, honey." She found the box and cooed to the bird through the holes in the top. She looked up with a frown. "I hope he'll be okay here. I might have been too hasty in wanting him back. It's not the greatest environment to breathe in with all this ash. Wouldn't be so bad if the wind would just die down."

"You want, I can keep him a few more days."

"Let's see how he does."

Leaving his golf clubs to drip-dry, Dad followed Mom and me into the house through the back door. The kitchen was a sight. The countertops were filled with cartons and jars and a couple of large half-filled trash bags sat on the floor.

"The power was out for a long time," Mom explained. "I'm having to toss out most of what we had in the fridge. We're having Chinese delivered for dinner."

"They deliver out here in Rancho?"

"For a price." Dad rolled his eyes and turned back to the window, looking out toward the Fieldings' place again. "Now I regret not knowing them better," he said.

"Randy Twain gave me a profile on the Fieldings that ran on *Hello, San Diego* a while back. Want to see it?"

"Why would he give you that?" Dad was instantly suspicious.

"He knows I'm investigating the case and I think he's genuinely rooting for me to find the boy." I reached for my canvas bag, grabbed a tape, and popped it into the VCR.

Randy Twain appeared on camera. In the background, a strong wind was blowing through a eucalyptus forest. Behind him was the iron gate of the Fielding estate, an image that made me shiver.

". . . child has been missing since last Wednesday, when he disappeared from the property. Police report no breaks in the case but there's a lot of activity at the Fielding home this morning as investigators come and go."

We were seeing what Randy Twain and Jane Sharpe had been taping yesterday morning at the Fieldings'.

"Oops. Wrong tape. Sorry." I pushed the stop button and got up to change tapes.

"No, wait. I want to see that," Mom said.

"Me, too," said Dad.

I punched it on again. This was the uncut master tape, complete with a window burn marking the time in the upper right-hand corner. There wasn't much left to see. Twain finished his update and the camera panned from the grounds of the Fielding estate around to the road. The segment ended with a slow dissolve. Just as the picture began to go out of focus, a white Fire Department Bronco drove by.

"Whoa." I hit the stop button. "Let's see that again."

I rewound the tape, hit play, and paused it on the truck. "Well, isn't this interesting. That looks like the guy who was blocking Camino del Norte yesterday morning."

Mom and Dad weren't getting it, and looked at me blankly.

"Look at the time." I pointed to the right-hand corner of the set. "This was taped at ten thirty-eight. The fire was estimated to have started at around one. What's he doing here now, before the fire breaks out?" I scrambled to remember the name of the firefighter who'd been manning the roadblock in his Bronco. Something with a Z. Zanuck. Zevnik. That was it, Zevnik.

"It's a Rancho Santa Fe Fire Department vehicle," Mom said. "I often see them driving around here."

Coincidence? I supposed it was possible. The tape began again at 13:25—one twenty-five—showing yesterday's fire and the much-aired footage of the Fieldings' driveway with its blazing tunnel of flaming eucalyptus. Dad picked up the remote and turned off the tape just before the camera panned to the iron gate.

"I've seen enough of that burning Jaguar already. Let's see that piece on the Fieldings."

I put in the tape of *Hello, San Diego,* this time examining the video carefully for details I might have missed. Again the image that struck me most powerfully was Matthew clutching his stuffed Scooby-Doo.

The tape ended. My father stared at the blank screen.

"Are you making headway, finding the boy?"

"Doing my best."

I got up to retrieve the video from the VCR when the doorbell rang.

"I'll get it," I said.

It was our Chinese takeout. Dad followed me into the kitchen and helped me dump the cashew chicken, Buddha's vegetable delight, and kung pao beef out of the white cardboard boxes and onto plates. Washing my hands at the sink, I could barely see through the filmy glass of the kitchen window.

"Jeez, why are the windows so dirty?"

Dad looked around and shook his head.

"Ash. It's all over everything. We tried to clean them today but it's pointless until this wind dies down."

We ate at the table in the kitchen, where McGowan and I had often shared meals with my folks. All through the meal I couldn't help looking at the empty fourth place. I hadn't had anything but a smoothie since breakfast, and expected to be starving. But the knots in my stomach made eating a chore.

Dad insisted on helping Mom with what few dishes we'd made. I put on water for tea and went into the living room, thinking I might play the piano. I didn't have the heart. I picked up one of the framed photographs Mom kept on the piano top. It was a picture of McGowan and me, taken on a Christmas morning three years ago.

"You okay, honey?" Mom stood behind me, drying her hands on a dish towel.

"Yeah, fine. You should pack this up and put it away, Mom."

She took the framed photo from my hands and dusted it with the dish towel. She held it out at arm's length, staring at our smiling faces with a wistful smile of her own.

"I'm not ready to put it away."

For the first time I realized that McGowan's death had been her loss, too. Realized that she wasn't just hurting for me, but for the friend she was missing, as well. As she returned the picture to the top of the piano I noticed brown spots covering the thin skin on the back of her hands. At that moment I felt the full impact of how deeply I loved her—my father, too—and how close this fire had come to destroying them. There was a strange palpitation in my heart and my head felt light. I lowered myself onto the piano bench.

"You sure you're okay?" Mom lined up the edges of the dish towel and folded it with care. She was holding back, giving me plenty of room, but I could feel her concern.

"We're all so fragile, Mom."

She sat down on the bench with me, put her arm around my shoulders, and squeezed.

CHAPTER 19

It was well after dark by the time I pulled into my own driveway. An overturned trash can loomed in my headlights and I stomped on the brake just in time to avoid a collision. A fallen soldier in the Santa Ana wars, the plastic can had blown in from who knew what neighbor's yard. I got out and rolled it aside with my foot. The wind kept right on rolling it across the lawn and out of sight. The two days of Santa Anas felt much longer. The constant turbulence had an insidious way of wearing on me. I pulled the truck into the garage and got out. The garage was hot and stuffy. I could hear my big Rhodesian Ridgeback scratching from the other side of the door leading into the kitchen.

"Down, Nero, down." It was useless. The dog assaulted me as soon as I opened the door, covering my clothes with slimy slobber. McGowan had never been able to break him of the habit and damned if I could, either. I stumbled past the tail-wagging dog and into the kitchen, where I saw the insistent light of my answering machine. I knew without thinking that it would be Loebman. I pushed the play button, eager for news.

"Hey, it's Bruce. I'm calling to thank you for tracking down Bonnie McBride—or should I say the Acid Queen?

I caught up with her at the playhouse. Great information source, since she worked for Fielding at his office and his home. Not a suspect at this point, though. Twelve witnesses say she was in rehearsal the day of the fire. Ditto the day of the kidnapping. But if you get any other leads like this, keep passing them on. Oh and, uh, we're still looking to confirm whether or not Matthew talked. Okay. Stay in touch. Thanks again."

Good for you, I thought. Some cops hate PIs on principle and would sooner wear skirts than hand out kudos like that. Loebman was one of the good guys.

I went into my office to write up my notes for the day. Dead tired or not, I was meticulous about updating my case files every night. I sat at my desk and switched on the computer. While I waited for the hard drive to boot, I sat back in my chair and let my gaze wander around my office. It stopped at a picture on a nearby bookshelf. Me and McGowan, dressed to the nines at a wedding reception for a good friend.

"You should pack that up and put it away," I said in a bossy voice, mimicking the lecture I'd given my mother this evening. *Talk about projection,* I thought. I was demanding that my mother let go, but all the while I was still holding on. I came out of my chair and snatched up the frame. I had a box for memorabilia in the garage. It was time.

The garage had become even hotter and stuffier during the few minutes I'd been in the house. I found a half-empty banker's box on the shelves along the garage wall, and placed McGowan's picture inside.

If there was a theme for this box, it might be called Things I've Had a Tough Time Parting With. My Etch-a-Sketch was in there. So was the raggedy stuffed lamb I'd had since age three, once snowy white, now an ashy gray. As I tucked the picture frame alongside the lamb, I thought of Matthew Fielding's Scooby toy. I'd left it on the credenza with the other stuff I'd dumped there when I came home from the Fieldings' yesterday.

I walked to the front hall. Scooby was propped on the credenza, looking at me with friendly eyes and a goofy, forgiving smile. He seemed to be guarding a stash of bills and change I'd emptied out of my jeans pockets. I scooped up the cash and found the card Frank Fielding had given me. I picked it up, thinking I wouldn't be needing it now. That's when I noticed a handwritten phone number on the back side.

The mobile phone number he'd given me? Probably not, since that number was already printed on the front of the card. Then what was this? There was one way to find out. Carrying Matthew's Scooby toy, I returned to my office, picked up the phone, and dialed.

Three rings. Five rings. On the sixth ring, a machine picked up and began: *Hi, this is Randy* . . . Then the real Randy picked up.

"Hello."

No doubt about it, the voice was Randy Twain's. I was speechless. In the seconds that followed I made a quick decision to deal with it head-on.

"Hey, it's Elizabeth."

"Hi!" Very friendly.

"Why did Frank Fielding have this number on the back of his card?"

I could hear the sound of a radio or television in the background, tuned to a football game.

"Oh, that. I met with him briefly at Starcom a few days ago and tried to get a statement from him about the kidnapping. I thought there was a good chance he'd cooperate, since the station has been running special reports on Matthew. You know, asking for the public's help. Frank couldn't talk right then but he gave me a card and asked me to put a number on it where he could reach me later that night. That's how it got there."

"Oh."

"Were those videotapes useful?" he asked.

"Maybe. I'll see I guess."

He made a sound like someone had just punched him in

the stomach. "That would have been a first down . . . sorry. You've got my divided attention at the moment. But I'm glad you called. Phone anytime, okay? Whatever I can do."

I thought about it after we hung up. It wasn't so extraordinary that Fielding would have had the reporter's number. Still, I made a note of it in my case-file diary, along with a detailed summary of the other events of the past day. As I wrote, I kept the Scooby toy in my lap. More than ever I had the feeling Matthew was alive.

I turned off the computer and continued to sit, holding the stuffed dog and closing my eyes. Breathing slowly and centering my attention at a spot in the middle of my forehead, I coaxed my mind into a meditative state and waited for any images that might come.

The elements seemed to be conspiring to keep me earth-bound. Outside the wind gusted, sending up a host of unfamiliar noises. It took several minutes before the noise receded into the background and my consciousness stayed in an alpha state.

On my inner movie screen I caught a glimpse of a small, darkened room with wood paneling. Another image came through, a television set.

Nero started to bark. The next thing I knew, my front doorbell was ringing. I opened my eyes and let out a groan. Would I ever find time to meditate?

Feeling irritated, I walked to the front hall, wondering who it could be. The hour was too late for door-to-door solicitors. Sequoia was out of town. I tried to think of who else might drop by without calling first, and came up empty. I put my eye to the peephole and saw a familiar face.

"Toby," I said as I opened the door, "how are ya, buddy?"

Toby has been my next-door neighbor for his entire high school career. I've seen him go from little skater dude to tall surfer dude to young white man rapper dude. He'd recently morphed into a new phase, which I could only call searching dude. He wasn't following anyone's drumming lately. Just wearing classic, almost preppy clothes and working to finish a few senior year credits.

"Hey, Elizabeth." He'd even stopped calling me "Psi," the nickname he'd given me to goof on my chosen profession. "You wouldn't have any work for me, would you?"

I often threw odd jobs at Toby, mostly tedious runs to the courthouse for paperwork. Occasionally I'd have him baby-sit a post office box or street address under investigation.

"No work at the moment, but I'm sure I could cough something up by tomorrow. Why, you need some cash?"

"Redundant. I'm a teenager. I always need cash. Could you front me, um, say twenty bucks?"

"Yeah. Let me get my purse."

Nero was delighted to see Toby, who always had more patience than I did when it came to scratching the dog's ears. I left Toby in the hallway with Nero while I went to get the cash. When I returned there was a girl kneeling at Nero's side, massaging his chest while Toby continued to scratch his ears. *Where'd she come from?* I wondered.

"Hello," I said.

"Oh, uh"—Toby looked from me to the girl—"this is Sue. Sue, this is Elizabeth."

Sue was small, with a pixie face and short dark hair. She wore a long floral skirt with a denim jacket. Her fresh face needed no makeup and she wasn't wearing any. The teeniest rebellious ring was looped through her left eyebrow.

"We're on our way to the movies," Toby said.

Ah. That explained the need for cash. While Sue was preoccupied with petting my dog, Toby stood above her, mouthing something to me. I think the gist of it was that Sue's coming into the house with him had not been his idea.

"Are you really a detective?" Sue asked.

"That I am."

"That must be such a cool job." She stood up and dusted the dog hair off her fingers.

"When the bad guys get caught and the bills get paid, yeah, it's all right. What movie are you guys going to see tonight?"

"A Hitchcock retrospective," Sue replied, "playing at the Ken. I love Hitchcock, don't you?"

"Love him. Master of the stylish thriller."

"No doubt." Sue smiled wide, as if she were getting a thrill just talking about Hitchcock. Meanwhile, Toby was looking sheepish. I knew he didn't want me to hand him the cash in front of his date.

"So Toby," I said, "you wanted to borrow that Jimi Hendrix CD."

He got it right away.

"Yeah, man," he said, looking relieved. "If I could."

I went into the family room, found the CD, slipped thirty bucks into the jewel case, and walked back to the front door.

"Here you go."

Toby snatched it up, a huge smile on his face.

"Thanks, man."

"We'll talk about that job tomorrow."

"Okay, right." He was opening the door for his date, eager to go.

"Nice meeting you, Sue."

She turned at the doorway and waved good-bye. "Same here. Have a nice night."

A Winona Ryder look-alike with a thing for Hitchcock. Toby definitely had scored.

CHAPTER 20

So deep was my sleep that I don't even remember picking up the phone. By the time I was fully awake, the person on the other end of the line had been speaking for some time.

"They're blocking off access from the Five, so if you decide to drive down be sure to come the back way, through Mira Mesa Boulevard."

"Can you start from the beginning again?" I looked at the clock. Two forty-seven in the morning.

"There's a fire in Sorrento Valley, right by Starcom." It was a woman's voice, cutting in and out, obviously on a mobile phone. "It just broke out but it's already threatening to go out of control. I'm down here working with the Wildfire Arson Strike Team. Thought you should know. Two minds against one, remember?"

It was the arson investigator, Carolyn Arnold. I was awake now and beginning to understand the implications of what she'd just told me.

"Thanks, Carolyn. I'm on my way."

The connection had already cut out, which happened frequently when people called from that part of town. Ironically, the deep canyons around Starcom's wireless headquarters wreaked havoc on air transmission.

If property talked, I was beginning to hear quite a tale. A fire had destroyed Frank Fielding's home and now a fire was threatening the corporate headquarters he'd established. I thought I'd better let Loebman know what was happening. I found his business card in my wallet and called the second number listed, hoping it was either his home or cell phone. He picked up on the first ring, sounding wide awake. I identified myself and began with "there's a fire" before he interrupted me.

"Near Fielding's company, I know. I've been advised. You saw it on TV?"

"No. Carolyn Arnold called me."

"It was on Channel Three almost as soon as the dispatch came in. You going down there?"

"I'd like to, yeah. If this fire is related to the one at the Fieldings' there's a possibility Matthew's kidnapper will be hanging around. Think I can get past the perimeter?"

"Don't know. Depends on conditions. If you have problems, call me on my cell when you get there and I'll see if I can pull some strings."

"Can you give me your cell number?"

He let out a laugh. "It's the one you just called."

"Sorry," I said. "Still waking up."

"I suggest coffee. See you later."

I made a last-minute check in my wallet to make sure I had Carolyn Arnold's card. Chances were good that she, as an arson investigator, would be more likely than Loebman to get me past any roadblocks I might encounter on my way to the fire.

I grabbed the first pair of jeans and T-shirt I could find and put them on as I turned on the TV. Loebman had been right—Channel Three already had a news helicopter at the fire and viewers were getting a bird's-eye view of what was happening. Flames covered the west side of the canyon facing the freeway. Firefighters were making stands above and below. Those at the top were sending streams of water over the edge of the burning hillside. Those below were dousing from the bottom up. The arcs of water looked futile; mere dribbles into the flaming mouth of a fire monster. Cars on 1-5 became front-row seats to the conflagration. Despite the wee hour, traffic bunched up as drivers slowed to gawk at the spectacle. In the few minutes I'd been watching, the flames had gained in strength. The Starcom building at the crest of the canyon was sitting directly in their path. Fire-fighters on the canyon's edge were giving it all they had, but their efforts looked increasingly hopeless against the growing inferno.

It was difficult not to become mesmerized by the fire-fighters' battle to keep the building from being overtaken. The Channel Three voice-over reported that air support had been summoned but had not yet arrived. Extremely low humidity was feeding the unusual night wind, which in turn was driving the blaze to the top of the canyon. The news helicopter dipped in for a closer view and I could see the reflected flames glowing brightly in Starcom's glass wall of windows. I thought of the melted blob of glass in the Fieldings' charred dishwasher and wondered how well Star-com's tempered windows would hold up against the thousand-plus-degree heat.

I didn't have long to find out. As I was pulling on my boots, flames reached the top of the canyon. The smoke grew increasingly dense, obstructing the view of the build-ing. Angry billows rose into the night sky. In my mind's ear I could hear the glass windows exploding. The news-caster wasn't admitting it yet, but I felt certain that the fire had entered the Starcom building.

Traffic along I-5 had come to a standstill. I switched off the TV, grabbed my backpack, and hurried downstairs, stopping briefly at the refrigerator to get a large bottle of water. At the last minute I went into my office and scooped up the Scooby toy. It had become my connection to Mat-thew and, indirectly, to his kidnapper.

Nero trotted ahead of me to the garage door, cutting me off at the pass.

"You gotta stay here, boy." I scratched his ears. He was

accustomed to joining me on most of my jaunts outside the house. Not this assignment.

I took the inland freeway, I-15, south to Mira Mesa Boulevard, and headed west to I-5. So many geographically inspired street names are bogus—Heights that aren't high, Meadows that don't exist, Ranches that are really subdevelopments. But Mira Mesa is genuinely that—an elevated flatland that stretches for miles in mid–San Diego County. Approaching the mesa, I could see the fire's smoke from miles away. Traffic was glutted along the boulevard and I wondered where people were going at three in the morning. To see the fire, probably. When forward progress came to a halt, I made an exception to my pull-over rule and dialed Carolyn.

"Where are you?" she asked.

"Mira Mesa Boulevard. Looks like I'm about a mile from the fire."

"Okay. Real soon you're going to hit a CHP roadblock. Just pull over and park. I'll come get you."

Within minutes I reached the roadblock. A CHP officer in a glow-in-the-dark vest was using a glow-in-the-dark baton to redirect traffic away from the fire. I pulled off the road and waited. And waited. About three minutes before I lost all faith, a gigantic Suburban came into view and pulled to a stop on the other side of the roadblock. It took me a minute to recognize Carolyn behind the wheel, as she was wearing a fire helmet. I got out of my truck, locked the doors, and walked around to the passenger side of her hulking vehicle. I practically needed a ladder to climb into it.

"You know what they say about girls with big SUVs, don't you?" I said as I slammed the door.

She shot me a bored look.

"I don't give a damn what they say."

I smiled. It was a good answer. With her blond hair tucked under the helmet, her no-nonsense face was even more so. Her gloved hands spun the wheel and we headed back into the fire zone. The night air was smoky, but not nearly as bad as what I'd experienced during the fire in Rancho Santa Fe. The winds out of the east were blowing most of the smoke over the freeway and toward the ocean. Up ahead I could see a multistory building—it looked like an apartment complex—burning along the edge of the canyon.

"How bad is it?" I asked.

Carolyn turned down a side street, heading toward the burning building.

"Could be a lot worse." She nodded toward the building up ahead. A piece of the flaming roof hit the ground, scattering sparks for several feet. "This is the only residential structure the fire has taken so far. We're pretty sure it was fully evacuated when it went up."

"When did the firefighters get here?"

"The first units were here about two minutes after the apartment building caught fire, but they probably couldn't have saved it anyway. These brush-filled canyons are pure fire fuel. Creates conditions that make the fire impossible to stop."

I looked toward the canyon, where smoke swirled in the tangerine-colored light created by the fire. "What happened to the Starcom headquarters? One of the buildings was just catching fire when I turned off the TV."

"The building that faced the canyon was hard hit, but it's not completely woofed. Plenty of damage, but nothing the company can't afford. A few hundred thou and change, maybe."

I could hear the throbbing of a helicopter and peered up through the windshield. The aircraft went right over us to the canyon's edge, where it dropped a load of water on the flaming brush below.

"Thanks, Huey," Carolyn said.

"Huey?"

"Huey-1. The CDF helicopter up there. Between air support and the fact that we got a jump start on this one, we're in pretty good shape. The fire's mostly contained. There's really no place for it to go now."

"Any casualties?"

Carolyn pulled to a stop along the street, about fifty yards from the burning apartment building.

"Not that we know of."

The street was crowded with fire trucks. Hundreds of yards of hose lines stretched toward the building. I counted five stories. The fire was burning languidly now, mostly spent.

"You saw an explosion at the Fielding place," Carolyn said as she watched the firefighters working. "Do you have any sense of what happened here?"

I flashed back to sitting at the edge of this very canyon yesterday afternoon and hearing Sequoia's voice, urging me to pay attention. It was the second time I'd missed an intuitive clue before a fire had broken out. I didn't feel good about that.

"I'm not certain what started the fire," I said, "but I'm fairly certain *where* it started."

"That'll be pretty easy for us to determine, but I'm curious. Where do you think it started?"

"Right over the canyon's edge, where the Starcom building looks out."

"You may be right. The first reports of the fire were from drivers passing by on the freeway. Said they saw flames at the bottom of that hillside. It'll take a while for the area to be cleared, but I'd like you to be around to help Buster look for the ignition device."

"Buster?"

"Our arson canine."

"You're assuming it's arson, then."

"Not assuming anything. Just being thorough. Like these guys."

She nodded toward the firefighters working on the burning building. There was no saving it now, but they were hosing down what was left of it and putting out any hot spots started by stray sparks. One of the firefighters took off the department-issued yellow helmet to reveal a head of pale blond hair. He swiped his flushed face with a red bandana.

"Hey," I said. "I know that guy."

"Which?"

I pointed out the towheaded firefighter.

"He was manning the roadblock at the Rancho Santa Fe fire."

"Yeah, that's Zevnik," Carolyn said. "He's with our unit in Rancho Santa Fe."

I remembered the Channel Three video Twain had given me, the one he'd taped at the bottom of the Fieldings' driveway the morning before the fire had broken out. I remembered seeing a white Fire Department Bronco that had looked very much like Zevnik's.

"If he's with the Rancho Santa Fe unit, what's he doing fighting fires down here in central San Diego?"

"Dispatch called in all of the area strike teams. Didn't want to take any chances with this fire. Not with these weather conditions. Zevnik's on active rotation."

A small crowd of civilians were clustered on the sidewalk to watch the firefighters put out the flames. I realized these were probably the displaced residents of the burned apartment building.

Carolyn pointed to a silver-haired man who was talking with some people in the crowd.

"That's my captain. I'm going to see if he can give me an update. You okay here?"

"I'd like to get out and nose around."

"Stay on the sidewalk and out of the burn area. And take your phone. I'll be here at least until daylight, so page me when you need a ride back to that big truck of yours." She gave me a wink as she slid out.

I stepped out onto the sidewalk. At three-thirty in the morning it wasn't hot, but it was a long way from cool. And dry enough to make my skin itch. The smoke-scented air stirred up anxiety in me, even though I knew this fire was under control. Post-traumatic stress left over from the Fielding fire, I supposed.

I stood with the band of civilians watching firefighters douse the burning apartment building.

"Hey, Zevnik!" He turned at the sound of my voice and I waved him over. He didn't recognize me.

"I'm that woman who gave Randy Twain a ride behind the perimeter at the Rancho Santa Fe fire, remember?"

He nodded. "Oh, yeah. You were worried about your parents. Is their house okay?"

"Yeah, it was spared. Thanks for asking." I felt touched that he'd remembered.

"What about that woman photographer? Was she okay?"

"Yeah. Her Ford Explorer was pretty much roasted by the fire, though."

He shook his head and wagged a scolding finger.

"That's not good. She violated rule number one: Never give up your equipment."

"I don't know about that," I said. "I saw what happened to that Explorer. Pretty scary. I think she was wise to abandon it."

Zevnik had been keeping his eyes on the other firefighters as they doused what remained of the apartment building.

"Was anyone hurt here?" I asked.

"No, we got everybody out."

"That's a blessing."

"Yeah, that's one of the things I love about being a firefighter. Always a hero, no shades of gray. Cops sometimes gotta wonder if they're even on the right side. Me, I'm always a good guy."

"So what's rule number two?" I asked.

"Huh?"

"You said rule number one was never abandoning your equipment. What's rule number two?"

He paused to think about it.

"Be brave and never admit you're afraid. You're not doing your job unless your eyebrows are burning."

A firefighter nearby was struggling with his hose, not realizing that it was kinked near the street.

"Hey!" Zevnik called out. "You gotta unfuck that line!" He gave me a distracted look. "Gotta go."

As Zevnik walked away, a wave of blinding white swept over the block, throwing the firefighting scene into a surreal light. I turned and squinted into a megawatt floodlight moving slowly up the street. As my eyes adjusted to the intrusion, I recognized an oversized white van painted with the garish letters: Live News—KFEC—Channel Three.

CHAPTER 21

"I heard all this yelling in the courtyard. There was a police officer knocking on doors, telling us to put on clothes and grab our kids and get out as fast as we could."

The interviewee was in her early thirties, with the tangled hair and bare face of someone who'd been roused from sleep. In the unflattering glare of the television lights, her bewildered face appeared haggard. She was in a state of near shock, too preoccupied with the crisis to be self-conscious about her appearance. She looked to Twain obediently, waiting for the next question.

"Was that the first time you were aware your apartment building was on fire?" Twain extended his microphone closer to her so that she could be heard above the helicopter flying overhead.

"Yeah. It wasn't until we were out of there that we could see that whole canyon on fire and our roof starting to go up and stuff."

Twain stretched the mike toward a man standing beside her. "Were you able to salvage your belongings?"

The man was wearing a windbreaker over his pajamas. His face was sullen and his tone was angry.

"Just the clothes on our backs, our daughter, and our

bird." The news photographer panned the camera to the man's left, where his daughter stood holding his hand. At her feet was a small birdcage with a green parakeet inside.

"Where will your family go now?" Twain asked.

The man shook his head in disgust. "We're outta here. Leaving California. Forget about it. Sunshine's nice, but this is bullshit."

I wondered if there was a tape delay, or if "bullshit" had made the airwaves. Twain thanked the couple and turned to the camera.

"Well, there you have it. Mira Mesa Apartments, which you see burning behind me, has been hardest hit by this fire that started a little over a hour ago on a steep canyon in Sorrento Valley. That blaze is mostly contained now. The fire burned out of control for well over an hour early this morning, causing significant damage to an office building owned by the Starcom corporation and, again, completely destroying this apartment building. For News Three, this is Randy Twain."

I looked at the residents who'd been displaced from the building and turned to a man standing next to me.

"I feel for these people."

He was perhaps fifty, with a philosophical air and a slow smile.

"Then feel for me. That was my home, too."

A Red Cross truck had pulled up next to the fire engines on the street and a pair of volunteers began to circulate through the crowd, announcing that food, water, transportation, and telephones were available for residents who needed them. A few people walked toward the truck. I heard the popping of soda cans and wondered if I could bum a Coke. My throat was parched. Stupidly, I'd left my water bottle in my truck.

As I was heading for the Red Cross truck, I walked past a woman sitting on the sidewalk, arms crossed over her knees, rocking herself slightly as she gazed at the burning building. She looked up at me as I passed and I recognized her face. It was the employee I'd met at Starcom yesterday afternoon, the woman who'd escorted me through the shipping department. The one with the name that conjured up images of monks and nuns.

"Hey. Aren't you Abby?"

She looked at me the way you look at a lunatic who accosts you on the street.

"I'm the one who was trying to find the back door to Starcom yesterday. You showed me in through the shipping department, remember?"

Her expression softened as the memory registered.

"Oh, yeah. Right." She turned back to watch the fire.

"You didn't live in that building, did you?"

"Who me? Nah." Her voice was thick with sarcasm. "I always sit out on the sidewalk of a strange neighborhood at four in the morning." She sounded angry but I couldn't really fault her for it.

"You did live there."

"Yes."

"Gosh, I'm sorry. That's awful."

She shrugged.

"What do you expect? I told you this place was hell."

"The Red Cross is up the street, if you need any food, water, transportation, whatever. And I've got a phone here if you need one."

"Thanks. I'll be okay."

I looked at the smoldering building, trying to put myself in her shoes. "I can't imagine what it must feel like to lose a home like that." The statement sounded so lame that I regretted it the moment it came out of my mouth.

She got up from the sidewalk, picking up the soft knapsack sitting beside her and tossing it across her back.

"I'm looking at the bright side. The freeway noise was getting worse all the time. Starting to drive me crazy. Besides, I've got family I can stay with."

Two hours after it began, the canyon fire was nearly out. I was anxious to get over to the Starcom compound to see what I could see, but it wasn't going to be easy. The Mira

Mesa Apartments were the nearest neighbor to Starcom along the canyon's edge, but a half-mile away by road. That road was still blocked off to traffic, so I had to go on foot.

As I walked the deserted highway I felt oddly detached, as if each step were bringing me into someone else's lonely dream. The darkness around me closed in and for a moment I felt as frightened as a motherless child. Whether I was picking up on Matthew's mental state or sensing my own mortality, I couldn't tell.

I finally reached the entrance to Starcom International. A dozen or so fire engines were gathered in a circle out front and vehicles from a dizzying array of departments— police, FBI, CDF, Sheriff, City of San Diego, you name it—fanned out in all directions. I found Carolyn and her captain behind one of the fire engines, where a folding table and chairs had been set up on the sidewalk.

"You found me," Carolyn said with a smile. "Welcome to our command post." She pointed out three men sitting nearby: Fred Harvey, an arson investigator from the San Diego Fire Department who reminded me of a young Jimmy Stewart; Jeff Serra, a burly investigator for the San Diego Police Department; and Dale Blades, a field agent from the FBI who bore an unfortunate resemblance to Adolf Hitler. Somebody, I thought, should tell him to lose the moustache.

"They're the guys who form the core of San Diego's Wildfire Arson Strike Team. Along with me, of course."

"What happens next?" I asked.

"We're mapping that out now. We'll be starting our investigation as soon as the area's safe enough to walk through. Probably another two, three hours from now. Can you hang?"

"Sure." I found an empty folding chair and pulled it up next to her. "I talked to your buddy Zevnik back at the apartment fire. Looks like that's all the way out now."

"Pity they couldn't save it," she said.

"You guys are both from the Rancho Santa Fe Fire Department. Did you ride down here together?"

"No, Zev came down separately. Which is a good thing, because I'm going to be here for a while." She studied my face. "You haven't had much sleep tonight. Want to catch a few winks in the back seat of my Suburban?"

"No, I'm fine." I was too wired for sleep. Something was happening here, something more sinister than a fire. I felt it like a presence. My nervous system was on red alert but I couldn't pinpoint the source. Not knowing what to look for, all I could do now was wait. And watch. "I'm going to stretch my legs. I'll be back in a few minutes."

I wanted to see what kind of damage the fire had done to the Starcom building that faced the freeway. I headed in that direction, going past the entrance. The electricity had gone out—or been turned off—so there were no outdoor lights to brighten the predawn darkness. The Channel Three news van was parked out front. I was walking past when I heard a familiar voice.

"Hey, Elizabeth!" Twain came around from the back of the van, where station hands were packing away camera and audio equipment. The crew was on their way out.

"Hey yourself," I said.

"What a night, huh? Gotta fly now, but call me later." He climbed into the passenger side of the van. As it pulled away he rolled down the window and leaned out. "Seriously, call me. I have important info for you."

CHAPTER 22

"Forty-two acres." Carolyn stood at the canyon's edge, boots planted firmly, hands on hips. She nodded toward the vast expanse of blackened landscape. The smell of the burn was everywhere, thick and sharp. "Ever processed a scene this big?"

I shook my head no. I'd stayed awake through the night, waiting and watching to put a face on the sinister presence I'd felt at the scene. The opportunity seemed to melt away as the sun came up. Below us, commuters rolled at a steady pace along the freeway. Last night's orange-red flames had stopped cars in all four lanes; this morning's gray-black hillsides were barely worth slowing for. Behind us, the first stirrings of early morning traffic were audible along Mira Mesa Boulevard, which the CHP had opened an hour ago. I studied the charred acreage.

"Whatcha think?" Carolyn asked.

Think wasn't the word. It's what I was sensing that had struck me dumb. A feeling emanated from the torched landscape, lingering here like something left behind. If I had to reduce that feeling to a single word, the word would be *hate*. Carolyn, still waiting for my reply, gave me a verbal nudge.

"Well?"

"I think the person who did this is the same person who torched the Fieldings'," I said.

"Because of the proximity to Fielding's company, sure. It's a tempting conclusion to jump to."

"For me it's not that logical. It's more about the vibe."

"The vibe." She looked at me evenly, without judgment.

"Yeah. It's familiar."

"Could be." Her lips curled into a wry smile. "We'll see what tales the property tells. Want to see why this area burned so fast?"

"Sure."

"Hand me one of your business cards." She took the card I offered and fired up a cigarette lighter. "Here's fire burning on flat land." She held the card horizontally and ignited the edge. "Here's what happens on a hillside." She tipped the card up and the flame disintegrated it almost instantly. "If it gets big enough, a fire like that can create its own wind."

The fire had leveled the chaparral, exposing a series of gopher holes on the ash-covered hillside. I was reminded of cannonball holes in a battlefield.

"Might as well have been nuclear war for the plants and animals who lived here, huh?"

"Not really," Carolyn said. "They're well adapted to fires. It's a normal part of this ecosystem. Fire actually recycles nutrients in the old plants. Clears things out so new stuff can grow."

"Yeah, but the animals—"

"You'd be surprised. Most big mammals outrun fires like this and come back after the flames pass through. The snakes and rabbits burrow underground or hide in rocky areas during the fire. Their habitat grows back in a season or two. They fare a lot better than, say, corporations."

I considered this as I looked at the job ahead of us.

"How *do* you process a scene this big?"

"With a lot of help. It would take forever if I didn't have

the assistance of the strike team. We divvy up the tasks and go at it bit by bit."

The long night was catching up with me and I couldn't suppress a yawn. Carolyn frowned.

"Hey, don't crap out on me now."

"Never," I said when I was able to pull my jaws back together. "We'll be looking for the same kind of things we found at the Fielding house, right? Like a cigarette tucked into a book of matches."

"Yep. The 'fusee' as we call it."

I scanned the forty-plus acres of charred territory, trying to remember how many square feet were in an acre. Forty-three thousand-something stuck in my head. I multiplied by forty and came up with over a million square feet. *That couldn't be right—could it?*

"It's a daunting job," she said, guessing my thoughts. "Glad I have you and Buster to help me."

"The arson dog."

"Yep. Star member of the Wildfire Arson Strike Team. Come on, I'll introduce you."

We walked across the burned ground and onto a sidewalk that led to a cul-de-sac. The official vehicles were still gathered like a ring of covered wagons at the Starcom entrance. Due to the fire, the company would be closed for the day.

"So these are all arson investigators?" I asked.

"Not exactly. The idea with the strike team is to pool talent and resources. We've got photographers, chemists, city cops, feds, you name it. Hey, there's Craig."

She pointed to a man stepping down from the driver's side of a SDFD Explorer. A big yellow Labrador retriever jumped out behind him.

"Craig!"

He looked over and waved. Carolyn motioned him to come join us.

A handsome man with a friendly face, Craig approached us wearing the same half-smile I saw on the muzzle of his dog.

"Like you to meet Elizabeth," Carolyn said.

Craig and I nodded our hellos.

"And this is Buster," Carolyn said as she patted the dog, "our accelerant canine."

"Your what?" I wasn't sure I'd heard it right.

"He's a trained arson investigator in his own right," Craig explained. "That nose there is highly sensitive to hydrocarbons. He's a lot better at finding traces of gasoline and whatnot than we are."

Buster broke away from Carolyn and walked over to me. When he pushed his wet snout against my legs I concluded that his nose was highly sensitive to the fact that I had Nero scent all over me.

"Accelerant canine," I repeated, scratching the dog's chest. His tongue lolled out of his mouth and dripped heavily in the heat. "What a great idea. I didn't even realize such things existed."

Carolyn looked at her wristwatch. "Between his nose and your psychic ability, I figure we'll have this scene processed in time for breakfast."

Craig looked confused.

"She's a psychic detective working with the Sheriff's Department on the Fielding case," Carolyn explained.

The dog handler's face lit up.

"Cool. Like on TV."

"Not quite," I said. "A TV psychic would come up with your arsonist by the next commercial break. Things are a little harder in real life, I'm afraid."

Craig's face lost its little-boy glow.

"You're destroying my fantasy," he said.

"So sorry."

All members of the Wildfire Arson Strike Team met briefly in the cul-de-sac before splitting off into smaller teams to process the burn area. Carolyn and I teamed up with Craig and Buster, riding to the bottom of the canyon near the freeway. We pulled off the road along the edge of a burned-out brush area, where the fire was reported to have started.

I got out of the car with the others and stared up at the canyon.

"It all looks the same," I said. "Gray sticks and stones. Looks like a million burned match heads out there. How do you know what to look for?"

Craig unhooked Buster's leash and let the dog go.

"He'll know," he said.

We walked along the edge of the road. After about an eighth of a mile, Buster got excited. He headed for a spot about fifteen feet up the canyon and began digging, letting out a series of sharp, insistent barks. Craig was right on his heels.

"Take a look at this, Carolyn," he called.

We hurried to join them. When Carolyn got to Buster's side, she peered at a small, dark object at his feet.

"That would do it," she said, opening her black canvas bag. She pulled out her video camera and taped what she was seeing, then took a picture with her still camera. That done, she pulled out a large pair of tongs, grabbed the object, and studied it. It looked like the broken neck of a beer bottle, charred completely black.

"What is it?" I asked.

"Molotov cocktail," she said with a frown. "What's left of one, anyway."

"How do you know it's not just a piece of broken bottle?" I asked.

"I don't know for absolute certain. I'm taking Buster's word for it. The lab will tell us for sure." She bagged the bottle piece and continued searching the ground. "You know what a Molotov cocktail is, right?"

"Sort of. Isn't it a bottle filled with gasoline or something?"

"With an ignition device stuck inside, like a long wick. The wick is the built-in delay factor. Gives the arsonist time to get away. I'm guessing that someone tossed this out the window of a moving car. Not terribly sophisticated, but it's effective. As you can see." She gestured to the scorched acreage.

Buster was still sniffing and digging around the area.

"Check out the radical leaf freeze," Craig said.

"What's leaf freeze?" I asked.

"See how what's left of the burned brush is all slanted, like it's going that way?" Craig was right; there did seem to be a pattern in the ashes. "That tells you the direction the fire came from. Get some samples from here, Carolyn. I'm guessing we'll find gasoline evidence. We might be able to trace where it came from."

"You can trace gasoline?"

"Chromatograph technology. Every batch of gas has its own distinct pattern, almost like a footprint."

Carolyn turned to me with a smile.

"See? Told you this wouldn't take long with Buster's help. We could wrap this up by noon."

I was listening to her but looking at the canyon ridge a hundred feet up. The edge of the damaged Starcom building jutted against the sky. Yesterday its roof had cut a sharp architectural line; this morning it was burned and jagged.

Carolyn followed my line of sight.

"Whatcha looking at?"

"I want to go up there," I said. "To the top of the canyon by the Starcom building."

Craig stared up at the sixty-degree incline.

"Let's take the car," he said.

Most of the buildings in the Starcom compound had been unaffected by the fire. The company would not officially open for business today but the security staff was on duty. We checked in with the guard at the front desk to let him know that we'd be surveying the burn area near the executive building.

Once again I crossed the cement patio that wrapped around the western edge of the corporate compound. I looked for the place I'd been sitting the day before, but the fire had burned away any familiar landmarks. The three-foot hedge that once ringed the patio had been reduced to a band of black ash. The open space at the top of the canyon had been burned bald. Again I remembered Sequoia's words.

Pay attention here.

"What are we looking for?" Craig asked.

"Not sure," I replied as I headed for the canyon's edge. I was trying to remember what I'd been sensing here yesterday before Randy had come along and interrupted my thoughts. I stared out over the canyon, straining to think. I *felt* something just beyond my line of sight.

"There's something down there," I said, pointing over the edge.

Craig looked dubious.

"Buster doesn't seem too interested."

That was true. The dog sat on his haunches, panting heavily. If anything he looked sleepy.

"Buster's trained to sniff out accelerant. Maybe this is something else."

"Like what?" Carolyn asked.

"Only one way to find out," I said. "I'm going to check it out."

"Want help?" Craig asked.

"No, let me do this alone, feel it out."

"Careful," Carolyn said. "It's pretty steep there."

I took my time descending over the canyon's edge. The fire had burned away most of the handholds, and my palms were soon black from grabbing for purchase on the remains of the ash-covered brush. Twenty feet down I turned and looked up. From this vantage point I had a direct view of the damaged executive building. One of those blown-out windows had been Frank Fielding's old office. When I turned back around to continue my descent, a man-made object caught my eye.

"I see something," I called.

"What is it?" Carolyn called back.

"Looks like a box. Just a minute."

I inched closer to the thing, which had lodged against a rock.

"I think it's one of those fireproof safes," I called up. "With the key still in it."

"How big is it?" Craig called down.

"Small enough to tuck under my arm and bring up. Want me to do that?"

"Leave it there," Carolyn called. "I've got to take photos and preserve any fingerprints."

Carolyn skidded expertly down the hillside and reached the spot in half the time it had taken me to get there. She photographed the safe and picked it up with gloved hands.

"This could be something . . . or nothing at all," she said as she placed it into her evidence bag.

I knew it was something. I got a vibe from that safe, the same vibe I got from the ruins of the fires. Hate, emanating in concentrated form, as if the little box were the very source of the destruction.

We climbed back up to the top of the canyon. Carolyn removed the safe from her evidence bag and photographed it again. With gloved fingers, she turned the key and opened the lid. Craig and I craned our necks to see.

Inside was a note typed on a single piece of white paper. Immediately I was reminded of the unburned page I'd found at the ruins of the Fieldings' house. The three of us bent closer to read the words silently to ourselves. Carolyn was the first to comment.

"Aw, shit."

The message, neatly printed with extremely wide margins, looked as if it had been produced by a word processor.

> Clue for the Clueless
> Let's see if this fireproof box is worth the ninety bucks I paid for it. I know you'll analyze this printer, so let me save you some time: it's a Hewlett-Packard 5LP, set at 600 dpi. But on to more important matters. This insanity must end. There'll be more fires until you people get the message. That's a promise.

CHAPTER 23

"You people," the note had read. *Who people?* I wondered as I headed home along the inland freeway, I-15. "There'll be more fires until you people get the message." Frank Fielding and Starcom International seemed to be the obvious targets. The moustachioed FBI agent, Dale Blades—I couldn't help but think of him as Der Führer—had jumped all over the note when Carolyn brought it to the attention of the strike team. When she presented what she believed to be the remnants of a Molotov cocktail, Blades called Washington for Alcohol, Tobacco, and Firearms backup. It was starting to feel like an interdepartmental talent show by the time I'd left, all of us trying to perform the same trick: find the arsonist.

The cool air inside my house was a welcome caress after eight hours of exposure to the hot, dry wind. The bright light of early afternoon poured through the windows. Not exactly bedtime, but the hour didn't matter. After the adrenaline workout of responding to two fires in three days, my body was screaming for sleep.

Sleep would have to wait. As any homicide cop will tell you, the first seventy-two hours of an investigation are critical. Taking time out to sleep can mean the difference be-

tween closing a case and letting a killer walk. No one had
died in last night's fire, but I felt certain the arson was
related to the Fieldings' deaths and even more certain that
whoever was involved knew what had happened to Matthew.

I went right to my office, Nero padding behind me. I
turned on my computer and sat back in my chair, waiting
for the software to load. My clothes reeked of smoke and
ash. Nero pressed his muzzle along my pant legs, making
wet sniffing noises. My attempts to push him away failed.
In the end I went upstairs to strip off the soiled clothes and
change into a clean nightshirt.

Back at my desk, I logged on to the Internet to begin
my search.

You people.

Starcom was the keyword I punched into the search engine at the *San Diego Union-Tribune* archive site. After a
forty-five-second search, the computer told me that 3143
documents had been found under my query. I began scroll-
ing through headlines. Most of them had to do with stock
offerings, acquisitions, new wireless technologies, and
earnings reports. I was looking for something alive, something controversial. It took until document number 2901 to
find anything even remotely interesting:

150 RALLY AGAINST STARCOM EXPANSION

An environmental group gathered on Sorrento Mesa at
dawn yesterday, determined to save the sage-covered habitat from development, even if it meant standing directly in
the path of oncoming bulldozers or being hauled off to jail
for trespassing.

They lost their battle by noon.

With police officers stationed nearby, construction
workers forced the protesters to retreat and erected a chain-
link fence around the property. When the bulldozer engines
roared, shouts and tears erupted but there was no overt violence. As the protesters looked on in despair, the hilltop
was graded to make way for an industrial complex that will

serve as the headquarters for Starcom International, a leading manufacturer of wireless communication systems.

The article went on to recount the city council actions that had led to the development and the environmentalists' ongoing battle to preserve the area. The piece concluded with a telling quote:

"People say they're concerned about the destruction of the environment and that they want to change the system," said Ken Fender, 27, a Sorrento Valley resident and organizer from the San Diego chapter of the EarthNow League. "But for all their good intentions, nothing happens. What we're doing is identifying the perpetrators and targeting our actions against those people."

The article was nearly three years old. I couldn't count on being able to track down Mr. Fender, but figured I'd give it a try. I typed his name and city into an on-line phone-number database. The computer spat up a number, which didn't surprise me. If it was the number for *the* Ken Fender I was seeking, then I'd be surprised.

I dialed and got a ring. Several rings. No answering machine. I was about to hang up when a man's voice answered.

"Hi," I said. "My name's Elizabeth. You don't know me, but I was wondering if you could talk to me about taking an active role in saving the environment."

"You a journalist?" His tone was friendly but tinged with caution.

"No. I read about you in the paper and I wanted to find out more about your organization."

"You're a concerned citizen, then."

"Yes, very concerned." As indeed I was.

"Great. We've got a meeting coming up next week."

"I was hoping I could talk to you before that. It's about a particular, uh, perpetrator, you might say."

"Ah." He mulled it over for a few seconds and said, "I

usually have breakfast at Miracles Café. Know where that is?"

Miracles was a beachside bungalow that had been converted to the most casual of restaurants. In summer shirts were optional and customers often went barefoot. The place offered organic food and a knockout view of the Pacific.

"I know it well," I said. "What time?"

"Is eight tomorrow too early? I like to catch the morning surf."

"Eight's fine. I'll be the woman in the green baseball cap."

I hung up with the vague sense that I'd made headway. By the time I'd updated my daily log, the words on the computer monitor were going in and out of focus. I went into the living room and collapsed onto the sofa, closing my eyes. My Himalayan, Whitman, jumped on my abdomen and did his best to nudge me into petting duty, but in spite of his pawing, purring, and head butting, I started to drift. I thought about getting up and putting myself properly into bed, but couldn't muster the energy. Fearing I'd fall into a Rip Van Winkle coma, I fought to stay awake. What resulted was that curious half-sleep that produces the most vivid dreams.

I saw myself traveling along a narrow dirt path. Up ahead was a dip in the ground. Walking toward me from the opposite direction was a boy I knew to be Matthew. I stepped aside so that we could pass each other on the narrow trail. After he walked by, I realized I'd missed an opportunity. I spun around.

"Wait!"

I don't know whether it was my own voice calling out or the ringing phone that woke me. Still groggy, I got up off the sofa and lumbered into the kitchen to answer it.

"You didn't call me," a male voice complained after I'd said hello.

I had no idea who was talking, or what he was talking about.

"I'm serious," the voice said. "This could break your case."

It was Randy Twain. I flashed back to the employee parking lot at Starcom after last night's fire and remembered him leaning out the passenger window of the news van, saying something about having important information for me.

"I just got home a little while ago." Not entirely true. According to my kitchen clock an hour had elapsed since I'd walked in the door.

"I told you it was important and I meant it. I've got information you need."

It seemed odd to me that a reporter in the middle of a big story would take the time to update a secondary investigator on the case—a mere PI, for crying out loud. It wasn't the first time I'd questioned Twain's motives, but I couldn't afford not to hear him out.

"Information's always welcome," I said. "Fire away."

"I'm covering a seven-o'clock press conference at Starcom. We'll be parked in the employee parking lot. Meet me there at six forty-five and I'll fill you in. By that time I'm sure I'll know even more."

I looked again at the clock. Five minutes to two. I could set my alarm, get three or four hours of sleep, and squeeze in a wake-up shower before driving down to meet Twain.

"All right, I'll meet you at Starcom at quarter to seven. What's this about?"

"Can't go into it now but you'll want to know, trust me. Gotta go. See ya."

I hung up the phone and hauled my tired bones up the stairs. Fatigue aside, I was feeling good. The images I'd seen during my brief nap had reassured me. I might not know where Matthew Fielding was—might even have passed him by—but I was more certain than ever that the boy was still alive.

CHAPTER 24

Five hours later I pulled into Starcom's employee parking lot. Randy was standing at the entrance, gesturing in a circular motion: *Roll your window down.*

"You're late," he said through my open window. "They're starting any minute."

"Sorry. I had to get gas, and of course there was a line. Ever noticed how there's always a long line when you're late, but if you're early the place is empty?"

He ignored my excuse.

"Park in that spot." He pointed to a nearby space that had been painted Reserved. As I got out of my truck he handed me a laminated green press pass. "Jane's already set up in the conference room. You're going to be my intern. Let's go."

We headed to the conference room at a jog and burst through the doors with two minutes to spare. Twain and I maneuvered through the throng of reporters to a space near the front, where a table had been set up with a nest of microphones. I saw the Channel Three photographer, Jane Sharpe, standing at the side of the room next to a tripod mounted with her television camera. The room was buzzing with conversation, giving us privacy in the crowd.

"I take it you don't have any new leads on Matthew," Twain said.

"I might," I said, thinking of the note I'd found in the fireproof safe. "Too soon to say." *You people* could have meant Starcom. Starcom was connected to Frank Fielding, and Frank Fielding was connected to Matthew. The strike team had admonished me to keep quiet about the note. So far, no news media, including Channel Three, had reported anything about it. I certainly wasn't going to say anything.

Twain bent toward my ear and spoke in a low voice. "I think the arsonist is right under everyone's nose. Take a close look at Larry Gandle when he comes out."

"Why Gandle?" I asked.

"I was out late last night. Happened to be driving through this part of town when the fire broke out, so I got to Starcom almost right away. When I arrived, Gandle was already here." He looked at me intently. "At two-thirty in the morning." His implication was clear.

"Gandle's the chief executive now. I'm sure the security people called him immediately. Being here in a crisis is kind of his job, isn't it?"

"I told you before, Gandle and Fielding had a long-standing rivalry. I'm suspicious of the guy. See what you think when you hear him talk. Test his vibrations or read his aura or whatever it is you do."

A door at the side of the room opened.

"There he is," Twain whispered. He gave me a meaningful look.

The man I'd seen briefly on the news walked out and took a place at the table in front. He was shorter than he'd appeared on television, but also better looking. He seemed intense and determined, the way you'd expect a person in authority to be during a crisis.

Following behind Gandle was Pamela Jaffer. The Vice Demon of Misinformation, as one Starcom employee had called her. Looking more elegant than devilish in a fire-engine-red suit, she walked to the front table and took a seat next to Gandle.

"Good evening," she began. "My name is Pam Jaffer, and I'm the vice president of marketing and publicity at Starcom. To my left, as many of you know"—she smiled at some faces in the crowd—"is Larry Gandle, our chief executive officer.

"We're here tonight to answer your questions regarding the fire that broke out near the company early this morning. I'd like to begin by thanking the San Diego Fire Department, whose prompt response got the fire under control almost immediately. Is Fred Harvey here?" The SDFD investigator who reminded me of a young James Stewart stood up. "Take a bow, Fred."

Pamela began the applause and the rest of the room followed suit. Harvey blushed and sat down.

"Thanks to Fred and the other firefighters, Starcom suffered relatively little damage. Our product inventory was completely unaffected by the fire and all of our corporate documents are secure."

The room erupted in a shouting match, with reporters calling Jaffer's name. She pointed to the most vocal one, a raven-haired woman in the front row.

"Stephanie Lamba, Channel Eight News," she announced. "What is the estimated dollar amount of the damages to the company?"

Gandle took the question.

"Most of the fire damage was to the office building at the northwest edge of the property, along the canyon," he replied. "As Ms. Jaffer stated, no product inventory was destroyed. Most of the hardware—the in-vehicle computers, PC software, cell phones, et cetera—is stored in a warehouse in Nevada. So while it looked quite dramatic on television last night"— like Jaffer, he smiled to the audience—"there really wasn't a large dollar amount involved. We won't know the exact figure until the insurance company has done an investigation, but early estimates are under a million dollars."

Again the audience erupted into shouts. Randy joined

the throng this time but Jaffer called on a reporter from Channel Ten.

"Do you know the cause of the fire?" the reporter asked.

"That's a question for the fire and police departments," Jaffer said. "But no, we don't have word on that yet."

Again Randy joined in the shouting. This time Jaffer called on him.

"Randy Twain, News Three. Have the police identified any suspects yet?" Randy gazed intently at Larry Gandle as he asked the question. Gandle met his gaze and shot back an answer.

"Again, that's a question for the police department. But no, I'm not aware that any suspects have been identified at this time."

"Has last night's fire been linked to the fire that took Frank Fielding's life?" Randy got the question in quickly, almost before Gandle had finished his last sentence.

Gandle and Pamela Jaffer exchanged a lingering glance. After a pause, he answered.

"Once again," he said slowly, "that's a question for the police."

The press conference was over by seven-twenty. Randy asked me to stick around while he threw his story together, a process that involved going over what Jane had shot and cutting some sound bites with her to round out the story. Jane was a completely different woman from the one I'd met the day of the Rancho Santa Fe fire. She was breathing evenly, for one thing, and her skin tone was normal.

"Have you made a full recovery from that smoke inhalation?" I asked.

"Yeah," she laughed, "pretty much. But my Explorer got fried."

"So I saw."

Twain put his hand on Jane's shoulder.

"Could you do me a big favor?"

From the put-upon look she gave him, I guessed that Randy often asked for favors.

"What now?"

"Can you take that tape to the station and tell Cliff to put it into editing? Elizabeth's going to give me a ride home."

"I am?" This had not been discussed. Twain gave me a bold look.

"So we can go over those important developments on the case, remember?"

I went along. Maybe he did have something useful for me.

"Okay, Twain," Jane said as she hopped into the driver's seat, "but you owe me. Remember that."

As soon as the news van pulled away, Randy started in on the press conference. "Did you see the look that passed between Gandle and Jaffer when I asked if the fires were connected?" His eyes were wide, his tone full of innuendo.

"What are you implying—that there's some sort of corporate conspiracy going on?"

"Why not? Weirder things have happened."

We walked to my truck. I opened the passenger side door and cleared away a week's worth of junk before Twain got in.

"Where are we going?" I asked as I started the engine.

"Right across the street from Balboa Park, downtown. Take 163 to University."

I turned on my headlights, feeling strange. I'd woken up just a couple of hours ago. My sleep schedule was completely discombobulated.

"Explain to me," I said as I drove toward the freeway, "why you have it in for Gandle. Maybe it made sense when Fielding died in the Rancho Santa Fe fire, but now Gandle's taken his position at Starcom. Why would Gandle burn up his own company?"

"I don't know. But don't you get a slimy feeling from the guy? You're supposedly a psychic. Surely you pick up that he's a jerk."

"I pick up that Larry Gandle's an ambitious man. That doesn't necessarily make him evil. What I really pick up is that you hate him for some reason. Why? Did he snub you on an interview?"

"Several. But that's not why I don't trust him."

I suspected Twain's history with Gandle was coloring his judgment, but didn't say so.

"Why don't you trust him?" I asked.

"I've got a friend who's been an engineer with Starcom since it was just a start-up."

"Ah," I said, "an insider."

"For years he's been telling me about the rivalry between Gandle and Fielding. Just about everybody who works for the company knows about it."

"So what are you saying? That Gandle kidnapped Fielding's kid and burned his house down to move up in the corporation? And why would he kidnap the kid? Sorry, I don't see it."

"I'm not saying he has anything to do with the kidnapping. I'm also not saying he killed Fielding single-handedly. Maybe he hired a professional."

My response came immediately, without thought.

"No, this isn't a professional matter. This is personal. Whoever's setting these fires is filled with hate."

"That could be Gandle. He loathed Frank Fielding. I've got an old tape at home that shows the two of them at a press conference after the Starcom stock went to three digits. It was a happy occasion, right? But you could see the animosity, even that day."

We drove in silence for a while.

"Shoot," Twain said out of nowhere.

"What?"

"I forgot my briefcase in that conference room."

"Want me to turn around?"

"No, there's nothing in there I can't live without. I'll pick it up tomorrow."

We lapsed into another silence. The surreal scenes from last night's fire played in my head. I saw the shocked expressions of the apartment residents who'd suddenly found themselves homeless.

"I'll tell you whose vibes seem weird," I said.

"Whose?"

"One of the firemen I saw last night. He was at the roadblock, the first day I met you."

"Who, Zevnik?"

"Yeah. If I get a dicey vibe from anyone, it's him."

"Dicey?"

"Dangerous."

"That's no wonder. Zevnik's a maniac. I've known him for years."

"What do you mean, a maniac?"

"He's gung-ho, man. He takes crazy risks and gets reprimanded for it. That's why he had road duty that day at the Rancho fire. The last fire he fought, he stayed in a burning barn after everybody was ordered out. Roof nearly fell on him. But he saved a horse and the family dog, so he became a hero in the news. Yeah, Zevnik's a wild man."

"Hero syndrome," I mused.

"You could put it that way."

"Remember that tape you gave me that shows you reporting from the bottom of the Fieldings' driveway? I saw something kind of suspicious on that tape."

"What?"

"A white Fire Department Bronco driving down the road before the fire broke out. Looked just like Zevnik's."

"Rancho Santa Fe Fire Department vehicle seen driving on Rancho Santa Fe road. Not exactly scandalous."

"That's what my mom said. But still. Something about Zevnik sets off my inner alarm. It's that danger vibe."

"Like I said, there's a rational explanation for that. Zev's a daredevil." Randy shifted in his seat. I could feel his eyes on my face. "Tell me you don't really believe this vibe stuff, Elizabeth. You seem so intelligent and down-to-earth. The psychic thing's just a gimmick, right? A publicity ploy you use to set yourself apart from the pack."

The temptation to brag about finding the fireproof safe and the arsonist's note was great, but I kept my mouth shut. As Sequoia might say, the truth would out.

"It's my reality, not a gimmick. The last thing I want during this case is publicity."

"It's tempting to let the public know that a psychic detective is trying to find the Fielding boy."

"Please don't." I took my foot off the gas and looked him in the eye. "You say you care about Matthew. Outing me could really screw up my chances of finding him."

"Don't worry." He raised a hand in surrender. "I won't. But it's tricky deciding what to report and what to leave out. Frankly, I'm not all that keen about covering these fires. There's a contagion effect a lot of times. Am I informing the public, or am I inspiring the next pyromaniac?"

"I think you're boosting your career. A lot of people have tuned in to watch you narrate this drama."

"I know," he said. "It's kind of sick the way disasters pump up ratings. I mean, who ever heard of Wolf Blitzer before the Gulf War?"

We'd hit traffic on the freeway. To help me relax I popped in one of my CDs. Booker T. and the MGs, mellow and retro. A few minutes later Twain burst out:

"Quick. What number am I thinking of?"

I was about to tell him that my ability didn't work that way, that I couldn't read minds on command. But the number 88 appeared in my mind, strong and clear, impossible to miss. If the image had been sound, I would have had to turn down the volume.

"Do you have a pen and a piece of paper?" I asked.

"I'm a reporter. Of course I do."

"Write it down. Don't show it to me, just write it down."

"Okay," he said as he turned away and scribbled, "it is written." He folded the paper and held it behind his back. "Now, tell me the number." He stared at me, smiling smugly.

"Eighty-eight."

His smug smile vanished.

"Let me see." I extended my hand. "Give me the paper."

He passed it to me, looking shocked. I unfolded it and

wasn't surprised to see the number 88 scribbled on the front.

"How in the hell did you do that?"

I shrugged. "There's no formula. It just happens. I can't control it. I get these visuals sometimes."

He furrowed his brows, trying to figure out how I'd tricked him.

"Weird," he muttereded, more to himself than to me.

We drove for several miles just listening to the music. Twain finally broke the silence as I turned off 163 at University.

"People tell me my house is haunted," he said.

"Really?" Now this intrigued me.

"Yeah. I've had a few friends—several, now that I think about it, tell me that they think my house is haunted. I think it's crap, of course. Just keep going straight here, down Sixth Avenue."

"What do your friends say they sense?"

"I haven't really paid much attention to what they say since, again, I don't believe in any of this. But, uh, people seem to have creepy experiences when they use my bathroom."

"A haunted bathroom. That sucks. Bathrooms should be off-limits for ghosts, you know? There's a privacy factor, and I think ghosts should respect that. Where is this house?"

"Just take Sixth to Olive. You want to come in?"

"To your haunted house? How can I resist?"

CHAPTER 25

Twain and I continued down Sixth, the avenue that runs along the western edge of San Diego's beautiful Balboa Park. In the night shadows beneath the park's historic eucalyptus, two men and a woman huddled together and passed a bottle. To the south, the lights of downtown sparkled against the clear October sky.

Halfway past the park I turned onto Olive Street. My attention was riveted to a three-story brownstone in the middle of the block.

"That's it, isn't it?"

Twain's eyes followed my gaze. "What?"

"Your haunted house. The fourth house from the park there."

"What makes you think that's my house?"

"I can feel the negative energy from here." I shuddered visibly, and it wasn't all an act. "How can you even *live* there?"

Twain laughed. "Negative energy. Come on—you're kidding, right?"

"No, not at all."

I found a spot along the street and impressed myself with a flawless parallel parking job. When we stepped out of the truck I noticed that the wind had finally died down, although the air was still hot and dry. It made for a strange atmosphere, as hot nights are unusual in San Diego. I followed Twain to the house, where we stepped up three narrow stairs to his front door.

The house wasn't particularly old. From the hardware on the door, I guessed the place was built sometime in the 1940s. Twain put his key in the lock and swung the door open.

"Please, come on in."

Crossing the threshold, I felt as if I were stepping inside someone's migraine headache. Even though the ceilings were easily ten feet high, I felt pressure at the top of my head, as if some unseen force were trying to push me to the floor.

"Good Lord," I said.

"What?" Twain's boyish face was questioning, innocent.

Thanks to movies like *The Amityville Horror,* years ago I would have turned tail and run. My parapsychology field work had taught me that astrally charged environments like this might be uncomfortable, but they were rarely dangerous. I stepped through the small entryway and into the living room.

"Good thing you don't have any psychic sensitivity," I said. "You'd have to move."

"Why? What is everybody talking about? What am I missing here?" He sounded genuinely baffled.

I was too overwhelmed by the surroundings to answer. The walls were paneled in old mahogany, dark and deep. It felt as though they were closing in on me.

"All right," Twain said, "let me get you that videotape of Gandle and Fielding. This-a-way."

He led me to another wood-paneled room, this one dominated by a large wooden desk. The rest of the space was packed with video- and book-filled shelves, a TV/VCR setup, and a jumble of office equipment. I noticed Twain had an HP printer. Of course, thousands of other computer owners did too; still, I couldn't help but remember the arsonist's note: *I know you'll analyze this printer, so let me save you some time: it's a Hewlett-Packard 5LP, set at 600 dpi.*

Randy found the video on a low shelf. As he handed it to me, the phone on his desk began to ring.

"Excuse me," he said, pulling the receiver to his ear.

I stuffed the videotape into my backpack. "Mind if I use your restroom?"

"Go right ahead. All the way down." He pointed to the hallway and got back to his call.

Steeling myself, I made my way toward the back of the house. I was getting used to the atmosphere now, feeling less intimidated by it.

I opened a white painted door at the end of the hallway. Like most bathrooms of the era, this one was small, with a high window that opened to the alley. The floor was covered with tiny square tiles. The sink and toilet were new, but the claw-footed bathtub looked original. I stepped inside the room and closed the door. At the risk of over-sharing, I really did need to use the facility.

I nosed through a nearby magazine rack and, to my great surprise, found a trade paperback book entitled *The Complete Idiot's Guide to Being Psychic*. The very sight of it made me laugh. I picked it up, scanned the table of contents, and laughed some more. Clairvoyance, Telepathy, Precognition. Was this some kind of joke Randy had planted for me? Or had it been a gift from one of his more sensitive friends? I put it back, still chuckling. And suddenly gasped.

There was a body in the bathtub.

When I turned to look at it directly, the body was gone. My heart began to race and I made an effort to remain calm. *Apparition,* I told myself. *Apparitions can't hurt you.* I could no longer *see* the person but the presence was palpable. I flushed the john, ran my palms under the water faucet, and bolted out of the bathroom without drying my hands. I rushed into the office, where Randy was still talking on the phone.

"Yeah, I know you want the story now. And people in hell want ice water." He looked up and beamed a smile my way—dimples everywhere—then finished up his call. "Go find your namesake and jump off it, all right? See you later." He hung up and shook his head. "Cliff," he explained, "my coworker."

"Definitely haunted," I said.

"What?"

"The bathroom. It's haunted. No joke."

Randy threw up his hands. "What the hell is going on in there?"

"You're a reporter, right?"

"I've fooled people into believing it, anyway."

"Why don't you investigate and see for yourself? Do a title search. Check out the history of this place. I guarantee you'll come up with a murder story or a suicide—something."

"You're quite serious, aren't you?"

"Yes. Quite."

"Tell me what you saw back there."

"Tell you what. Since you're a nonbeliever, I'll write down what I saw and send it to you in the mail. That way it will be postmarked. Don't open it until you've done your research. When you find out from the archives what happened here, then open my envelope. That way there'll be no confusion about what I said or what you heard."

He looked at me blankly.

"You do know how to do historic investigation, don't you?" I asked.

He nodded. "Yes. I investigated your history, in fact."

"Oh, really."

He nodded. "To see how legit you were."

"And?"

"You're rock solid. I wasn't expecting that." His face softened. "And then I came across that cult case you were involved in. I remember when the story broke. It was big news around here, an FBI agent shot down in the flower

fields of Leucadia. I didn't realize that was your partner.
I'm really sorry."

As always, the subject brought a lump to my throat.
"Appreciate your sympathy." I waited for the stinging in
my nose to pass. "And that wasn't my partner, exactly. That
was my fiancé."

Twain walked over and put his arm around my shoulder,
an unexpected move that took me by surprise.

"I know," he said softly. "That's what I meant."

His hug felt genuine. One human being comforting another. Part of me wanted to burrow deeper into his arms,
take shelter in them. The other part of me pulled away and
spoke up.

"Gotta go."

"So soon? Can't I at least offer you something cold to
drink before you leave?"

"Thanks, but I'm afraid I can't stay." I headed for the
front door.

"Am I that repulsive?" he joked.

"Not at all," I said as I turned the doorknob, "but your
house is."

CHAPTER 26

I grabbed my green baseball cap and headed out the door before seven the next morning. A good night's rest had restored me. No more dreams, but I was feeling optimistic that I was on the right track toward finding Matthew. Roxanne Fielding had denied that her husband had enemies, but the construction of his company headquarters had pissed off a lot of environmentalists. Ken Fender of EarthNow was as good a lead as any I'd had so far.

I spent the entire drive to the coast sandwiched in a queue of impatient commuters along Del Dios Highway. Apparently the driver of the Dodge Caravan behind me failed to realize that riding my tail would not speed the progress of the dozens of cars creeping along in front of me. When had so many droves of people moved to North County? It was feeling more like L.A. every day, and that was not a good thing. I picked up speed once I passed under I-5 near the beach but by the time I pulled up to the bluff by the restaurant, I was nearly late.

Miracles Café was the Anti-Starbucks. The hand-painted sign on the roof and the tables on the porch were the only indications that the coastal cottage was even a business. I walked in, ordered a cup of breakfast blend, took a table in the corner and waited for Fender. He hadn't described himself but I imagined I'd be looking for someone with suntanned skin, sun-faded hair, and subcasual clothing. I was still looking for this person when a gentleman carrying a steaming mug approached my table.

"Elizabeth?"

"Yes."

"I'm Ken Fender." He put down his mug and extended his hand. With his collar-length dark hair and small round glasses, Fender looked like a thirty-year-old John Lennon. Except for his clothes.

"You always dress like that for surfing?" I asked, taking in his pressed trousers and tailored shirt.

He held up a well-worn athletic bag. "I change into my board shorts at the beach. After an hour or so of surfing I go in to the office. Clears my head." He settled into the chair across from me and opened the bag. "I brought you some literature." He tossed a few brochures onto the table.

"Thanks."

I picked up the flyers, which featured photos of local lagoons and beaches. The text design was tasteful and sedate. I'd see about the copy later.

"You said on the phone that you read about me in the paper, but my name hasn't been in the news lately. Not that I know of, anyway."

"It was an old article," I said.

"You also said you were interested in a particular perpetrator against the environment. Who were you talking about?"

"Starcom." I stated it flatly, staring right at him. Fender's only reaction was to blink.

"We don't take credit for yesterday's fire, if that's what you're wondering. EarthNow doesn't condone that kind of thing."

I continued to study his face. Was it the story he was sticking to, or was it the truth? "Why not?" I asked.

"Defeats our primary purpose. What we're all about is protecting San Diego's endangered habitats. If people go

off and start committing violence, the media's going to focus on the criminal conduct and not on the environment.
Totally undermines our effectiveness."

"Does the whole group feel that way, or just you?"

"The group agrees on this."

"So what if a member doesn't agree?"

He shrugged and took a sip of his brew. "They'll have
to find another group. Do you have a grudge against
Starcom?"

"No, but someone does. I'm trying to find that person."

He studied me through the steam of his coffee.

"You're not interested in joining our group, are you?"

"I wouldn't say that."

"But that's not your primary purpose in meeting me."

"Well, no."

"Who do you work for?" he asked.

"I was about to ask you the same question."

"I'm an environmental lawyer." He reached into his
pocket and handed me a card printed with the name of a
law firm: Lippman, Schell, and Comparetto. "And you?"

"Private investigator." I gave him my card and he looked
it over.

"Three years ago," I went on, "you were involved in a
protest against the development of the land where the Starcom headquarters is now located. Is there anyone in your
organization who felt extremely passionate about that particular issue?"

"Lots of people. We hated to lose that ridgeline."

"I mean passionate enough to sabotage the company."

He considered it a moment. "On the extreme side, there
are those who think that Starcom produces a cancer-causing
product."

"What—you mean cellular technology?"

"Yes," he said, "although there's no scientific evidence
to support that theory."

"Are any of those extremists in your chapter?"

"I couldn't say." He took another sip of coffee.

"Couldn't, or wouldn't?"

Steam from his coffee had fogged his glasses. He took them off and began wiping the lenses with his napkin.

"Wouldn't. We weed out the radicals from our group, but we don't go so far as to turn them over to the police. That would put a damper on free and open discussion, as you can imagine."

"So what do you do after you weed out a prospective member who you can see might be really dangerous?"

He gave me a hard stare before slipping his glasses back on. "Nothing. I'm a lawyer, not a cop."

Rick Wong sat in the conference room of the Encinitas sheriff's station, taking notes with one hand and drumming his small fingers on the cheap laminated tabletop with the other.

"That's all one word," I said as I read Wong's handwritten notes. "EarthNow, with a capital *N*. I think it's worth pursuing but I may need some help getting my hands on their membership list."

He sighed and looked up at me.

"Listen, we appreciate the work you've done with the strike team. Finding that fireproof safe was a major breakthrough. Without your help, the team most likely would have missed it." Wong paused, letting his words sink in. "It's just that this department hired you to assist Loebman's investigation and find the Fielding boy. Frankly, it seems like you're giving more attention to the arson investigation than to the kidnapping."

"I can understand how it looks that way." I paused as Wong had done, hoping my words would also sink in. "But finding Matthew is my primary goal. As I told Detective Loebman, I strongly feel that the fires and the kidnapping are connected. To investigate one is to investigate the other."

Wong used his pen to tap a restless rhythm on his notebook. "Can't you just . . . I don't know . . . *focus* on the boy?"

"You mean like put my fingers to my temples, mumble

a few mantras, *et voilà,* come up with his whereabouts?" I smiled. "I wish I could. I really do. Unfortunately, this is the best I can give you today." I pushed a slender folder across the table to him.

"What's this?"

"That's an updated report of my investigation since Sunday morning, when I interviewed Roxanne Fielding. It doesn't include this morning's interview with the EarthNow lawyer, but that'll be in the next report."

He opened the folder and took out the pages, reaching into his breast pocket for a pair of reading glasses. Wong took his time reading through my report. When he reached the fourth page, he looked up.

"I thought you might want to pay a little more attention to the sister, Debbie Fielding-Cross."

"She's not off my list. Logically, she makes such a great suspect. She's a close relative who desperately wants a child. Her brother named her as the person who got custody of Matthew in the event of his death. Believe me, I was eager to check her out. But once I interviewed her she seemed less likely."

"Why?"

"Wrong energy."

Wong looked predictably amused. "We're looking at a little more than her, uh, energy. We ran her phone bills for the last few months and tapped her phone line."

"And?"

"Nothing yet."

He went back to reading the report I'd given him, turning the pages. He'd almost finished when he looked up again.

"What's this about passing the Fielding boy on a path? What path? Where was this?"

"First, understand that you're reading what I call my dailies. I put everything in those notes, every impression I get during an investigation. When I wrote that I saw Matthew on that path, I didn't mean it literally. As I said in the opening paragraph there"—I pointed to the page in question—"that was a psychic impression. A dream, more or less."

"I get that," Wong said with a shrug. "But where? Where was this path?"

"The dream didn't take me that far."

Wong scowled and returned to his reading. When he finished the last page he straightened the papers and slid them back into the folder.

"You think the boy's alive, though."

"Yes. Very much so."

"Now I have something for you." It was Wong's turn to slide some paperwork across the table.

"What's this?" I asked.

"An updated list of the Fieldings' next of kin. We'd like you to help us follow up on these names."

I scanned the list. There were at least a dozen and a half names and addresses here, many of them out-of-state. I gave Wong my most sincere face.

"With all due respect, I don't think this would be the highest and best use of my time."

"Why not?"

"Whatever's going on here isn't a family matter. There's a palpable hate behind these crimes—"

"Hate's a family matter. Family members kill each other far more often than strangers do. Surely you know that."

"Of course. But what's going on here is an impersonal hatred. I'm getting that Fielding was targeted the way politicians and movie stars are targeted. He was killed for what he represented, not for who he was as a man."

"What makes you think that?"

"It's the feeling I get. Plus, the tone of that note we found in the safe. The message was directed to 'you people.' "

" 'There'll be more fires until you people get the message,' " Wong quoted.

"Right. 'You people.' Not Frank Fielding."

"It's a decent theory. But remember, the boy didn't

make any noise when he disappeared. That's a strong indication that he knew his kidnapper."

"I disagree. The boy didn't make any noise because he was a selective mute." I pointed to my report. "Interview with Bonnie McBride, page eleven."

Wong chewed the end of his pen.

"Taking a man's child, burning his home, burning his company—you ask me, that's pretty personal," he said. "Let's let the FBI look into the environmental groups."

In other words, Wong was steering my investigation. I felt frustrated but it was his department, after all, that was paying my bill.

"You'll pass Ken Fender's number and the EarthNow info on to Dale Blades?"

"Yes, but I want you to stick closer to the Fielding family."

I was thinking about the White Bronco I'd seen on the video of Twain's report from the bottom of the Fielding driveway.

"All right," I said. "I've got a lead in Rancho Santa Fe I'd like to follow."

CHAPTER 27

Carolyn Arnold sat at a small desk in the Rancho Santa Fe Fire Department, dwarfed behind the mountain of files stacked in front of her. It had been only twenty-four hours since we'd stood together on a burned canyon ledge, opened a fireproof safe and read the arsonist's note, but when I greeted her by name she looked up and stared blankly, as if she didn't quite know where she'd seen me before.

"You awake?" I asked.

She ran a hand over her face and massaged her bleary eyes. "Barely. I'm trying to read through insurance-company reports. I think English is a second language for these people."

"Which insurance company?"

"Companies," she corrected. "Starcom's insurance company, the Mira Mesa Apartments' insurance company, and about a dozen automotive insurance companies."

"Auto insurance?"

"The carport at the apartment building burned down, too. Took out five Hondas, three Toyotas, a couple of pickup trucks, and a 1970 Mercedes."

"No wonder you look tired."

"I'm beyond tired. I'm headed for the zombie zone. These reports are only the beginning. Over here"—she patted a fat, messy stack on her left—"I've got the Department of Forestry, FBI, ATF, and Sheriff's Department reports waiting to be integrated into my analysis."

"And you need to get this done by—"

"Yesterday. But fuck it. Pull up a chair and tell me what brings you to this neck of the woods."

I pulled out her desk chair. "Oops. Looks like this one's occupied." A silver lump of cloth was sitting on the seat. "What's this?"

"That's my 'shake and bake.' Observe." She came over and scooped up the silver thing. With one good shake it sprang into something that resembled a pup tent.

"Oh, yeah," I said, recognizing the fire shelter now. "Last-ditch fire protection. What's it made out of?"

"Aluminum foil and fiberglass. Hear it works pretty well, but I hope I never have to find out." She collapsed it back into a compact lump. "I'm sure you didn't come for a fire-equipment demonstration. What's up?"

"I was wondering what you could tell me about Tim Zevnik."

She smiled knowingly. "All the girls eventually get around to asking that question. He's single, if that's what you want to know."

"But a troublemaker, right?"

"Tim? Nah. He's a good boy."

"I heard Zevnik was reprimanded for . . . how should I put this? *Overzealous* behavior at a fire not long ago. True story?"

"Who told you that?"

"Randy Twain, that reporter from Channel Three."

She gave a noncommittal shrug. "It was a mild case of hero syndrome. Well intentioned, though. There was a stable fire over on Via de la Valle. Zevnik held the line in a burning barn against the captain's orders. Nearly got his ass killed, but he saved some animals. Captain took him off active firefighting for a while, for his own good."

"That's why Zevnik wasn't pulling line the day of the Fielding fire?"

"Off the record, yes. It's kind of shitty Twain's spreading that story around."

A bell went off inside the building somewhere.

"Break time," Carolyn said.

"I don't want to keep you, but do you have access to Zevnik's work schedule?

She looked at me carefully, realization dawning in her eyes. "Oh, I get it now. You're interested in investigating him, not dating him."

I didn't deny it.

"What's this about, Elizabeth?"

"I saw a Channel Three video that shows a Bronco looking very much like Zevnik's driving along the Fieldings' street the morning *before* that first fire."

"So what? It is Rancho Santa Fe Fire Department territory, you know."

"I know. I just want to make sure." I didn't mention the dicey feeling I got from Zevnik. I liked Carolyn and trusted her judgment, but she and Zevnik had fought fires together. I didn't underestimate the loyalty they were bound to share.

"It's true," she said, "that there's a fine line between firefighters and fire setters. You're probably thinking about that case a year or so ago where that reserve firefighter started a string of brushfires so he could go play hero."

"It crossed my mind."

I could have guessed what Carolyn said next.

"You're chasing down the wrong hole with Zevnik."

"Could be," I said.

"I can tell you're not going to stop until you're satisfied. So what do you need from me?"

"Let's take a look at his schedule, for starters."

"All right."

She jiggled the mouse to awaken her sleeping computer and pulled up a program. Peeking across her desk I saw a spreadsheet on the monitor, with fire department employee names listed on the left and two weeks' worth of columns stretching to the right. Carolyn scrolled to the last name on the page, where Zevnik was listed.

"Everybody works in twenty-four-hour shifts. Zev was working Sunday the fifth, the morning of the Fieldings' fire. I'll have to check the dispatch record but I'm sure he had a legitimate reason to be driving along Camino del Norte that morning."

"What was he doing at the Starcom fire?" There were no marks on the spreadsheet to indicate that Zevnik was on duty for either Monday the sixth or Tuesday the seventh.

"Like I said last night, he's on active rotation. He probably heard about it on the scanner and called in. Again, the dispatch record can tell us that." She sighed. "Look, I'm not so sure we're even dealing with the same arsonist for these fires. The device used to start the Fielding fire was different from the device used to start the Starcom fire."

"But they were both crude and amateurish."

"True."

"And it seems to me like they were designed to fit each scenario. A cigarette slowly burning in a matchbook is the kind of low-key device someone would need to start a fire at a residence without getting caught. On the other hand, a Molotov cocktail is better suited for tossing from a car window and making a quick getaway."

"Maybe."

"Somebody gave each of these fires some thought. Somebody who knows how fire behaves in Santa Ana conditions. Both fires were started downwind from the fuel supply. In the Fielding fire, downwind from a propane tank. In the Starcom fire, downwind from a canyon overgrown with dry brush."

Carolyn clicked the computer mouse and closed out the file. Her computer screen returned to the main menu.

"That's true. But I hope you have other suspects besides Zevnik."

"I'm looking at a lot of things," I said.

"Like?"

My eyes were drawn to Carolyn's computer monitor,

where her screen saver had kicked in. It was an image of a raging forest fire.

"An environmental group protested the building of the Starcom headquarters three years ago. I'm thinking there might be a connection here."

"Ecoterrorism?"

"Yeah. You read that note. 'There'll be more fires until you people get the message.' What do you think?"

"If you're talking about the Starcom fire, could be. But if you're talking about the fire that killed the Fieldings, I don't know. Those groups usually go out of their way to see that people aren't harmed."

I got up out of my chair.

"I'm keeping you from your lunch. Thanks for the co-operation. I appreciate it. Don't go cross-eyed over those insurance reports."

"What?" She gave me a goofy, cross-eyed grin.

I laughed and fired one more question before going out the door. "Does Zevnik live around here?"

"In Cardiff, I think." Her face was serious now. "He's off today."

"Thanks."

I found Zevnik's address in the white pages. Three-oh-two Munevar was a small house on a narrow street perpendicular to the coast highway. I drove slowly past Zevnik's place, until I found an empty parking spot two blocks up. The day was hot and I was grateful for the slight offshore breeze. When I reached the mailbox marked 302, I turned up the front walk and rang the bell. I hadn't called ahead, preferring the surprise visit.

Nothing stirred inside. I was pretty sure no one was home but waited a few minutes and rang again, just in case.

A lot of cars passed by, most of them probably headed for the beach. Whatever privacy this neighborhood had once upon a time was gone now, wiped out by its proximity to the ocean. Residents had to share the street with a year-round influx of tourists.

I sneaked around the back of the house to find a small yard, surprisingly well tended. I took a peek in the back window. The interior of the firefighter's home was small and sparsely furnished but neat, almost Zen-like. Other than that, looking through the windows told me nothing.

At the rear of the backyard was a storage shed. It had no windows, just small vents under a tar roof. The door to the shed was padlocked.

Could Matthew be inside? I walked up to the shed and knocked on the door. "Hello. Is anyone in there?"

I felt a tingle on the back of my neck and turned around. A man, seventyish, was looking over the backyard fence. He was wearing a green and white golf cap and carrying a matching pair of hedge clippers. He looked at me as if I were a few cards short of a deck.

"That's just a storage shed, honey. The man you're looking for lives in the house up front."

"I was looking for a little boy. You haven't seen him, have you?"

"Nope. Just the big boy. Haven't seen much of him lately, either. Not with all these fires around. He's a firefighter, you know."

"Uh-huh," I said vaguely. "Thanks." I smiled and nodded, heading back to the street, hoping he wouldn't mention the incident to Zevnik. Which was kind of like hoping the IRS wouldn't notice that you hadn't filed your taxes.

CHAPTER 28

The oleander trees lining the driveway were more green than gray today, now that the wind had blown off most of the ashes from Sunday's fire. Still, the landscape surrounding my parents' place looked wretched. It was the middle of the day in the middle of the week, but I hoped someone would be home since I'd left the videotapes I'd borrowed from Twain on my parents' VCR Monday night.

For years—decades—this had been my home, too, and I'd barged through the front door, usually without remembering to wipe my shoes. As I rang the bell, I tried to remember when I'd decided that ringing the bell was the thing to do. When the door opened, Mom stood before me, a pair of videotapes in her hand and a cockatoo on her shoulder.

"Hello, Mr. Poe," I said to the bird.

"Looking for these?" Mom held up the videos, proud of herself.

"How'd you guess?"

She stepped back and opened the door wider. "I know you can't stay, but it's my duty to tell you that there's a portobello mushroom quiche in the oven."

"No fair, Mom. You know I can't say no to quiche."

"Nevermore!" Mr. Poe screeched.

"Silly bird," I said. "You're a cockatoo, not a raven."

Mr. Poe fixed a liquid black eye on me and blinked his wrinkly white eyelid.

"Pretty boy. How cliché."

I cracked up.

"It'll be about twenty minutes," Mom said. "I was just finishing up my column for the newsletter. Make yourself at home."

The newsletter was *Watch Your Assets*, an eight-page monthly that my mother, Suzanne Sarah Chase, has been publishing for a decade or so. When the subscriber base topped fifty thousand last year, she turned the newsletter's production over to a small staff of Wall Street whiz kids, but she still keeps a hand in by writing an editorial column. Her readers study each paragraph as if it's sacred text. For good reason. Mom foresees market trends with uncanny accuracy. Yet she swears she's not psychic.

I went into the living room and sat down to play the piano, tinkering around with Gershwin but settling on Beethoven's *Moonlight Sonata*. The piece was overplayed, and certainly many played it better than I. But I was in a minor-key mood today and hoped that the sonata's slow chord progressions and subdued harmonies would soothe me. I ran through the piece and started again, getting deeper into the music the second time around.

"I love to hear you play."

I looked up to see Mom standing behind me, listening. I faltered for a beat, then continued to play. She walked around and leaned against the piano. When I was done there were tears in her eyes.

"My playing's that bad, huh?" I joked.

She laughed and dabbed at the corner of her eye. "I was just thinking how grateful I am to still have this old piano. If it hadn't been for a shift in the wind and the fire department, this thing would be a pile of ashes now."

"True."

"But mostly I was thinking how grateful I am to have this beautiful daughter to play it."

"Easy on the sugar, Mom." She always embarrassed me with overt statements like that. Not that it didn't feel good.

"Could use a little dusting, couldn't it?" She ran her hand along the piano's smooth black top.

"I see you took the picture down," I said.

"I decided you were right. Like it or not, life goes on without our loved ones."

I nodded in agreement.

"Kind of like living under a president you didn't vote for. You hate it, but you get used to it."

The timer in the kitchen went off.

"Quiche is done." She hurried into the kitchen as the timer continued its insistent buzzing. "That reminds me," she called over her shoulder. "You got a call here this morning."

"Here?"

"Yeah, from your friend Sequoia. He was calling to remind you about your archery practice today. I didn't know you'd taken up archery."

Damn. I'd forgotten all about my next session with Sequoia. "I just started recently," I said as I followed her into the kitchen. "Why'd he call here?"

"I don't know. Guess he couldn't reach you at home."

"But I have my cell with me."

She gave me an exasperated look, as if figuring out the whys and wheretofores of my generation were far beyond her. She put on a pair of hot mitts and slid the quiche out of the oven. The cheese pie filled the kitchen with a tantalizing aroma.

"I don't know if you realize this," she said as she placed the pan on a cooling rack, "but I won second place in my college longbow competition."

"You're kidding."

"There's an old picture of me and my bow in a box around here somewhere. I'd almost forgotten all about it."

"Do we have to wait for that to cool?" I hadn't had breakfast and was so hungry it felt as though my stomach were beginning to eat itself.

"Of course we don't."

I went to the cupboard for some plates. My parents had recently installed a television above the kitchen counter, a development I believed to be degenerate. That didn't stop me from turning it on.

The station was tuned to Channel Three and we were catching the top of the midday news broadcast. A logo in the corner let me know that it was a follow-up story on the Starcom fire. I turned up the volume.

". . . the company formerly headed by Frank Fielding, who died last Sunday in a fire that destroyed his Rancho Santa Fe home. Authorities are still seeking to resolve the mysterious disappearance of his son, four-year-old Matthew Fielding, who was last seen one week ago today, playing in the woods near his home."

The now familiar picture of Matthew flashed on the screen.

"The FBI is offering a reward for information leading to the boy's whereabouts. Meanwhile, a local law-enforcement agency has enlisted the aid of psychic detective Elizabeth Chase to help find Matthew."

To my horror, a videotape of me getting into my truck at the bottom of the Fieldings' driveway flashed on the screen.

"Chase is the daughter of Dr. Alfred Chase of Rancho Santa Fe, a neighbor of the Fieldings' whose home narrowly escaped being destroyed in Sunday's fire."

The picture changed again, this time treating viewers to a panoramic sweep of my parents' fire-ravaged neighborhood. Then it was back to Bill Bainsley, who was on to another story.

Mom snapped off the TV and turned to me for comment but I was too angry to speak.

"Let's not mention this to your father."

"I'm going to kill him," I said.

"Kill your father?"

"No, Mom. Kill the bastard who leaked my name to the media."

CHAPTER 29

I was still seething as I pulled up to my house. When I saw Sequoia's Jeep parked in my driveway I experienced two feelings: guilt, immediately supplanted by self-righteousness. Sequoia was leaning on the hood of his Jeep, waiting for me.

"I can't possibly keep our appointment today," I said as I got out of my truck.

Sequoia stood and nodded. "Uh-huh."

"Sorry, but I've had too many delays already in finding this child. I've got to review some videotapes and get started on some surveillance work. I'm racing the clock here."

Sequoia followed me up the walk. He wasn't getting the hint.

"I really don't even have time to explain it to you right now." I unlocked the door and hurried inside. He stepped in after me, putting me in the awkward position of having to send him away.

"I brought you the fifty-pound bow this time," he said.

I turned and stared at him, feeling vexed. He was supposed to have said, "Oh, sorry. I'll come back another time." Instead he was acting as though he were deaf.

"Did you even hear me? I can't play bow and arrow today. I have leads to follow and things to straighten out and not enough hours left in the day."

"Sounds like a lot of running around."

"Yes, a lot."

"Probably be more effective to stand in the center and let what's important come to you."

"Huh?"

"You heard the words. Now let them sink in."

I looked at him—really looked at him—for the first time since I'd arrived home. His face was calm, his eyes clear. For a split second I was able to see the world as he saw it. I'd been on the outer edge of a merry-go-round watching life go by in a blur. Now, standing at the center where Sequoia lived, I got some perspective.

"You're not going to let me give you the brush-off, are you?"

"Nope." His obsidian eyes radiated serenity, wisdom, and affection. "Remember when I accepted you as my student, I told you there would be times you'd have to take instruction you wouldn't necessarily want to take?"

"Yes."

"This is one of those times."

The committee in my brain broke into a chorus of objections involving time, responsibility to the case, the foolishness of getting sidetracked by some woo-woo Native American medicine man. I weighed their objections against what I knew about my teacher. Never once had a session with Sequoia been a waste of time. He was a man who did not fritter away actions or words. If he wanted to continue with our session today, he had a good reason.

"Fifty-pound bow, huh? Really think I can handle that thing?"

He looked at me tenderly and smiled. "Yeah. You're ready for it now. We can go out to Lake Wolford. Not such a long drive from here."

"Let's take my truck. Nero needs to get out."

*   *   *

We drove past the Lake Wolford Café, which serves the best catfish and hush puppies in the county. Sequoia instructed me to turn onto a one-lane road of hard-packed dirt. We drove through some brush-covered hills, where an occasional cypress tree waved its paper-dry leaves in the hot wind.

"Pull over and park in this clearing," Sequoia said.

It felt good to get out, away from the crowded city. Nero jumped from the truck, put his nose to the ground and trotted happily down a tiny rabbit path. He was well trained and came when called; I wouldn't have to worry about him.

Across the field, a bull's-eye was mounted on the trunk of a tree. Sequoia lifted the bow from the truck bed and handed it to me.

"Whoa," I said as I felt its heft. "Substantial." The recurve was nearly as tall as I was. "What is this, sixty-six inches?"

"Sixty-four. Try it."

I notched in an arrow and pulled back. It was harder than the bow I was used to.

"I'm going to stand closer."

"Don't think you need to, but okay."

The truth was, I wasn't ready to shoot. I talked as we walked. "I've been looking for this kid, I think I told you that before you went back East."

He nodded.

"His parents were killed in that fire Sunday, did I tell you?"

"I heard it on the news," he said. "Heard about you on the news, too."

I felt my blood boil.

"I'm not happy about that." I stopped. We were about ten yards from the tree. I strapped on my armguard and wriggled into my glove.

"Makes you mad, doesn't it?"

"Yeah, it makes me mad. Everyone who paid attention to the news today knows I'm working on this case now. I have enough obstacles without people knowing who I am."

I pulled back the bow and let the arrow fly. It went low and landed in the trunk beneath the target.

"This reminds me of the way the wind was pissing you off the other day."

"This is worse."

He looked up at the sky and laughed, a high-pitched sound that was so lighthearted I couldn't help but smile.

"You're straight up about it," he said, putting a hand on my shoulder. "That's good. Remember what I told you about using the energy around you, like the wind? You can use this, too."

"Use what?"

Sequoia handed me another arrow.

"This situation that's making you mad. You use it by shifting your point of view. Try to see your name in the news as a good thing."

"Lemons to lemonade?" I rolled my eyes. "Spare me the Pollyanna sermon, Sequoia."

"Hey," he said quietly. "This ain't no pop psych seminar. I'm teaching you how things really work."

Sometimes Sequoia is so humble that I forget what he's capable of. He is what Native Americans call a shapeshifter. Years ago at Stanford I'd researched case studies of rare individuals who were able to achieve bilocation— the ability to appear in physical form in two places at once. When Sequoia came into my life, I witnessed the phenomenon for myself. During an investigation last year, Sequoia's sudden appearance outside a window caused me to step out of the path of gunfire. How his form appeared there remains a mystery, but I literally owed him my life.

"Okay. My name in the news is a good thing. I'll work on that."

I concentrated on my next shot, raising my bow and drawing the string in one fluid motion. I locked on the center of the target and released the arrow. It landed in the second ring, a respectable hit. Suddenly I remembered what had led up to my finding the fireproof safe.

"Sequoia." I looked him in the eye. "I heard your voice

when I was sitting overlooking the canyon the other day, before the Starcom fire broke out. You really helped me out there. Thanks."

He looked confused. "I don't know what you're talking about."

"I heard you saying to me, 'Pay attention.' I figured you were sending me some kind of telepathic message."

He shook his head. "Wasn't me."

"But I heard a voice. Where'd it come from?"

"The wiser place in you."

"Why did I think it was your voice?"

"You associate the wise place inside yourself with me. But it's really you, your spirit self. I'm just your teacher here. What was the voice telling you to pay attention to?"

I picked up another arrow. "That area of the canyon, I guess. It's where the fire broke out a few hours later. It's also where I found some key evidence."

Sequoia nodded. "That's good." He squinted at the bull's-eye. "Try again, but shift your point of view. Go right inside the center of that ring. Travel there with your spirit."

I looked at the bull's-eye. The very center was deep black, a void surrounded by the bright colors of a California autumn afternoon. As I traveled into that void I drew back the string with a contented sense of how good the tension felt against my arms. A gust of wind came up and pushed against my back. Infused with a sense of peace, I let the shot happen. The arrow hit the center of the eye, dead-on. I turned to Sequoia with glee.

"A miracle!"

"Not a miracle. You're just paying attention now, and using the energy around you."

I was anxious to do it again.

"Let's go," Sequoia said.

"But we've only been here five minutes."

"We only needed five minutes. I thought you had a lot to do."

"Oh, yeah. I do."

*   *   *

My session with Sequoia, including transportation, had taken less than an hour. He hopped out at the driveway, got into his Jeep, and drove away with a cheerful wave good-bye.

I pulled into the garage, cut the engine, and let Nero out. It had been a busy week and a lot of junk had accumulated on the floor of the cab. I leaned over to straighten things up: an empty Starbucks latte grande, a stack of mail, a couple of stray CD jewel cases, and Matthew Fielding's Scooby toy.

Scooby's glass eyes silently implored: *Hold me.* You had to admire the cleverness of a manufacturer who could design a toy so irresistible. I picked up the stuffed dog by its soft, floppy ears and looked into its pupils, deep black and lifelike. They were like the void at the center of the bull's-eye.

Go right inside the center . . . travel there with your spirit.

What came next was like a brightly colored newsreel playing in my mind.

CHAPTER 30

"Matthew is being held in a place—I think it's a house, but I'm not sure—near a narrow path that runs along a chain-link fence. Kind of like this." I did my best to re-create the image I'd seen in my mind's eye onto a piece of paper. "The inside of the place has wood paneling. It's dark and he's scared. But here's the most important thing: somewhere nearby is a shopping mall with a Kmart. The path leads beside or behind the Kmart. It's in San Diego County somewhere." In the margin of my drawing I wrote the words "near a Kmart" and shoved the paper across the desk to Dale Blades.

The FBI agent looked down at my drawing but avoided touching it, as if it might contain some communicable disease. He frowned and looked over at Loebman.

Loebman returned Blades's gaze with a hopeful look. "A Kmart. That narrows the field quite a bit. There can't be that many Kmarts in San Diego County."

I'd come in from the garage and called Loebman immediately to tell him about the vision I'd seen while holding Matthew's stuffed dog. He'd foreseen the need for more manpower and had arranged to meet with Blades at the FBI field office in Carlsbad. It was getting toward quitting time—almost five—and Blades had agreed to the meeting with some reluctance.

"I've been in law enforcement for eighteen years and in all that time I've never seen a psychic help out on a case." Blades took a small packet of tissues from his shirt pocket, pulled one out and blew his nose. "Allergies," he grumbled. I wondered if perhaps his moustache had become a pollen magnet. "What I have seen is people who call themselves psychic coming in and tossing out a hundred vague clues— like 'you'll find the corpse near a body of water'—and then when the case gets solved, the so-called psychic takes credit for it. Retrofitting facts, basically."

He was making an excellent point and I nodded my agreement. "Yeah, that's true. Happens a lot. Most of the time, probably."

"She's the one who found that safe with the arsonist's note the other day," Loebman said. "I think it would behoove us to pay attention to this Kmart thing."

Blades honked his nose into another tissue.

"Seeing as how we're running out of time and what we've got is diddly," Loebman added.

"Not true." Blades sniffed and wadded his tissue into a ball. "We got a twenty-four-hour turnaround on the analysis of the gasoline in that Molotov cocktail. We've narrowed down the gas that was used to one of five suppliers."

Loebman smirked. "Give me a break, Dale. Who's going to ID a drive-through, self-serve gas customer?"

"And we have a profile," Blades continued. "Male, mid-twenties, dysfunctional family, poor academic record, unmarried. We're trying to find a match from a list of nearly two thousand Starcom employees. Plus the eighteen residents who lived in the Mira Mesa Apartments. It may take a little time, but we'll get a hit." Blades cocked an eyebrow at me. "See, I believe in doing investigations the old-fashioned way."

I didn't respond. I was thinking about Tim Zevnik. I didn't know anything about the firefighter's family history, but he didn't strike me as a Rhodes scholar. The rest of the profile fit, as well. Zevnik was an unmarried man in his mid-twenties.

"Not to be disagreeable, but we've got five agencies working twenty-four/seven the old-fashioned way," Loebman said. "So far they've turned up zero viable leads from the missing-persons bulletin. Zero viable leads from tracking down every damn purchase the Fieldings made on their credit cards in the last three months. Zero leads from analyzing Fieldings' bank records, and zero leads after calling every damn number on Frank and Roxanne's phone records."

There was a tension between the two today that hadn't been there the last time I'd met with the strike team.

"Our cyber investigator," Blades said in a raised voice, "has tagged at least two suspects who've been posting on the bulletin boards from the National Center for Missing and Exploited Children Web site."

"Suspicious, maybe. But actual suspects? They're in the southeast, Dale. I haven't seen any evidence that links those guys with the Fielding kid." Loebman turned to me. "I'm happy to take anything you can give us, Elizabeth."

"Did you follow up on that EarthNow contact I gave to Rick Wong?" I asked.

Blades frowned. "We're working our own sources on the environmental angle."

"I'd like to have a copy of the EarthNow membership list if you can get one. Also those other lists you mentioned—the Starcom employees and Mira Mesa Apartments residents."

Blades was shaking his head no before I'd even finished the question. "It'll be a while before we could copy all that. Don't hold your breath."

Loebman saw my predicament and jumped in.

"How about I just copy the files onto a disk for you?"

"Thanks," I said. "By the way, what did you mean when you said 'we're running out of time'?"

He and Blades exchanged a look, the way people do when they share a secret.

"She's part of the investigation," Loebman said.

Blades dragged his finger across his neck like an imaginary knife. His message was clear: *Shut up, Loebman.* He turned to me and crossed his arms over his chest. His eyelids were soft and swollen from his allergies, but his eyes were hard as stone.

"How is it you know about this Kmart?" he asked.

"The technical term is *psychometry*. It's a sensitivity to touch. Sometimes I can use an object that a person was deeply attached to as a transmitter to the original owner. I'm using the word *transmitter* here allegorically, not literally. There's no weird science involved that I know of."

"Then how does it work?" Blades asked.

"That would be in the To Be Determined file, Dale."

He stared at me intently, waiting for a better answer. I didn't have one.

"I spent ten years at Stanford trying to figure out how it works. I made up some bullshit for my dissertation, but I'm not going to bullshit you. I don't know how it works. I just know that it does, sometimes."

Blades turned his stony gaze to Loebman. They were carrying on a silent conversation and it was starting to bug me.

"What are you two not telling me?" I asked.

"Got a call from the op-ed editor at the *Union-Tribune* this morning," Loebman began.

"Hey," Blades said, cutting him off.

"Come on, Dale, she's part of the team. She's not going to leak anything."

Blades mumbled something that sounded like "better not," and riffled through the file folder in front of him. He pulled out a sheet of paper and slid it across the table.

"The editor got a letter that scared her and she called us. That's a copy, of course. The original's at the lab, not that we think we'll get prints. Whoever it is knows what he's doing."

It was a note, printed in a typeface I recognized immediately and formatted with the same superwide margins.

Dear Editor,

Regarding the recent arson fires, Diana Jordan of Carlsbad asks how a person "can unleash so much destruction." Ms. Johnson should look in the mirror and ask the same question.

I'll keep killing you until you stop killing her. She's bleeding under the wheels of your carbon-dioxide-belching SUVs, drowning in your shit-filled ocean, choking under your shit-brown skies. Your ticky-tacky houses are multiplying on her like cancer cells. There are way *too many of you. Warning: GET OUT. Grass and trees grow back but when your flesh burns, you're dead forever.*

The letter was unsigned. I read it a few times, committing the sentences to memory, and looked up.

" 'There are way too many of you,' " I repeated. "Motive seems clear to me. I take it you're checking out eco-terrorists and radical green groups."

"Yeah, obviously," Blades said. "Hey, I think I feel a psychic prediction coming on. There's going to be another fire." He smiled, delighted by his own joke.

I wasn't amused. The fear I'd felt at the beginning of the week was snaking through my abdomen again, accompanied by those motherless-child blues. I stared at Blades, trying to remember that at one time he'd been an innocent baby like the rest of us. I wondered what had hardened him into the kind of guy who joked about terrorism.

Loebman noticed my staring and gave me a sympathetic smile. "Come on," he said as he got up from the table. "I'll get those names onto a disk for you."

CHAPTER 31

It was after five o'clock—show time—at the Channel Three station in Kearny Mesa, so I knew Twain would be on duty. Last time I'd been here, he'd escorted me in through the back door. This time I came through the front, which was a more formal affair. With its thick carpet, neutral sofas, and graceful potted palms, the reception room was as hushed as the newsroom was hectic. Behind an imposing black Formica counter, a brainy-looking receptionist gave me the once-over.

"Who are you here to see?" Her voice was pleasant enough.

A glass partition separated us, with a narrow opening near the counter, not unlike a movie box office. I leaned down so that my voice would pass through.

"Here to see Randy Twain."

"He's in the edit room right now. May I have your name?"

"Elizabeth Chase."

I studied her as she made a call from her phone, trying to figure out what made her look so smart. It wasn't just the glasses. She wore a simple white shirt and the demeanor of someone with important things to do. Maybe an intern,

I thought, putting up with this job to get a foot in the door.

"It'll be a while," she said, hanging up.

I settled down with a magazine. Ten minutes into my wait a man came through the front door and greeted the receptionist by her name, Beth. She pushed a buzzer that let him through a door on the left side of the room. I watched him walk through, watched Beth's face. She looked at her watch and gave me a wan smile.

"Shouldn't be long now."

"This kind of reminds me of the new prison downtown," I said.

She let out a laugh.

"You have no idea."

A few minutes later Twain came through the door, breaking into a smile when he saw me. I put my magazine aside and got straight to the point.

"You burned me," I said. In my peripheral vision I could see that Beth was delighted by this diversion.

" 'A local law-enforcement agency has enlisted the aid of psychic detective Elizabeth Chase to help find the missing boy,' " I quoted from the newscast, giving him my sharpest dagger eyes. "Thank you very much."

He held up his hands in complete surrender. "I didn't burn you. I swear. You think I'd give them that, after you asked me not to?"

"Who else would have? Butthead Bainsley used the footage your news photographer shot of me at the bottom of the Fieldings' driveway." The receptionist was hearing every word but I didn't care. Over Twain's shoulder I could see her pretending to do paperwork.

"That tape belongs to Channel Three, not me. I didn't have anything to do with it going on the air. How could I, after you'd made it so clear you didn't want any exposure?"

"How could you? I don't know. Maybe you wanted to score points with your sensationalism-loving producer."

"That's ridiculous. I don't have anything to do with the midday show."

"So you're denying that you had anything to do with leaking my name."

"I'm absolutely denying it." He looked hurt.

"Randy, the story was broadcast on your station. Who else could have leaked it?"

"Maybe one of the sheriff's people shot off their mouth. Maybe the FBI. You've been at all the scenes, Elizabeth. People see you there and they ask questions. Secrets get out. Happens all the time."

I looked over at Beth. She shrugged as if to say she could neither confirm nor deny Twain's story.

"I'm sorry it aired," Twain said. "I'll spread the word here to keep it from happening again. Won't erase the damage but it might at least help."

"The whole story is getting out of control."

"Of course it is," he said with a cynical smile. "High-profile kidnapping plus raging southern California wildfires equals higher ratings. It's JonBenét Ramsey meets the Malibu fires of ninety-three. But I didn't out you. Honest. If I'm lying I promise I'll lick your toes for as long as you want me to."

Good eye contact, no twitching or other telltale body language. Either Twain was telling the truth or he was one righteous liar.

I sighed, feeling deflated. "Do what you can to keep it from happening again."

Twain touched me lightly on the elbow. "As long as you're here, could you come back to my office? I have some information that could be worthwhile for you."

"I've heard that before," I said without enthusiasm. But I followed him through the bedlam of the newsroom and into his office.

"It's definitely an arson case," Twain said when we entered the shelter of his office. "Did you know they found a note in a fireproof safe after the Starcom fire?"

"Yeah, I knew that."

He dropped his jaw. "You dog. You weren't about to tell me, were you?"

"No. Contagion effect of the news, remember? The last thing we need right now is a copycat. What are these?" I pointed to a pair of videotapes on his desk chair.

"Follow-up profiles on the victims of the Starcom fire, those people who lived in that apartment building that burned down. Human-interest-type stuff. Where they are now, how they're faring. Most of it won't ever be broadcast, but my producer wants to keep the pump primed on this story."

The labels were scrawled with last names. King, Locke, Stern.

"I'd like to have a look at these," I said.

"If you think it'll help, sure. I'll make you dupes. Machine's right here." He picked up one of the videos and put it into the left side of a duplicating VCR. His act—if it was an act—was perfect, but my jury was out on whether Twain was guilty of leaking my name to the station.

"Not that I owe you this whatsoever," he said as he took the cellophane off a new videotape, "but did you hear about the bizarre letter to the editor that the *Union-Trib* got this morning?"

"Is there any other kind?"

"Seriously. Someone wrote in and claimed credit for the fires. Ranted about pollution and overcrowding and SUVs. Promised more fires and ordered everybody out."

"Yeah, I heard. How'd you find out?"

"One of my best buds works for the *U-T*."

"Is Channel Three going to report the letter?"

His brows came together and he shook his head. "Not at this point. We'll see how the story develops."

He popped the new video into the duplicating machine and began making the first copy for me.

"You ever see *Ghostbusters*?" he asked.

"One of the funniest movies ever made. I was rolling in the aisles with laughter before the opening credits stopped running. Why do you ask?"

"Ghosts on my mind, I guess. I ran a title search on my house and got the names of the previous owners. Then I

ran those names through a news database. I have to admit
the results were very interesting."

I held up a hand to stop him from saying any more.

"Don't tell me. I haven't had time to write down what
I saw and mail it to you. We're doing a blind experiment
here, remember?"

"Write it down now."

I sat at Twain's desk and with pen and paper wrote an
account of the apparition I'd seen in his bathtub.

"Got an envelope?" I asked.

He dug up a Channel Three business envelope and a
stamp.

"What's your home address?"

He recited the address and I wrote it on the front of the
envelope, tucking my report inside. "I'll mail this on my
way out," I said. "After you've opened and read it, you can
show me what your research revealed." I got up and headed
for the door.

"Elizabeth."

When I turned around he was studying my face, looking
serious.

"What?" I said.

"You can't stop thinking about me licking your toes, can
you?"

I turned back around, hoping he wouldn't see me blush.
Randy Twain did not play fair.

CHAPTER 32

When I woke up on Thursday morning, death was hanging around.

A lot of PIs aren't acquainted with the Grim Reaper. Serving subpoenas and watching naughty spouses, their work is no more likely than a barber's to put them in contact with corpses. But a psychic PI gets called in as a last resort, when people are too desperate to be prideful. By the time I've been summoned, the Reaper usually has been, too.

Emily Dickinson imagined that Death "kindly stopped" for her. Very sweet. Not my experience, though. The times I've seen Death stop by, he hasn't been the least bit kind. More like inflexible; the collection agent from hell.

In a vain attempt to shake the visitor off, I went to the living room and did some yoga stretches. Started with the sun asana and moved into more strenuous positions, to work out that racing feeling in my heart. Amazing what a good lungful of oxygen can do for the nerves. By the time I was done I felt calmer, stronger, and more centered.

Death was still hanging around, though.

I knew from experience that getting to work would be the best way to deal with my anxiety. I went through my phone books, jotting down the addresses and phone numbers of San Diego County Kmarts.

It was a manageable list of twelve stores. FBI field agents could have handled these drive-bys in no time. I thought back to my last conversation with Dale Blades, remembering the cold reception he'd given to my report about envisioning the wood-paneled house and the narrow path running by a chain-link fence near a Kmart. Remembered his explanation that psychics threw out massive quantities of details and then—how had he put it?—retrofitted the facts of the case after it was solved. Given his cynicism, I didn't expect any help from the FBI.

I ran my eyes down the list, hoping to get a vibe off one of the addresses. But the typewritten information sat inertly on the page. In the absence of intuitive insight, I figured I'd go at it systematically. I kept a plentiful supply of San Diego maps in my office cabinet. I pulled one out and marked each Kmart location by number, starting with the store closest to me on Mission Avenue in Escondido. My plan was to survey each store, looking for chain-link fencing and a path. I would drive by the north county stores first and work my way south.

At five minutes to noon I pulled into the parking lot of number four on my list, a Kmart in Oceanside. Even on the coast, the air felt hot and dry. Here too the temperature was in the nineties.

The Kmart was in a new shopping center, with nary a chain-link fence in sight. Feeling hungry, I figured I'd take my chances at a small deli on the far side of the parking lot. I walked through the door and it slammed shut behind me with a bang like a gunshot.

"Sorry," I said when the guy behind the counter looked up with a start. "That was the wind, not me."

He was wearing an apron over jeans and tank top and his long hair was pulled back into a thick ponytail. A thin layer of perspiration covered his bare arms and shoulders, giving him a sheen.

"I know. It's a heck of a wind out there. What can I get for you?" His accent was Australian.

"How about tuna on wheat?"

I watched him put the sandwich together. A boom-box radio on the counter behind him was broadcasting lunch-hour news.

"You want cheese on that?"

"No, thanks."

Two teenage girls came in behind me, moving toward the glass display to see what they wanted. Their chatter blended with the sounds from the radio. The man in the apron took an enormous butcher knife and sliced my sandwich in two.

"Is that for here or to go?" he asked.

I paused to think it over. The girls behind me had stopped talking and the radio announcer's voice filled the silence.

"Did I just hear them report a fire?" I asked.

The girls behind me spoke up.

"Yeah, in San Marcos. We could see the smoke on our way over here."

"I'll take that sandwich to go," I said.

My original plan had been to continue south to the next Kmart, but I got in the truck and went toward San Marcos on 78, to get an idea where the fire was. It wasn't long before I could see a cloud of smoke rising from the hills. My stomach went into major jitters and my sandwich didn't look so appetizing anymore. I got out my cell and called Carolyn Arnold's mobile phone. No answer. I tried Loeb-man's number and was relieved to hear him answer.

"I'm looking at the smoke from the San Marcos fire," I said without preamble. "How bad is it?"

"Bad. Real close to a big development. Lots of houses threatened." From the background noise, it was obvious he was talking from his car. "I'm on my way there now."

"What development?" I asked.

"Sapphire Heights, off Rock Springs Road."

*   *   *

There was never a more perfect target for an arson fire than Sapphire Heights. The planned community was perched on top of a hill that rose from the valley like a monolith. The sides of the hill, too steep to build on, were blanketed in thick blue sage. The high oil content of sage helps it survive desert droughts but makes it one of the most flammable substances in the world. Combined with the kindling undergrowth of dry sumac and native grasses, the hillside was a fire waiting to happen.

From ten miles away on 78, I could see the isolated hilltop community of Sapphire Heights. In spite of their tile roofs, ocean views, and $400,000 price tags, the houses were packed together so closely that from this distance they looked like a bumpy pink rash on the land. Words from the intercepted letter to the editor came back to me.

Ticky-tacky houses multiplying like cancer cells.

As I drove closer I could make out the single road that led into and out of the development. It was jammed bumper to bumper with cars heading down the hill. Black smoke was muscling up from behind the hill, spreading over the community like bad news.

I'd lived through this scene too many times in the past few days. Once again the sky was dark and the acrid smell of burning filled the air. I didn't want to be one of those jerks who gets in the way of firefighters trying to access the area, so I exited the freeway and took the back roads. By the time I reached Rock Springs, I could see tall flames shooting up from the far side of the hill.

My cell phone rang. I pulled over to the side of the road and answered it.

"Where are you now?" Loebmen asked.

"I just reached Rock Springs, near Nordahl. This is unbelievable."

"Drive a mile west, to Woodland Park. That's command central for this fire. I'm parked near the restrooms."

I followed Loebman's instructions but couldn't get anywhere near the parking lot at Woodland Park. Commandeered by fire officials, the small public oasis had become a staging area where fire-engine teams checked in and received their assignments. The entire lot was crowded with big rigs, readying for fire-fighting action. I parked on a side street and walked. As I neared the park I could hear people shouting. The atmosphere was intense and frenzied. I located the restroom sign and scanned the area for a Sheriff's Department vehicle, then saw a silver Crown Victoria and remembered that Loebman drove an unmarked car. As I neared it I saw Loebman through his open driver's-side window, listening to his scanner and watching the fire through a pair of binoculars.

"Come on in and have a seat," he said.

I slid in and listened with him, picking up on several conversations.

"We're listening to Tactical One, the firefighters' broadband," Loebman explained. He handed me the binoculars. "You can see the engines taking position along the crest up there."

Voices, thin and ghostlike, cut in on one another over the scanner.

"The smoke's unbelievable up here. We've got a map but it's too damn dark to see the street signs."

"Having trouble evacuating residents who don't understand the situation here. Plus the road is covered with hose lines . . . it's a mess."

"Is Carolyn up there?" I asked.

Loebman nodded. "Her unit left from here about ten minutes ago."

"How about Zevnik?"

"Yeah, he's up there. His engine was one of the first on the scene."

Again, my dark feeling about Zevnik returned. I was about to comment when a woman's voice broke in on the scanner.

"We're in a bit of a jam here. We're not getting any water pressure. This hydrant's only discharging a trickle. It's worthless to us. We're getting a lot of flying embers."

Her voice was barely audible over what sounded like wind.

"We're laying hose line here but I don't know . . . it's getting close. I can feel the heat. We're not getting any water at all now. It's a real hazard situation."

"What's the deal with the water situation up there?" I asked.

"It's been like that for the last fifteen minutes or so. Some power lines went down and the commander thinks that's what's causing the water system pumps to fail. Takes a lot of energy to pump water up a hill that steep."

"We're seeing flame now. We need a water drop. Repeat: we need aircraft assistance and a water drop ASAP."

"Where's Huey when you need him?" I asked, referring to the CDF firefighting chopper.

Loebman looked up through the windshield at the smoky sky, worry lines covering his forehead.

"I don't know. All I've seen up there is a news helicopter."

A louder, clearer voice came over the airwaves.

"Engine 2610, don't hold your position. Abandon your position and get down off the hill. Repeat, get down off the hill."

"That's the commander," Loebman said. "Calling from right over there." He pointed to the staging area in the park.

"I can't get the engine started. There's so much smoke the engine has stalled."

Loebman and I exchanged a worried look. The commander barked orders to the stranded engine on the hill.

"Engine 2610, get that rig started and return to the staging area." There was no reply. *"Engine 2610, do you copy? Engine 2-6-1-0, come in."*

The only response was the sound of the wind howling.

My attention was on the hillside. Preheated by the hot sun, the brush might as well have been gasoline. In a matter of seconds the fire had made a run of five hundred feet, jumping the road into the development. Flames were rising more than a hundred feet into the air. Fire and smoke ob-

scured my view of the top of the hill, but the black plumes
told me that flames had begun to consume the houses. Even
from our position a quarter mile away, we could hear the
fire's roar.

The firefighters were cut off by the fire. My stomach felt
sick as I watched, powerless to help.

Again the commander's voice came over the scanner.

"Engine 2610, please verify if you copy."

I picked up the binoculars and focused on the road leading down from Sapphire Heights, which was crammed
bumper to bumper with cars trying to get out. As the fire
spread, people began getting out of their cars and running
on foot. I tried in vain to find Engine 2610 through the
binoculars, but the smoke at the top of the hill was thick
and black, visibility zero.

"Finally." Loebman pointed north.

A plane appeared out of the smoky sky, banking down
toward the flaming hillside. The pilot undoubtedly would
be having the same problem seeing his target as we were.
The wings dipped so close to the flames that I feared they
might ignite. The plane dropped a ruddy cloud from its
belly, but the winds picked up most of the fire retardant
and carried it off.

Over the scanner, there was no acknowledgment from
Engine 2610 that they could see the plane overhead. There
was no sound from Engine 2610 at all.

CHAPTER 33

The aircraft circled and made another run at the fire, flying low over the smoke that had gathered like a thundercloud around Sapphire Heights. Again the plane released a reddish cloud of fire retardant over the burning hilltop. I didn't notice that it made any difference. When a gust of wind created a hole in the swirling smoke, Loebman and I caught a glimpse of the fire eating away at the development.

" 'Your ticky-tacky houses multiply like cancer cells,' " I quoted.

His mouth was set in a grim line.

"And burn like cardboard boxes." He picked up the binoculars I'd laid aside and stared through the lenses. "Those are brand-new, code-approved, fire-resistant roofs going up in flames." He let out a groan. "We could use some rain. Can you make it rain?"

I shook my head.

"Don't know that trick yet. Sorry." I thought of Sequoia. "Can't make the wind die down, either."

The cell phone on the seat between us started to ring. Loebman scooped it up and carried on a conversation that seemed to be over before it started.

"That was the lieutenant. We need to set up a roadblock

near Sapphire Heights Drive, at the corner of Rock Springs and Woodland Parkway. They're going to land the Life Flight helicopter at that intersection and need to keep the area clear. Where'd you park?"

"I'm on a side street down the road a little ways."

"Let's get your truck. We could use an extra vehicle."

Loebman dropped me off at my truck and I followed his Crown Victoria down Rock Springs to Woodland Parkway. We fell behind a platoon of bulldozers, which made the going agonizingly slow. I called Loebman on his cell.

"What's up with these bulldozers?"

"They're on their way to clear brush on the other side of Sapphire Heights. If they can make a big enough dent, the fire may be contained. I'd turn on my emergency lights and go around them, but we're almost there. Hang on."

"Okay."

Loebman was right. We arrived at our designated intersection in less than two minutes. A single San Marcos patrol car was blocking the road, and a lone officer stood with baton in hand, doing his best to divert traffic. He looked relieved to see us. Both Rock Springs and Woodland Parkway were wide roads. By the time we'd boxed it off we had a good-sized area for the helicopter to land.

I stood by my truck in the middle of Rock Springs, noticing a change in the weather conditions. The wind was stronger now, constantly shifting directions. Fire creates its own wind, Carolyn had said. What had started as a blaze on Sapphire Heights had grown into a firestorm. Flying embers from the main fire were blowing north, east, south, and west, igniting new conflagrations around the main fire. A dusting of gray flakes fell on my shoulders. Ashfall.

The smoke was getting thicker. Under a darkening sky, Loebman, the San Marcos patrol cop, and I kept our positions at the roadblock, waiting for the helicopter. I got the sense that Death was waiting, too.

Three vehicles stopped at our roadblock at almost the same time. The first was a Sheriff's Department cruiser, klieg lights flashing, coming down from Sapphire Heights

Drive. The second and third were news vehicles, including the Channel Three news van. A pair of camera crews got out of the news vans.

Above the sound of the wind came the chopping of the approaching helicopter. I stood behind my truck to get away from the gale created by its whirling blades. The erratic winds buffeted the helicopter from side to side, a precarious sight that made me so nervous I had to turn my eyes away. As soon as the aircraft touched down on the street, the sheriff's deputy got out of his cruiser and opened the back door. There was a body inside, lying on a portable stretcher in the back seat.

Paramedics from the air ambulance pulled the stretcher from the back seat of the cruiser. A yellow tarp covered most of the body. A strong gust blew the tarp up and I saw it was a man. His skin was burned red, split in places. Most of his face was obscured by an oxygen mask, but what I could see of the rest looked like mottled plastic. His arms jerked spasmodically. As they lifted the stretcher into the helicopter I could see that the soles of his bare feet were charred black.

The news cameras were rolling on it. Randy Twain and I noticed each other at about the same time. He did a double take on me and jogged over.

"What are you doing here?"

"Right now I'm assisting with a roadblock," I said.

His eyes were bright and his cheeks were flushed. He had the look of a man rushing on adrenaline.

"Can you believe this? Jesus. We'll talk later—I gotta work." He jogged back to join his photographer, a young man. Jane Sharpe must not have been scheduled to work today, or perhaps she'd had enough of covering fires.

The Life Flight helicopter didn't take off right away as I'd expected it to. The people in charge seemed to be waiting for something. The sheriff's deputy was watching the road expectantly. Soon another car approached from Sapphire Heights Drive, this one a civilian vehicle, a minivan.

The driver's-side door opened and a firefighter in a badly

sullied yellow Nomex jacket and pants got out. The firefighter stood back as paramedics from the helicopter rushed
forward to open the back door. Together they pulled out
another stretcher. At first I thought the injured party was
wearing black clothes, but soon I realized that I was seeing
the remains of what had once been a Nomex suit. All that
was left of it now was half of a bright yellow pant leg. The
burned turnout coat hung from the body in shreds.

Remnants of a charred bandana hung around the victim's
neck. The face was too badly burned to recognize. The first
firefighter was murmuring encouragement to his fallen colleague as the stretcher was carried to the helicopter.

The wail of a siren filled the air as a Hartsman ambulance approached from Rock Springs Road. Two more civilian vehicles pulled out of Sapphire Heights Drive and
entered the roadblock area. More Nomex-clad firefighters
got out, looking dazed.

Microphone in hand, Randy Twain approached the firefighters. I moved closer to hear the interview.

"Can you tell us what happened up there?" he asked.

One of the firefighters pulled off her helmet and blond
hair fell to her shoulders. When I recognized Carolyn Arnold, tears of relief sprang to my eyes. Other than a bright
red face, she looked okay.

"We got trapped," she said, clearing her throat. "Fire
came up the hillside and our engine stalled in the smoke.
Fireball rolled right over us. Sounded like a jet engine."

"Can you describe the conditions up there?"

"It was bad. Huge embers kept raining on us. We could
see a wall of flame heading up the mountain. Our engine
wouldn't start. All we could do was lie down on the road
and deploy our fire shelters."

"What about the injured man?" Twain had to shout to
be heard over the helicopter.

"Right before the firestorm hit I saw him trying to open
his fire shelter. The wind up there was unbelievably strong.
His shelter got blown away. We found him after the firestorm passed. He was unconscious."

The helicopter was so loud now that continuing the interview was impossible. I turned my back against its wind as it took off, saying a prayer for the injured passengers.

One of the paramedics from the Hartsman ambulance began handing out oxygen masks to the remaining firefighters, telling them that he'd be transporting them to Palomar Hospital.

Carolyn looked back up at the smoke-shrouded Sapphire Heights and made a final comment before putting on her mask. "We had no choice but to abandon our engine. We had to borrow people's cars to get down the hill. It was hell up there. Excuse me." She put on her mask and stepped past Twain's microphone, getting into the ambulance with the others.

Twain turned toward the camera. "The critically injured are being transported by Life Flight helicopter to the UCSD Burn Center. We'll have more information for you when the helicopter arrives there. Meanwhile, the fire in San Marcos still rages . . ."

"Elizabeth!"

I turned around as I heard my name called. Loebman was standing outside his car, waving me over. As I approached I could see that he was on the phone.

"We've got backup coming in now," he said to me when I was within earshot. "You'd better get out of here. Word is the fire just leapfrogged past the defense line. It's heading west at about three miles an hour. This whole area is a hazard. I'd get back to Escondido if I were you."

"Do you have an ID on the critically injured firefighter from Engine 2610?"

"Yeah." His face was somber. "That was Tim Zevnik."

It all came together now. The dangerous vibe I'd been sensing around Zevnik had been a premonition. There was no official word on his condition, but I didn't need official word. I already knew. I'd known since Death had stopped by this morning.

On my way back to my truck I passed Twain again, this time doing a live feed, with the smoky hillside behind him.

"This fire continues to rage out of control. We just got word that it's crossed what firefighters had hoped would be its western boundary and is now threatening to destroy homes in the Carlsbad area. In the forty minutes since this fire was first reported at least four dozen homes have been consumed."

He's really in his element, I thought as I watched Twain ad-lib into the camera. *He loves this.*

"Mutual-aid companies are attacking this fire with everything they've got. An estimated three hundred firefighters are here on the scene, with more arriving every few minutes. Four fixed-wing aircraft are defending from the sky . . ."

Maybe he loves this too much, I thought.

He'd been at all the scenes. His reporting was winning him kudos and respect. For millions of southern California viewers, Randy Twain was the name behind this story. He was a hero.

We'd even talked about the star-reporter phenomenon earlier in the week. I felt a chill as I remembered Randy's comment: *Who ever heard of Wolf Blitzer before the Gulf War?*

Not only that. The inside of Twain's house had wood paneling.

CHAPTER 34

"You want me to do what?"

Thomasina Wilson stood before me with her arms crossed over her chest, giving me that glare of hers. I was standing in the doorway of her downtown condo.

"It's perfectly legal." I tried to keep the begging tone out of my voice.

She's my best bud, the one who hooked me up with my shaman teacher, Sequoia. They have the same great-grandfather—which makes them cousins or some such—although you'd never know it to look at them. Most of Sequoia's ancestors are Native American and he looks it; most of Thomasina's ancestors are African American and she looks it too. I love them both, but damn, they know how to intimidate me. Must be in the genes.

"Look," I said, "all you have to do is sit in the car, keep your eyes open, and let me know if you see anything."

"And if I do see something?"

"You let me know. We'll be in touch by two-way radio. I'll be wearing a headset so all you'll have to do is speak into the mike if you see anybody coming."

She didn't budge.

"If this is so legal, why are we going to be sneaking around like thieves?"

"We're going to be . . . *inconspicuous* because I don't want to be seen. Simple as that."

"You sure it's not burglary?"

"It's Dumpster diving, Thomasina. Once people put their trash out, it's fair game."

Her ebony eyes were doing their best to bore a hole through my confidence.

"Come on," I prodded. "Say yes. His place isn't even ten minutes from here." I glanced at my wristwatch. "You can cover me and be back in time for the Letterman show."

Behind her, a large-screen television was tuned to the local news. Harrowing scenes of the north county fire filled the screen. Seeing the fire's rampant destruction renewed my urge to see this thing through.

"Sequoia said you were working on the Fielding kidnap case. You think this person you're investigating has something to do with it?"

"I'm not sure. Maybe. That's why I'm investigating."

Her jocular mood toned down as she picked up on my vibe.

"What if he comes home?" she asked.

"He won't. He's otherwise engaged. Look." I pointed to the television. She turned and looked at the talking head.

"Randy Twain? That's whose trash we're gonna steal?" Her eyes went wide and I could feel her beginning to back-pedal.

"This is important, Thomasina. I can do it alone, but I'd rather have a partner. Please."

I thought I saw a trace of a smile as Thomasina took the keys off a hook by the door and stepped outside with me.

"I don't know why I let you talk me into these things."

"Because secretly you're bored with your proper bourgeois existence. You seek excitement, a taste of life on the edge."

"Oh, yeah," she said, rolling her eyes. "That's really the thing."

"Seriously, thanks."

We headed toward the elevator. As we walked, Thomasina glanced at my outfit. I'd changed out of my smoke-drenched clothes and into black pants, a black turtleneck, and black boots. My hair had disappeared under a black cap.

"You look like a cat burglar from one of those bad spy movies from the sixties."

"Pretty hard to see someone dressed like this in the dark, so never mind the stereotype. Is it okay if you drive?"

"It's not enough that I'm going along with this dubious scheme. Now you want me to drive, too."

"People know my truck. They don't know your car."

Thomasina's condominium, converted from an old mattress factory, is in the heart of the urban renewal area south of Market. As we drove north in her BMW through downtown San Diego, the atmosphere on the streets was festive, a carefree world away from the fires raging thirty miles north. We took Fifth Avenue up the hill and headed toward Balboa Park. Two blocks before Olive Street I spoke up.

"Park here."

Thomasina pulled into the next available space.

"Is that it?" she asked, pointing to a house across the street.

"No, Twain's house is the next block up. We're parking here because I don't want any nosy neighbors getting back to Twain about a strange car parking outside his house when he wasn't home."

I handed Thomasina her transmitter and headset, then strapped on my fanny pack and double-checked the tools inside. Mini-flashlight, Swiss army knife, a fine set of lock picks. Thomasina frowned at these last.

"Hey, you said you weren't breaking in."

I wriggled my fingers into a pair of thick latex gloves, glad she couldn't see the Glock in the holster concealed under my loose-fitting pants.

"The tools are in case the Dumpster is padlocked."

From the look she gave me, she might as well have come out and called me a liar.

"Never mind. I don't want to know."

Which is what I wanted to hear. Don't ask, don't tell. I also didn't mention that Twain's place was haunted. Thomasina was nervous enough as it was.

I clipped my transmitter to my belt, put on my headset, and got out of the car. As I walked up the block, I checked the two-way.

"Can you hear me?"

"Yeah," came Thomasina's voice in my earpiece. "You're breathing really loud. You letting yourself get out of shape?"

"Not really," I said under my breath. "I think I inhaled some of that smoke from the fire this afternoon."

I ducked into the alley that ran behind Twain's house. There was a large rectangular Dumpster back here, a communal garbage dump. Bummer. Individual trash cans are ideal. Dumpsters contain group goop, and it's hard to tell whose trash is whose.

The good news was that the Dumpster sat beneath Twain's bathroom window. I hoisted myself onto the top of the big metal bin. There were no bars on the window—with a ghost to guard the premises, perhaps Twain didn't need them. The window—an old-fashioned casement variety—was locked. The lock was nearly as old as the house and succumbed to my tools in a matter of minutes.

"You're awfully quiet," Thomasina said into my earpiece.

"Is anyone coming?" I whispered.

"No, you're fine."

I tried not to think about it too much. Just pushed the window open and crawled inside. The bathtub was directly below me.

Empty.

I dropped into the tub, landing with a thud. The room was completely dark. The presence I'd sensed two nights ago was right there to greet me.

Apparitions can't hurt you, I reminded myself.

If I'd tripped a silent alarm I had five minutes, tops, before the cops arrived. I knew from my first visit that the house was small. If Matthew was here, I'd find him. If he wasn't, I'd better get the hell out fast.

I searched each room—bedroom, sitting room, kitchen, bathroom, laundry room, office. Using all six senses I checked out every closet, every cranny. The boy wasn't here.

"I know what you're doing," Thomasina's voice said into my earpiece.

"No you don't," I replied.

"Lucky for you, not a creature is stirring."

"Except for this mouse," I said. "Now to get the cheese."

I went out the way I'd come in, which required balancing on the edge of the bathtub and using every ounce of upper body strength I had to pull myself up through the window.

Once I was back outside, the rest was easy. I opened the Dumpster and leaned in, feeling as if the rim were cutting my abdomen in two. I groped around, grabbing as many plastic bags as I could with my free hand. I slid back down and began going through the bags one by one, checking the contents with my flashlight.

I got lucky on bag two. A whole passel of Twain's mail, mostly junk, let me know I had the right garbage. Credit-card solicitations bearing his name. Pleas for alumni money from Northwestern University. Literature from every corner of the political spectrum, from far right to far left. If his junk mail was any indication, Twain was a reporter who liked to hear all sides of an issue, I'd give him that. Once I'd identified the first bag the rest was a cinch—literally. Twain was obsessive about his garbage, using the expensive brand of thick, cinch-sack bags. It was simple to spot which garbage was his. When my scavenging was through, I'd retrieved five bags from the Dumpster and lined them up in the alley.

"You there?" I said into my mike.

"I'm here," came Thomasina's reply.

"Come get me."

"What do you mean, 'come get me'?"

"I mean pull the Beemer into the alley. I'm not going to drag all this trash down an entire city block, for crying out loud."

I heard a *hmph* so disgusted that I thought she might abandon me. But two minutes later the BMW pulled into the alley. I opened the back door and started loading the bags.

"Whoa, whoa, whoa," came her firm voice from the driver's seat. "What do you think you're doing? Put that shit in the trunk."

"Oops, sorry." I heard a thump as Thomasina pressed the button that popped the trunk open. "I forget what it's like to have a civilized vehicle." When I was done loading the bags in the trunk I got in front with her. "You can just take me to my truck. I'll toss these bags into the back of my pickup and get out of your hair."

"You'll do no such thing," she said.

"Why not?"

"You think I'd go through all the trouble to be your partner in crime without getting the satisfaction of seeing what that damn news reporter throws away in his trash? Hell, no, girl. This is going to be the fun part."

CHAPTER 35

Fifteen minutes later I was helping Thomasina spread a paint-splattered tarp across her living-room floor. The dried dollops of red, yellow, and blue paint on the tarp matched the colorful network of pipes crisscrossing beneath the exposed ceiling over our heads.

"I see the last job this tarp was used for," I said as I craned my head upward. "You paint those pipes yourself?"

She looked up and smiled.

"It ain't the Sistine Chapel, but it still amazes me what I managed to do with a ladder and a paintbrush." She returned her gaze to the trash bags lined up on the floor. "Now what's the plan here?"

"Let's dump these out one at a time and see what we find. Hope you have an extra pair of plastic gloves. It'll make this job a lot more pleasant."

"Less revolting, anyway." Thomasina went to the kitchen, where I heard her rummaging through the cupboards. When she came back in, she was wearing a pair of pink dishwashing gloves. She picked up the remote and turned on the television. It was nine fifty-five; Channel Three's late-night newscast would be on in five minutes.

I dumped the first bag. Thomasina held her nose.

"What exactly is it we're looking for?" she asked.

"I'm not sure. I'm trusting I'll know it when I see it."

The discarded credit-card solicitations and sweepstakes envelopes that tumbled onto the tarp looked familiar. This was the bag I'd peeked into in the alley behind Twain's house. Thomasina took a tentative stab at the trash.

"Hey, this doesn't smell too bad." She began sorting through the refuse with an expression that almost looked like enthusiasm. We examined each piece of paper before tossing it aside.

"Uh-oh. Here's some stuff about you."

Thomasina handed me a stash of papers, articles printed off the Internet archives of the *San Diego Union-Tribune*. Apparently Twain had done a search using my name. The articles included a recap of the Bliss Project case in which McGowan had lost his life.

"Who's investigating whom?" she asked.

"Twain told me he'd checked up on me." Still, seeing the proof of it took me aback. Over Thomasina's shoulder I could see the late-night news coming on. "Here's the news. Turn it up."

Tim Zevnik's death was the top story. The ten-o'clock anchor recapped the details of the firefighters' losing battle with the Sapphire Heights blaze. So far, Zevnik was the only fatality. After a brief report on the current condition of the injured, the screen cut to Randy Twain, who was reporting live from north county. Bright orange flames were shooting dramatically into the night sky behind him.

"There's been no letup in this wind today," he announced, "which hasn't made the job any easier for the hundreds of firefighters battling to control the blaze that broke out around noon today in the Sapphire Heights area of San Marcos, where a firefighter lost his life and at least forty houses have burned. This afternoon the fire moved into nearby Harmony Grove and Carlsbad, destroying at least another thirty homes. More than ten thousand acres have burned today, with no immediate end in sight."

The camera zoomed in on the flames behind Twain.

"You can see the embers flying behind me," he said into his mike. "All it takes is one or two seconds for an ember lodged on a shake roof to ignite a house."

"He doesn't look like a kid snatcher," Thomasina said.

"How about a fire starter?"

The video cut to another view of the fire, this one from the sky. The audio switched to the female anchor's voice-over.

"The fire has caused power outages over a twenty-mile radius." From the sky, the camera panned over the blacked-out hillsides of north county. The flames stretched for miles like a neon yellow ribbon across the darkened landscape. Occasionally the camera would zoom down on a bright yellow patch, where a house was going up in flames.

I picked up the remote and started surfing. Almost every channel was covering the fire. Even CNN mentioned it in a brief national report. I flipped back to Channel Three. On the screen, Twain's face was flushed.

"Earlier today bulldozers cleared brush and fire person-nel used Terra Torches to set backfires, all in a desperate attempt to keep this fire contained." The camera zoomed in on burning hillside, the wind-whipped flames looking like waves rippling across the land.

I dumped out the contents of another trash bag and con-tinued excavating, coming across a startling quantity of empty bottles of hair spray, hair mousse, hair conditioner, and hair color.

"Ah-ha," I said. "So that ready-for-prime-time look isn't so natural after all. Check out all this hair stuff." I rolled one of the bottles in Thomasina's direction. She countered by tossing me an empty tube of very expensive makeup.

"I'll say this for the guy, he knows his cosmetics." She looked at the TV. "His hair products seem to be failing him tonight."

I looked up at the screen. The wind was really whipping now, completely flattening Twain's hair. He was holding his microphone down toward the face of a worried-looking woman who was busy packing three cats into a large wire cage. The cats, wild with fright, scampered in circles around the cage.

"The fire's just over the hill there. Have you been able to get everything out?" Twain asked.

The woman's breathing was fast and shallow.

"I don't know. I can't talk right now." She blew Twain off, calling for someone named Bill to come help her get the cage into her truck.

Thomasina shook her head."It's getting bad up there, isn't it?"

"It's been bad all day."

Thomasina looked up from her sorting. "You really think Twain's the one starting the fires?"

"I thought it might be that firefighter who died, Tim Zevnik. I was sensing all kinds of darkness around him. I'm not sure about Twain. Let's just say I'm trying to rule him out. I started suspecting Zevnik because he was at the scene of every fire. Twain has been, too."

"Well . . . covering fires is Twain's job, right?"

"In the case of the Rancho Santa Fe fire, he was at the scene when I met the Fieldings. *Before* the fire started."

"Covering the kidnap case, I remember. Again—that's his job, Elizabeth. I'm just not getting how you think he's some criminal."

I told her about my theory that Twain's motive would be the glory of reporting fires. I also told her about my vision of the place Matthew was being kept—the Kmart with the chain-link fence, the television in the wood-paneled room.

"Twain's office is wood paneled and has a television in it," I said.

"But there's no Kmart anywhere close to Twain's house."

"I know. That piece doesn't fit."

Several spiral-bound reporter's notebooks had been discarded in Twain's trash. I opened one up. It was filled with page after page of notes. It was tough to make out Twain's handwriting, but the pages appeared to be his draft of the profiles on the victims of the Mira Mesa Apartments fire. I'd watched the videotapes last night but nothing about them had caught my attention. A comment in Twain's handwritten notes, however, piqued my interest:

> Prop. purchased by Starcom—Apts. scheduled
> t/b torn down soon to make way for expansion
> of co. headquarters.

"This could be something," I said.

"What?"

"According to Twain's notes, the apartment building that burned down the night of the Starcom fire was purchased by Starcom and was scheduled to be demolished to make room for the company's expansion."

"I'm sure the insurance investigators will be all over that one."

"No doubt," I said. I looked up at the TV. Now Twain was interviewing a firefighter in a yellow helmet, a member of the mutual-aid team sent from Arizona.

"Last time I was here I was helping dig people out from the Northridge quake." The Arizona fireman's smile was incredulous. "I tell you, man. Living in California must be like having ringside seats to the Apocalypse."

I turned over the last bag, dumping out several empty packages of Lean Cuisine and an empty bottle of Mondavi cabernet sauvignon.

"That's disappointing," I said as the bottle rolled out. "I would have hoped Twain would recycle." We heard the sound of glass clinking as more bottles rolled out. One of them made my heart stop.

"Oh, shit."

Thomasina looked over. "What is it?"

I held up an empty bottle of Heineken. "Molotov cocktail, anyone?"

CHAPTER 36

The aluminum roll-up door to the shipping department of Starcom International was padlocked shut. I pushed the buzzer to the right of the door and waited. No answer. I checked my watch. It was early yet—seven-fifteen. Employees were just beginning to pull into the parking lot and most of the spaces were still empty. It was Friday, probably a payday. I hoped that Abby would be here soon, that the apartment fire hadn't forced her to leave her job. Most of all, I hoped she'd give me something I could use.

Earlier this morning I'd been wide awake when the *North County Times* hit my driveway, its front page headline screaming, WILDFIRE! During the night the fire had spread south and west, destroying several more homes in Olivenhein and Carlsbad. Photos of the flames and burning houses filled a two-page spread. My jaw had dropped when I'd recognized a familiar face and read the caption: "Pam Jaffer, above, returned from work late yesterday to find that her Sapphire Heights home had burned to the ground."

Another connection to Starcom.

It could hardly be coincidence that two of the company's top executives had lost homes to fire in the last week. Could the arsonist be someone on the inside, like Larry Gandle, as Twain seemed to think? Or was it Twain himself, for reasons that went beyond the glory of being a star reporter? I didn't have answers but knew that Starcom was the place to start asking questions.

I walked around the place to kill some time. Just three days after the fire, repair work was already underway on the damaged building near the canyon. The burned west wall had been knocked down and the new framing was in place. After watching the better part of an entire housing development go up in flames yesterday, seeing the repair work was heartening.

At seven-thirty cars began pulling into the parking lot in an increasingly steady stream. Most of the drivers got out and walked around to the front entrance, but a woman with cropped hair got out of a green Honda Civic and headed my way toward the shipping department.

"You again," Abby said as she jingled her keys and unlocked the padlock. "Just can't get enough of hell, can you?" She rolled the aluminum door open with a banging noise. "There is a front entrance to this place, you know. Or are you trying to sneak in again?"

"Actually, I came to talk to you. Did everything work out okay after the apartment fire? You move in with your relatives and all?"

She frowned, looking embarrassed. "I'm sorry. I forgot your name."

"Elizabeth," I said as I followed her into the receiving bay.

"Are you kissing up to me to get a job here or something?"

"No, I'm not looking for a job. I'm a private investigator. Here—" I reached for my wallet but she waved for me to stop.

"I don't need to see your ID. Frankly, I don't give a crap."

"Such refreshing candor," I said with a smile. I pointed to the aluminum roll-up door. "Do you keep this open most of the day, so that the UPS guys and shipping people can come in and out?"

"Uh-huh."

"So you probably have a pretty good idea of who comes and goes from this parking lot, is that right?"

She went inside and switched on some lights. "I keep my eyes open."

"And you have a pretty good view of the canyon over there. You keep your eyes on that?"

"If it weren't for that view I would have left this job a long time ago."

"Did you see anyone driving a Jaguar around recently?"

She gave me her best Village Idiot. "Duh, *yea-ah*. Everybody knows Frank Fielding drove a Jaguar."

"Not Fielding's Jaguar. This one was an older model. A forest-green Jag. You would have seen it the day before the fire here broke out."

She picked up a large bin of interoffice mail, a pensive look on her face. "I think I did see a car like that, now that you mention it."

"Did you see who drove it?"

"That I don't remember." She put the bin of mail on a countertop at the side of the receiving bay and began sorting the envelopes.

"You ever watch Channel Three news?"

"Sometimes."

"Did the driver of the green Jaguar look like that reporter, Randy Twain?"

"I don't even know who Randy Twain is. I'm not that devoted a viewer."

"Did you see *anyone* who looked like a television reporter hanging around here the day before the fire?"

"Before the fire? No. But I saw about a million reporters afterward. Bunch of pests. Between the news reporters and the cops, this place has been infested."

"How about anybody walking over to that canyon edge out there?"

"Lots of people walk out there, because it's such a nice view. It was nice before the fire, anyway."

My questioning was going nowhere but I wasn't ready to give up yet. Abby had the air of somebody who knew something and I'd learned from experience to pester such people until they clammed up or threw me out. I watched her weathered hands expertly tossing envelopes into the mail slots.

"You hear about the fire last night?"

She laughed."You must really think I'm stupid. A person would have to be in a coma not to have heard about that fire."

"I meant did you hear about Pamela Jaffer's house burning down."

"You're kidding." Abby paused in her sorting but didn't look up. "No, I hadn't heard. That's a shame." She resumed tossing envelopes into the slots.

"So you sort all the mail that comes through here, is that it?"

"Most of it, yeah. I have some coworkers"—she glanced up at the clock—"but as you can see, their attendance is spotty."

Fluorescent lights mounted under the cabinets gave the countertop a bluish glow. On the far right side of the countertop sat an old-fashioned typewriter. A Royal.

"You don't see too many of these anymore," I said.

"Still the best machine around for typing labels."

I walked over for a closer look. Several snapshots were tacked to the wall above the typewriter. The subject of most of the photos was a big brown Labrador retriever.

"This your dog?"

"Yeah."

"Nice-looking canine. I have a Rhodesian Ridgeback. Great dog."

I could see by the way her face hardened that she'd reached her limit with me.

"Look," she said coldly. "I'm not interested in your personal life, okay?"

"Sorry. Can you just tell me if Frank Fielding got any weird packages before he died?"

"Hate mail, you mean? The cops asked me the same thing. No, nothing like that."

"How about any packages that were out of the ordinary?"

She stopped sorting and turned to me with a smirk.

"You're way behind the game, honey. Those guys from the FBI have inventoried every piece of mail Frank Fielding got in the last few weeks. Why don't you go talk to them?"

CHAPTER 37

I sat in my truck in the Starcom parking lot, seething. Dale Blades could have shared the inventory of Frank Fielding's mail with me, or at least have let me know the FBI was reviewing it. Unless I begged for it, all the information had been flowing one way between us. Fine. I didn't need the FBI's stinkin' information. I had my own sources.

I reached into my backpack and pulled out my list of San Diego area Kmarts. Four stores down, eight to go. I decided to skip to number eight on the list, the nearest store to me geographically, a Kmart in Clairemont Mesa.

I started the engine and the AM radio burst to life, broadcasting news about the north county fire. Tim Zevnik's death was mentioned in passing. The ominous vibe I'd sensed around him had been no figment of my imagination. Theoretically, it was possible that Zevnik had been the one setting the fires, and was burned in his own self-inflicted funeral pyre.

Somehow I didn't think so.

I'd called the Sheriff's Department earlier and left a message for Loebman that another Starcom executive's house had burned down in yesterday's fire, just in case he hadn't picked it up from this morning's paper. I would have preferred to speak with someone there personally to get a sense of what was going on, but neither Loebman nor Wong had been in.

Wracked with self-doubt, I headed for the freeway. This morning I straddled a tightrope between two opposing forces: blind determination and a sense of utter futility. Gratefully, I had my list of Kmarts to pursue. When I'm feeling anxious, a to-do list can comfort me like nothing else.

I drove to San Diego's Clairemont Mesa community. The Kmart in question was the anchor store in an older shopping center. I cruised the neighborhood, finding lots of gas stations and fast-food restaurants. But no chain-link fences, no narrow footpaths, no Matthew.

"Five down, seven to go," I said to myself. It was still early in the day; if I really moved, I could cover the entire list. I headed north from the Kmart, looking for the entrance to the freeway. After about a mile it became evident that I'd gone in the wrong direction. I slowed, searching for a good place to turn around. That's when I realized I was driving past a chain-link fence.

By now I was at least a mile from the Kmart but I pulled over and parked anyway, figuring it couldn't hurt to check it out. A sidewalk led past the chain-link fence. I got out and strolled south in the direction I'd come from. On foot I was able to see what I hadn't noticed driving by: there was a narrow footpath on the other side of the fence.

My heart started to beat faster. I picked up my step, following the fence and the path running parallel behind it. At the end of a long city block, the fence stopped. I stood at the corner, trying to decide whether to keep going or turn back.

"Now what?" I said aloud.

Just stand here a minute. Listen. Notice the sounds.

Somewhere in the distance, a dog was barking. I crossed the street and followed the sound, heading down the sidewalk on the next block. The barking grew louder. Past a

vacant lot I found him: a big brown Labrador retriever behind another chain-link fence.

The dog looked a lot like the one I'd seen an hour ago,
in a photograph tacked to the wall above the Royal typewriter in the Starcom shipping department. The property he
guarded was a two-story, dilapidated Victorian with a
funky, faded orange-yellow paint job. The house—228
Jackson—was sandwiched between two others.

A woman came onto the porch of the house on the left,
probably roused by the barking dog. I walked on, pretending to be going somewhere. I turned at the end of the block
and circled back to where I'd come from. By the time I
reached my truck I had a plan. I would go back, but this
time I'd be prepared. I stopped at a 7-Eleven and bought a
bag of dog treats. When I returned, I parked on a street
parallel but closer to the house.

The dog started barking again when I came within half
a block of the house. I wound up my strong arm and hurled
a dog biscuit over the fence. It worked—for about a minute.
He barked again and I threw him another chewy. By the
time I reached the fence he might not have been my best
friend, but he wasn't trying to scare me off.

I walked around to the back of the house, hoping to get
a view into the rear window. The curtain was open. I was
looking through a family room that appeared to be empty.
The morning sun slanted through the glass, illuminating the
inside walls. They were covered in cheap imitation wood
paneling.

That was all the verification I needed. I threw the dog a
last biscuit and hurried back to my truck, breaking into a
run when I cleared the block. This was the place. I *knew*
it.

I called on my cell phone as soon as I was in my truck
and this time got an answer.

"Loebman," Bruce said.

"I've found the house. I'm almost certain of it. Matthew
Fielding is in there, but I'm going to need some backup."

"Where are you?"

I gave him the address.

"Can you see the boy?"

"No. But I can see the wood paneling, and there's a Kmart a mile down the road, and there's a chain-link fence along the street—"

"No boy, though."

"Not in plain sight, no."

"Let me call you back in a few minutes. I need to run this by some people. Don't go anywhere."

I seemed to wait forever in the truck cab. I rolled down both windows but the heat was becoming unbearable. Ten minutes later I was getting out, heading for the shade of a nearby tree, when my phone rang.

"I've been working on it, Elizabeth."

Loebman's tone indicated that it wasn't going well.

"What do you mean? What's going on?"

"Look, I'm going to need more than what you just gave me to get somebody down there. This fire up here is drawing down all our manpower. I'm not authorized to release a unit, and I can't get free to come down myself."

"No one's coming?"

"Blades ran that address through our suspect database and there's no match."

I was on my own here. The news was beginning to sink in.

"What database?" I asked.

"Starcom employees, the Fieldings' relatives, victims of the apartment building fire, et cetera."

"What kind of crap is that, Bruce? Maybe we're not looking for a Starcom employee. Maybe the employee has an alternate address. I'm seeing too many markers to ignore this. You hired me to do a job and now you're not backing me. This is bullshit." I stood in the hot sun, feeling a childish sense of abandonment.

"I'm not saying we're not backing you. I'm saying we can't get anyone down there right now. We'll check it out as soon as things lighten up on this end, okay?"

It wasn't okay but there was no sense in arguing. I had

my answer. Nobody gave a damn. I hung up and tried to think straight. Maybe I could go back to the house and find the "more" they needed to let loose a little manpower.

Keeping in mind the nosy neighbor on the left side of the house, I came around the right. I stopped at the mailbox and took a quick peek.

Empty.

The dog began barking louder than ever, doggy treats completely forgotten. I was down to three biscuits.

"Good boy," I said, tossing him half a treat. I went around to the back of the house one more time, taking mental notes of everything I saw. Chain-link fence running around the house. Side door on east side of house. Rusted wheelbarrow in yard. Small cement patio in back. No curtains on back window. Wood-paneled family room.

"Hey!"

The voice jolted through me like a current and for a second I couldn't breathe. I turned to see Randy Twain coming up behind me.

"What are you doing here?" I said when I found my voice.

"Following you. You are definitely where this story is breaking. I couldn't believe it when I saw you at the San Marcos fire yesterday. You beat me to that one. I'm beginning to think you might be the arsonist." He smiled and winked. The dog began to bark with a real sense of purpose. My heart was pounding.

"How did you find me here?"

"I went to Starcom this morning. It was the first chance I've had to pick up the briefcase I left there at the press conference. I saw your truck heading out and followed you. What's going on here?"

It was hard to hear him above the barking of the Lab. Twain yelled at the dog to quiet down. The dog responded by barking louder. Twain started to come closer. I had a strong urge to break and run but my legs felt paralyzed.

"Both of you, step away from the fence."

It was a man's voice and it sounded like it meant business. Slowly, I turned around.

A patrol cop in a khaki uniform and black sunglasses stood behind us, hand on the butt of his gun.

I put my palms out in plain view.

"I'm a private investigator working on the Fielding kidnap case. Credentials are in my pocket."

"Randy Twain, Channel Three News. How ya doin'." Twain was as casual as if he were meeting a dad at a PTA meeting.

"What's going on here?" the cop asked.

"Nothing yet," I said, "but maybe you can help. I think this house may be where the Fielding boy is being held." I got a card out of my wallet and handed it to the cop. "I'm working with North County Sheriff and the FBI on this, but with the fires and all it may take a while before they can respond. Maybe you could knock on the front door, check it out?"

He looked like an unintelligent bulldog. He was thick with muscle and fat, with blond hair and the florid face of a drinker. The question I'd posed was confounding him.

"The neighbor called to complain. You two are disturbing the peace." He came on tough. When in doubt, be a badass.

"Well, I certainly don't mean to disturb anyone, Officer. Could you just knock on the door and see if anyone's home? This house matches all the characteristics we've been looking for and in the suspect's location and a child's life is at stake."

I was offering him an opportunity for greatness, but he missed his cue.

"I don't know anything about your investigation. You got a warrant?"

"No, not yet, sir."

"Then I'm going to have to ask you to leave this property."

I looked longingly at the dilapidated Victorian. Matthew was being held in there against his will. I could *feel* it.

"Officer, please. What's at stake here is a kidnapped child. I have many reasons to believe that he's in that house, right now." Urgent but tough.

The cop had filed me under Nuisance and no amount of talk was going to get him to change his mind.

"If there's a kid in there against his will, how come he isn't yelling to get out?"

"Matthew Fielding is a selective mute," I said. The cop furrowed his brows, as if I'd lapsed into a foreign language. "He's dumb, sir. He doesn't speak."

"All right, that's enough." The cop put his hand on his baton and stepped toward Twain and me, herding us toward the street. "That's no way to talk, calling a little kid dumb. Get out of here before I book you for trespassing."

CHAPTER 38

"Now that," Twain said as we walked away, "was a world-class asshole. You'd think he'd know better than to pull that crap in front of a television reporter."

"Maybe he pulled that crap for the *benefit* of a television reporter. Didn't want to look soft in front of the media." I stepped away from Twain and headed for my truck. I needed some time to regroup, to think. Twain hadn't flinched when I'd asked the cop to check the house, but I still wasn't sure about his part in all this. His cooperative attitude could be a mask.

"Whatever the reason, it sucked." He looked back at the house but kept walking to keep up with me. "You really think Matthew's in there?"

I picked up my step. Much as I wanted to trust Twain, I wasn't certain about him yet.

"I can't discuss this now," I said.

"All right. Off the record, Randy to Elizabeth. What can I do to help?"

"I don't need your help."

"Look, I care about this kid as much as you do."

"Don't you have a fire to cover?"

Something like anger flashed in his eyes. "I worked

eighteen hours straight yesterday. I saw a firefighter, a man
I'd known for five years, who burned to death. I interviewed dozens of people who lost their homes. I'm not
ashamed to say that a day like that gets to me. This is my
day off and goddamn it, I need it. But finding this kid is
more important. If I can help at all, just say the word."

I unlocked my truck and got in, thinking that anyone
who makes a living in front of a camera knows something
about acting. I wasn't bowled over by the Mr. Nice Guy
act just yet.

"You really want to help? Let me do my job."

He backed away, shaking his head. "I'm too tired to
argue. You've got my number."

"Yes," I said as I shut the door, "I do."

I watched him walk across the street to where his Jag
was parked. If he was innocent, I hoped he'd forgive my
brush-off. He pulled away from the curb and made a U-y,
avoiding eye contact as he drove past.

The patrol car was still parked down the block. The cop
was waiting for my departure, no doubt. No way he was
going to let me sit on this house for the rest of the day. I
hated to leave and risk letting the suspect slip through my
hands. I needed help, somebody to survey the house while
I ran a paper chase after the owner.

I called Loebman again. "I just need a body to sit on
this address until we can cough up a warrant. Please?"

"Can't help you there, Elizabeth. We're in the middle
of a nightmare up here. Three new fires have started since
yesterday."

"Offshoots from the main fire?"

"No, new ones. Copycats, probably. The ODP declared
the area an emergency. Every body we got is on duty right
now."

"You mean you can't cut loose one single uniform to
knock on a damn door? Check with Blades. If he can't
come, maybe he can send someone."

"I did check with Blades. He doesn't want anything to
do with it." There was a heavy pause before Loebman

added, "Look, I think that publicity you got embarrassed some people."

"What people?"

"People who don't want it known that a psychic is working the Fielding case. Wong wasn't happy and Blades about crapped his pants."

Blades could stew in it for all I cared. I let out an exasperated sigh.

"He's probably the one who leaked it."

"Look," he said, "I'm sorry. Don't you have other sources you can use?"

"I don't know. Maybe." I hung up, too frustrated to say good-bye.

Who could I get to cover for me here? It was a Friday morning. I couldn't ask Thomasina; she was at work. I tried dialing Scott Chatfield's office. A top-notch PI, Chatfield was expensive but always worth the paycheck. Hence the name of his agency, Scott Chatfield's Value Added Investigations. He'd helped me out of a few jams and always made me laugh, no matter how dire the predicament. Unfortunately, his machine informed me that he was out of town until the fifteenth.

I tried Joanne, the financial services manager who raids databases for me. Her answer was classic Joanne, direct and unfiltered.

"Tracking down credit reports over the phone is one thing. But I'm not going to put my *body* into an investigation. Knowing you, you're probably trying to catch a mass murderer."

So far the only known dead were Frank and Roxanne Fielding and Tim Zevnik.

"Not mass," I assured her. "Just multiple."

She laughed, thinking I was kidding. "Well, then, what am I hesitating for? No, thanks, Elizabeth. Not for love or money." I heard the phone click. You never get a hello or good-bye with Joanne.

Then it hit me. Toby's senior-year class load was light and he had Fridays off.

"Toby," I said when he answered the phone. "Ready to earn that money you borrowed?"

"Yeah, sure. What's the job?"

"Surveillance. This isn't a PO box, this is a real house. And you might have to tail a real criminal. Think you can handle it?"

"When?"

"Now."

"How long will this take?"

"Not sure. Until I can get back here with a warrant. Could be as late as tomorrow morning."

"Oh." His tone was disappointed. "Sue and I were supposed to go out tonight."

I was beginning to have second thoughts about Toby, anyway.

"Forget about it," I said. "Sue's great. I don't want you breaking a date with her. This is probably not something you should be getting wrapped up in anyway."

"Sorry I couldn't help out. You know I love doing secret-agent stuff for you."

There was a commotion on the other end of the line.

"Elizabeth." A female voice. "It's Sue. What's this about secret-agent stuff?" Apparently she'd been right there, listening in on Toby's conversation.

"Nothing, really. Sounds like you guys are going to have fun tonight. What's the plan? Another Hitchcock flick?"

"Don't listen to Toby," she said. "We can be your secret agents."

"I don't think so. It's some serious surveillance work, watching a house while I try to get a search warrant issued."

"Are you kidding? We're *perfect* for the job. If anyone notices us we can just pretend we're necking."

"This isn't a game, Sue. We're talking long hours without access to a bathroom, the whole nine yards."

She hissed. "Like I don't know how to pee in a can." I didn't know what to say to that. "Don't be so shocked," she said. "We're *eighteen*, Elizabeth." As if that explained everything. I'm a full-grown adult and the thought of urinating in front of anyone mortifies me. Sue's ballsy tone pushed me to make a decision.

"You absolutely cannot get out of the car or risk interaction with the suspect," I said.

"Understood," Sue replied.

"All you have to do is watch, and call me when she gets home."

"It's a woman?"

"I think so."

A half hour later Toby and Sue pulled up to the corner of Jackson Street and Firestone Court. I pulled out of my parking space, which had a clear view of the Victorian at 228 Jackson, and Toby pulled into my vacated space. As we'd planned on the phone, we didn't wave, exchange greetings, or let on in any way that we knew one another.

Forty minutes later I was back home, starting my paper chase. I logged onto KnowX.com, a member-paid database that hooks up addresses with title holders. I plugged in 228 Jackson Street, San Diego, California, and waited for the match. When the title holder's name came up I stared blankly.

John Paul Glinski.

My phone rang and I let the machine pick up.

"Hey, Elizabeth, it's Randy. I know you want to be left alone, but I just did a title search on that house you were checking out this morning. I have recent practice and all, since I just checked the title on my allegedly haunted house. Results were very interesting, like I said. Anyway, 228 Jackson is registered to John Glinski."

Yes, I thought, *I know.* Unfortunately the name meant nothing to me.

I entered John Paul Glinski into another search engine, this time seeing if I could match any obvious public records. Bingo. I pulled up a death certificate. Dated two months ago, the death certificate informed me that John Paul Glinski had lived to be seventy-five years of age before succumbing to brain cancer.

Now that was interesting.

I popped the disk Loebman had given me into my computer and clicked on the file that contained information on the employees of Starcom International. It was a large document listing the names in alphabetical order, then giving date of birth, job title, and number of years with the company. I clicked the search command for Glinski but the software reported no such listing. I scrolled through the entire document, running my eyes down the addresses, searching for 228 Jackson.

Blades had been right about one thing—there was no Starcom employee living at 228 Jackson.

I'd have to find her by first name only.

I scanned the list again, this time instructing the software to search for "Abby." The first hit came up:

Landon, Abby, 4/18/53, Shipping Manager, 3 yrs.
8946 Mira Mesa Boulevard, #6, San Diego, CA 92117

I recognized the address as the apartment building next to Starcom that had gone up in flames. A light went on, shining so bright in my brain I wondered how I could have missed it before. *Better double-check before I get too excited,* I thought.

I pulled up the file that listed the Mira Mesa Apartments residents who'd been displaced by the fire. There was no Abby Landon on that list. There'd been no profile of her, either, on Twain's videotapes of the victims, or in his notes on that story.

I flashed back to the night of the Starcom fire, when I'd seen her sitting on the sidewalk, watching the last of the apartment building burn. She'd told me she would be all right, that she had family she could stay with.

I called the main number at the FBI field office and got transferred a couple of times before I was put through to Dale Blades.

"I'm looking at the list of Mira Mesa Apartments residents. You interviewed all these people, right?"

"Yeah, so?" Blades's voice made it clear that I was interrupting something and he barely had time for my questions.

"Do you remember a woman named Abby Landon?"

"Name doesn't ring a bell, but there were several women we talked to. If she was living there, she'd be on that list."

"On the Starcom employee database, Abby Landon's address is listed as the Mira Mesa Apartments, but she's not on the list of Mira Mesa Apartments residents who were displaced by the fire."

With all their computing power and dedication to old-fashioned investigation, the FBI should have picked up on the discrepancy. I admired myself for not throwing that in Blades's face.

"We input a lot of employee names and addresses. Maybe something got mixed up."

Lame, lame, lame. Still, I held my tongue. I'd given him enough and he certainly had nothing to offer me.

"Just wanted to confirm with you," I said. "I'll look into it."

I called the human resources department at Starcom. A woman answered.

"Hi, this is Elizabeth Chase. I'm calling on behalf of Agent Blades, who I believe you know is investigating the Starcom fire."

"Yes, what can I do for you, Elizabeth?"

"What we need is a look into the personnel file of Abby Landon in your shipping department. All I need is a name for her next of kin."

"That's easy. Hang on."

She put me on hold, where I was treated to the Pachelbel *Canon in D*. Amazing how too much exposure can make even a brilliant piece of classical music sound trite. Three minutes later she was back on the line.

"Okay, next of kin for Abby Landon. That would be John Glinski, her father."

"At 228 Jackson in San Diego."

"Yep. You guys are good. Would you like the phone number?"

"If you don't mind."

"We've got her."

"Got who?" Loebman asked.

"Our arsonist. Her name is Abby Landon. Date of birth, April 18, 1953. She's living at 228 Jackson, which was owned by her father, John Paul Glinski, who died of brain cancer two months ago at age seventy-five. It all checks out. You missed her because she wasn't living at the Mira Mesa Apartments when they burned down. She probably moved into her father's house right after he died. Now can we please get moving on that warrant?"

"Spell Abby Landon for me."

I did.

"I'm going to run this through NCIC. I'll be back to you in five minutes."

The phone rang as soon as I hung up with Loebman. It was Toby, sounding a little frantic.

"You were right. It's a woman. She just got home. She went inside for a few minutes and now she's talking to the neighbor in the driveway."

Great. I knew that nosy neighbor would snitch on me. I glanced at the time. Twelve-thirty. Abby must have come home for her lunch hour.

"Now she's getting in her car. I think she's leaving."

"What's she driving?"

"A green Honda Civic. An old one."

"Are you close enough to see a license number?"

"No."

My heart sank.

"Fortunately," Toby said, "I brought a pair of binoculars." There was a pause before he said, "The license number is 2EKG568. Okay, we're going to follow her."

"Not too close. Don't be too obvious about it. Wait for

her to get to the end of the block. Let me talk to Sue. You just concentrate on driving."

My pulse was racing as Sue got on the line.

"Does the lady in the car have a little boy with her?" I asked.

"No," Sue said, "it's just the one woman. She's pretty far ahead of us right now. A couple of cars pulled between us. It looks like she's heading for the freeway."

This went on for seven excruciating minutes.

"Oh, no," Sue said. "The light ahead of us turned red and she just ran it."

Toby's voice came on the line.

"Hey, Elizabeth? The light was red, I had to stop. There's cross traffic coming through the intersection. It was too dangerous to keep following her."

"You did the right thing, Tob. It's okay. Just see if you can find her when the light goes green again."

But after ten minutes, it was clear that Toby and Sue had lost her. When Loebman's call came in I was bummed.

"Okay, Abigail Landon. DOB April 18, 1953."

"An Aries," I said. "That figures."

"Huh?"

"She was born under a fire sign. Impulsive. A law unto herself. Go ahead, I'm rambling."

"We ran her through NCIC and got some interesting hits, including a 455."

"Since I don't have the entire penal code memorized, could you translate, please?"

"Basically, it's attempted arson. Guess she tried to burn down an ex-husband's house a few years ago."

My stomach felt queasy.

"I'm not sure how she slipped under our radar. Maybe the guys just ran the names through county check the first time. This was an Oregon rap. Turned up on the national database."

You missed her because the FBI profiler was looking for a twenty-something guy, not a middle-aged woman, I thought.

"Hang on," Loebman said. "Someone wants to talk to you."

I heard the phone change hands.

"Nice work, Chase." It was Rick Wong. "I just tracked down a judge. We'll have a warrant in an hour. Meanwhile, we're sending a unit over to Jackson Street."

"Don't expect to find the suspect at the house," I said. "She just slipped through my net. You might want to put out an APB on a green Honda Civic, license number 2EKG568. That's what she's driving."

"*G* as in *geese*?"

"More like *g* as in *gone*," I said. "But I think Matthew might still be there."

CHAPTER 39

It was nearly two in the afternoon by the time I got back to 228 Jackson Street. An SDPD patrol car was parked across the street and I spotted an unmarked van—probably a SWAT unit—along the curb about ten yards from the house. I had no scanner and therefore wasn't in radio communication with these guys. Loebman, who was about ten minutes behind me, was keeping me posted via cell phone.

"Everybody's waiting for Wong and Blades to arrive with the search warrant," he said.

I parked at the end of the block and rolled down my windows. Nero lifted his head and sniffed as a breeze rushed through the cab. A breeze, not hot wind. While I wouldn't call it cool, it wasn't the stifling hot we'd been enduring the last several days. Luckily for Nero. I'd had reservations about bringing him, but he'd charged out the door and planted himself in front of my truck with such determination that I simply had to bring him.

An ambulance, lights and siren off, pulled up across the street. Its presence bothered me, enough so that I called Loebman's cell again.

"An ambulance just pulled up. What do you know about it?" I asked.

"Nothing. My guess is they're just coming prepared. We don't know what we might find in there."

I hadn't even considered the possibility that Matthew might be hurt. Or worse. I pushed the thought from my mind, focusing instead on the Sheriff's Department Explorer that was pulling up into the driveway. The doors opened and Rick Wong and Dale Blades got out. They opened the gate in the chain-link fence and started up the front walk.

The brown Lab had been out of sight in the backyard, but at the sound of footsteps he came around and began barking ferociously. Wong and Blades backed out. Seconds later a pair of uniforms emerged from the unmarked van. Wearing heavy protective clothing and thick gloves, they entered through the gate, collared and muzzled the dog in just a few economical moves, and whisked the Lab into the van.

Wong and Blades went to the front door. I could see Wong rapping his fist against the door, saw Blades pressing the doorbell. Through my open window I could hear Wong shouting verbal commands.

"POLICE. OPEN THE DOOR." Wong repeated the order a few times.

Finally Blades shouted: "OPEN THE DOOR OR IT'S COMING DOWN."

The doors of the van opened again and the SWAT team emerged. It took them about fifteen seconds to blow through the front door, which caved in as if it were made of balsa wood. The men disappeared into the house.

Again I called Loebman, who by now had pulled up and parked across the street.

"What's going on?"

"I know as much as you do. They're searching the house."

We hung up and watched. A minute or so later, two SWAT guys reappeared at the front door. Loebman's voice came through my cell phone.

"Initial search found the house empty," he said.

My heart sank, then rallied. "They're wrong. Matthew's there, I *know* it."

"We'll soon see," Loebman said.

We waited and watched, anticipating the discovery.

"Let's hang up," Loebman said. "No point tying up the line. I'll call you when something happens."

The truck cab grew hotter and Nero's panting grew louder. After fifteen minutes, the SWAT team reemerged from the house. My phone rang.

"That's it," Loebman said. "No kid."

"He's in there, Bruce. Let me go in. I'll find him."

"I don't know, Elizabeth. These guys generally know what they're doing."

"Call Wong, tell him I need to talk to him."

A few minutes later, Wong was walking to my truck. I did my best to describe the certainty I felt about Matthew being inside the house and practically begged him to let me search. He started to object.

"I'm not sure I can authorize—"

"I'm licensed, bonded, and insured. It's okay." I was also armed with the Glock concealed in my thigh holster, but that was something I didn't think he needed to know.

It took Wong a few huddles with Blades and SWAT before they let me in the house and then only on the condition that the SWAT team commander accompany me. I had no problem with that. He led me to the door and we stepped inside. We walked from room to room. I searched every corner, every closet. The house appeared to be empty.

"We need to make one more walk-through," I said. "But with a little more help this time. Wait here."

I didn't waste time discussing the matter, just went back to my truck. Now I understood why he'd been so insistent. There was a reason for everything, I thought. I opened the door and called Nero.

"Come on, boy."

Matthew's Scooby toy was still sitting on the passenger seat. I grabbed it and let Nero have a good sniff. He wasn't wriggling or wagging his tail now. His muscles were taut, his ears alert. He knew this wasn't a game.

"Let's find him."

Nero put his nose to the ground and trotted up the front walk. Before the SWAT commander could object I explained that the dog was a trained tracker K-9 retired from the Escondido Police Department. He smiled and stepped back to let the dog through.

Nero made a beeline for the cramped hallway that led past the stairs. In the middle of the hallway he stopped at a closet door and started barking.

"What is it, boy? What?" I looked back over my shoulder at the SWAT commander and shrugged.

My dog was barking at the linen closet that was directly across from the downstairs bathroom. I'd already checked it and I knew the SWAT team had, too. Far as we could tell, it was empty.

"He's barking for a reason," I said.

The SWAT commander dumped out the sheets and towels and tossed the shelves to the floor with a clatter. He leaned in, his torso disappearing into the closet.

"There's a door back here," his muffled voice called out. "I'm too big to get through it."

"Let me."

He backed out and let me in.

Cut into the wall behind the shelves was a tiny door—maybe two feet high and eighteen inches wide. I pried it open. The door led to a crawl space under the stairs. I was staring into the opening, figuring out the best way to crawl through, when Nero nudged me aside and slipped past, disappearing into the blackness.

"Nero, heel!"

We heard his muffled barking.

"Nero, come!"

Being a well-trained dog, Nero came back as I'd commanded. A dusty cobweb clung to his coat. His eyes were bright with excitement and he continued to bark. A sharp, unpleasant odor came through the opening.

The SWAT commander handed me a flashlight.

"Are you up for this?"

For a moment I saw Frank Fielding's eyes. *Will you promise me you'll do everything in your power to get my son back?*

I understand. I promise.

Holding my breath, I grabbed the flashlight and wriggled through the opening on my belly. I beamed the light from left to right across the crawl space and stopped.

Two big blue eyes were looking back at me. I recognized the odor now. Worse than dirty diapers but not nearly as bad as a corpse.

"Hi, Matthew." My voice was shaking. "Am I ever glad to see you. It's okay, honey, everything's going to be all right. You can come out now."

He didn't move; didn't speak. Just sat there, frozen, about five feet from me. I realized that all he would be able to see was the glare of my flashlight. I turned the light around and shined it at myself, hoping I didn't look too creepy.

"I'm Elizabeth. That was my dog, Nero. He won't hurt you."

I turned the light back around, checking him for signs of injury. "Are you okay?"

He didn't respond.

"The bad lady is gone now. Just friendly people are here. Can you come out?"

Again, no response.

I was still holding the stuffed Scooby. I held it out under the beam of the flashlight.

"I've got your Scooby toy here."

I heard scuffling as he came forward. I backed out through the closet and sat in the hallway. Matthew crawled through the opening right after me. I handed him his toy, which he clutched to his chest. His hair was oily, his skin was filthy, and his pants were soiled, but to me he was the sweetest-smelling kid in the world. The temptation to take him into my arms was tremendous, but I held back. After all Matthew had been through, a stranger touching him could be traumatic. But he huddled next to me on his own, burrowing against my body. This was a child who, until the last week, had not been abused. Adults were for protection, for hugging.

I looked up at the SWAT commander. Tears were standing in his eyes. He clicked on his radio and static filled the air.

"We found him," he announced. "Matthew's fine. Ten-four." The team outside copied ten-four and the radio went off, leaving us in happy silence.

"I think you might be scaring him in that garb," I said. "Hell, you're scaring me."

The SWAT commander lowered himself into a squat. "Hi, Matthew. My name's Mike. I'm a policeman. This is just my uniform. I'm not really this big."

Matthew was clutching his Scooby and clinging to me, but he was looking at Mike with wide-eyed curiosity. Nero wormed his way into the middle of it all, sniffing at Matthew.

"This is my dog, Nero," I said to Matthew. "Want to pet him?"

That was a yes. As the boy reached for him, Nero stopped panting and sat stone-still, head high. Just as Matthew's hand touched the top of Nero's head, Mike's radio burst to life again.

"All right, out of the house. Now!"

CHAPTER 40

The staticky command coming through the radio made my heart leap. I looked to Mike for reassurance.

"Standard procedure," the SWAT commander said. "The house could be rigged with explosives or the suspect could come back." He looked at Matthew and chose his next words carefully. "There's no telling what that person might do."

I took Matthew's hand and together we followed Mike out of the house. As we walked outside, Matthew shielded his eyes from the bright sunlight. I saw a television camera trained in our direction. I didn't see the Channel Three news van among the crowd of law-enforcement vehicles that had crowded the street, but I had no doubt Twain was around somewhere.

Rick Wong stood at the end of the front walk, waiting for us.

"Hey, Matthew," he said. "How about a ride to the San Diego Police Department headquarters?" He was trying to make it sound fun, like a trip to Disneyland. Wong looked over at me. "You know how to get there?"

"Yeah. Can Matthew ride with me?"

"No can do. He has to be in police custody until we turn

him over to next of kin. Standard procedure."

Matthew clutched me tighter and looked up with an expression that was far too worried for a kid his age.

"Can Nero ride with him?" I asked. Wong looked dubious. "He's a trained K-9," I said. "He won't give you any trouble." I turned to Matthew. "You want my dog to ride with you and Scooby in the police car?"

His eyes lit up and he nodded.

"All right," Wong said.

I helped Matthew into the back seat of Wong's Explorer. When he was settled in I called to Nero. My dog is often wary of little kids, who have a habit of using his ears as handles and socking his nose just for the fun of it. But Nero behaved protectively toward Matthew, jumping into the car and curling up against him. I reached in and buckled Matthew's seat belt.

"Take good care of my dog, okay?" He looked at me, wide-eyed, and nodded solemnly.

Randy Twain intercepted me on my way back to my truck. Jane Sharpe was right beside him, catching me on camera. Twain turned to her and put up a hand.

"Jane, stop taping."

I gave Twain a grateful look. "Thanks."

"You rock, Chase. This was an amazing job here."

"The real credit goes to my dog."

"Don't be so modest. I told you you're where this story is breaking."

I looked back at the house. The cops had hauled out the next-door neighbor and were starting to grill her. I pointed it out to Twain.

"I'd go get the neighbor's story on camera if I were you. I even have a prediction about what she's going to say."

"What's that?" he asked.

"She's going to tell the cops what a nice, quiet neighbor Abby Landon was." They always did. Antisocial personalities apparently made the best damn neighbors.

When I got to my truck I searched my wallet for the piece of notepaper on which Wong had written Debbie

Fielding-Cross's phone number. I dialed her on my cell, hoping she'd be home.

"Hello?" came her tentative greeting.

"Debbie, this is Elizabeth, the investigator you met on Monday. I have the happiest news in the world for you."

"You found him?" Her voice was a prayer.

"We found him, and he's just fine."

She shrieked so loudly that I had to hold the phone away. When I put my ear back to the phone she was half sobbing, half laughing.

"We're taking him down to the police headquarters on Broadway," I said. I gave her directions and the address. And my phone number, in case she'd been too excited to get it all down right.

Forty-five minutes later Matthew was sitting in a seat next to me in a conference room at the SDPD headquarters. He'd been cleaned up, had a change of clothes, and was eating a Happy Meal, compliments of the SWAT team. Nero, lying at Matthew's feet, was keeping his eyes open for any stray French fries that might fall his way.

The door to the conference room opened. Wearing ill-fitting brown Dockers and a shirt that didn't quite match, Dale Blades strutted in and gave Wong a congratulatory slap on the back. The FBI agent completely ignored Matthew and me. There's a song somewhere, done by an obscure renegade band, called "High Fivin' Motherfucker." I wondered if perhaps the songwriter had known Blades.

Matthew had information the police desperately needed. Patsy King, an SDPD officer who specialized in family law and dealing with children, sat next to him at the table. I'd told the officers about Matthew's selective mutism, explaining that interviewing the child would probably be fruitless. Nonetheless, Patsy was giving it her best shot. At first Matthew had been entirely unresponsive to questioning, but he'd warmed to her in the last few minutes and was now answering yes and no questions by either nodding or shaking his head.

"Did the woman who kept you in the dark room take you away from your house?"

Yes.

"Did you know her?"

No.

"Do you know where she is?"

No.

"Did she say when she was coming back?"

No.

"Did she keep you in that house the whole time?"

Yes.

"Were you locked in that closet all this time?"

After a pause, Matthew shook his head. Again I saw the image of a small, dark room with wood paneling and a television set.

"Did she let you watch cartoons?" I asked.

He bobbed his head and his eyes lit up. *Yes!*

Officer King gave me a frown to let me know that my interruptions weren't appropriate.

"Did she lock you in the closet when she went to work or left the house?" she asked.

Yes.

"Did she hurt you?"

Matthew's face darkened and after a pause he moved his head from side to side. It was a halfhearted *no*.

After a few more questions, King wrapped up. "Thank you, Matthew, for helping us."

"I've got a lot more questions," Blades said.

"No." Officer King was adamant. "He's had enough for now. He needs rest and lots of hugs."

Blades frowned.

"Yeah, I suppose he does," he said with a sigh. "Let's contact next of kin."

"I already called Debbie Fielding-Cross," I said. I looked at Matthew. "You want to see your aunt Debbie?"

Matthew nodded eagerly as he stuffed another ketchup-drenched fry into his mouth. A few minutes later she arrived, escorted into the conference room by another officer.

When she caught sight of her nephew, she hurried to greet him.

"Matt!"

He jumped down from his chair and ran into her arms, hugging her legs as if he'd never let go. Debbie leaned over and scooped him up.

"Thank God. Thank you so much."

I stood to go. Matthew's kidnapper was still at large and much as I would have loved to stay and chat, I was anxious to see if the task force had made any progress toward finding her.

"We're going to go now, Matthew. Want to say goodbye to Nero?"

He nodded and squirmed down from his aunt's arms. Nero held his head still while Matthew gave him a farewell pat. I squatted down and patted him, too.

"This dog used to belong to a police officer," I said to the boy. "He's helped out a lot of people who were lost or in trouble. Now he's my pet. I love him very much." I put my arms around Nero's chest, hugging him for a job well done. Matthew hugged him, too, putting his face next to mine.

"Can I ask you one more thing?" I whispered.

The boy's face grew serious and he nodded.

"Did the bad lady say where she was going?" I whispered.

Matthew stared at me with big blue eyes. Slowly, he nodded his head.

I leaned close and turned my ear toward Matthew's face.

"Can you whisper it to me?"

To my surprise, he did.

CHAPTER 41

"She's going to burn down the witch's house."

Matthew's words were barely a whisper, more like puffs of breath shot through with meaning.

I searched his face.

"The witch's house?" I whispered.

He nodded solemnly. Again I found myself thinking that he possessed the eyes of a soul much older than four.

His aunt, seeing our exchange, came over and joined us.

"What'd he say?" she asked.

"I asked him if his kidnapper told him where she was going. He said she was going to burn down the witch's house."

Blades stepped forward. "What'd he mean by that? What do you mean by that, son?"

Blades was scaring him. Matthew clutched his Scooby toy and burrowed into the shelter of his aunt's dress. When it was clear that he wasn't going to speak, his aunt Debbie stepped in.

"I'm taking him home. If you need to question him again, it's going to have to be tomorrow."

No one was about to argue with her. I thought about the job ahead of Debbie and didn't envy her; she'd somehow have to tell Matthew that his parents weren't coming back.

I watched them walk out. As I thought about Matthew's whispered message, a dread took hold, starting as a tightening in my abdomen. When the door closed behind them Wong came over to talk.

"The witch's house. Hate to say it, but you know what I'm thinking."

I nodded. "Bet you're thinking the same thing I am. I'm Abby's witch, right? The psychic detective. She probably saw that story about my involvement in Matthew's case on TV."

"Where do you live, Elizabeth?" Wong asked.

"At the corner of Juniper and Tenth in Escondido. I run my agency out of my home office. Anybody can find me in the Yellow Pages under Investigators."

"I'm going to get a task force out there, stat." He turned to Blades. "Let's go."

All was normal when Nero and I pulled into my driveway, if you didn't count the unmarked law-enforcement vehicles that had descended on the block. The task force was using Abby's threat as an opportunity to set a trap. I'd called Toby at his house across the street, to fill him in on what was going down.

"Too cool," he replied.

"Don't get in the middle of anything. Just thought you should know."

"I'll keep my eye on your place from our backyard," Toby said. "Nobody's going to burn down your house, not if I have anything to say about it."

Rick Wong had followed me to Escondido and was now pulling his Explorer into the driveway behind me. As the garage door opened, Wong got out of his Explorer and tapped on my window. I rolled it down.

"We don't want you going in. You got someplace else to stay tonight?"

"I need to get my cat out of there," I said.

"We've got this place surrounded," Wong said. "Your

cat will be fine. You don't have to worry about a thing."

"Repeat: I need to get my cat out of there. This is non-negotiable, Rick. I'm going in."

He bit his lip. "Okay, five minutes. I'm going in with you."

I left Nero in the truck and Wong followed me through the garage. As I searched the garage shelves for Whitman's pet carrier, I ran across my box of Things I've Had a Tough Time Parting With. This would come, too, I decided.

"I could use some help here," I called out. Wong came over and I dumped the box in his arms. "You take this and I'll take the cat."

I found Whitman upstairs sleeping on the bed. I put him in the carrier and was just headed back down the stairs when I caught sight of the fifty-pound bow Sequoia had given me this week. I picked it up, along with a quiver of arrows, and carried the lot outside to my truck, where Wong was waiting with his arms crossed over his chest.

"Okay," I said as I slid into the driver's seat, "now I'm set."

"If Abby attacks, she's probably going to wait until after dark to do it. Where will you be staying?"

"With my mom and dad." I gave him the number.

"We'll keep in touch," Wong promised. "Meantime, you've got my number."

I nodded and took a last look at my house. The place had survived more than a hundred twenty years of human and natural disasters. I had faith it would get through this.

On my way to my parents' house, I called Mom to warn her that she'd be having guests for the night.

"You're coming with the dog and cat? Why?"

"I'll explain later, Mom. The good news is, I found Matthew Fielding and he's fine."

"I just heard it on the news. I never had the slightest doubt you'd find him."

"That's good, because I sure did."

"Your only problem, Elizabeth Merry Chase, is that you

underestimate yourself. See you when you get here."

I spent the half-hour drive to my parents' house thinking about the wise-cracking shipping department manager. I hadn't guessed that Abby's sarcasm masked a lethal rage.

Mom must have heard my truck coming up the drive, because she was coming out to meet me when I drove up to the house. I opened the passenger door for Nero, who galloped across the driveway to greet her.

"Can I help you carry anything?" she said as she dodged Nero's slobbering kisses.

"No, that's okay." I pulled out the cat carrier and Whitman's yowling filled the air. "I can get everything."

But Mom was already rummaging around in my truck bed.

"Oh, hey, look at this. *Nice*." She picked up the fifty-pound bow and pulled back the string. She looked like someone who knew what she was doing. "I didn't realize you were at this level yet."

"I'm not. Sequoia just started me on that."

"It's a beauty," she said as she carried the bow and arrows into the house. "Sequoia must think a lot of your potential to give you a bow like that."

"Yes, Mom. Like you, Sequoia has great faith in me. Where's Dad?"

"He's in surgery. Called in on a trauma case just before you got here. I don't expect him back for dinner, so it'll be just the two of us."

I opened the cat carrier and Whitman took a few tentative steps into the living room. Nero had already disappeared into the kitchen, hunting for scraps.

"You mean the four of us," I said.

"Carpe diem!" It was Mr. Poe, squawking from the kitchen.

"Five," Mom corrected.

Four o'clock stretched to seven. I gave Mom a blow-by-blow of Matthew's rescue. After that we filled the time preparing and eating dinner. I volunteered to do the dishes while Mom settled down for some television watching. I needed something to do with my hands, something to keep me busy.

When the last dish was done I broke down and called Loebman, who was stationed at my house.

"What's new?" I asked.

"Nothing here."

"Any word on Abby Landon?"

"We've got an APB on her green Honda Civic. Nothing's turned up yet."

"I take it she didn't report back to work today."

"No, but we checked out her time-card record at Starcom. She clocked in pretty regularly all week. The Fielding fire, as you know, happened on a Sunday. And the Starcom fire started in the wee hours. But what do you know, yesterday's San Marcos fire started during the lunch hour and Abby Landon clocked in late back from lunch. What really went bada-bing was when we looked at her attendance last week. Abby Landon called in sick on Wednesday, the day Matthew was kidnapped."

"How about the house on Jackson Street? Any evidence turn up there?"

"The techs found gas cans in the garage. Plus a bunch of environmental literature and a diary that described her plan to burn down the houses of the people she was working for. She's loony-tunes, man."

"Not that loony. Otherwise you'd have her in custody by now, don't you think?"

"Well, maybe."

"Why did she take Matthew?"

"We don't know that yet. Maybe she was planning to use him as some kind of hostage if she got in a jam. Maybe she couldn't bring herself to torch him. As you like to say, that's in the To Be Determined file."

"You should get ahold of that EarthNow guy, Ken Fender."

"We already have. He's cooperating real well and seems to be genuinely appalled about the fires. He gave us copies of the group's membership records. Abby Landon was never a member of EarthNow or any other group we know of. At this point it looks like she was acting alone."

"You'll call me if anything happens at my place?"

"Promise," Loebman said.

I hung up and joined Mom in the family room, where the television was tuned to Channel Three's evening news. Tonight Bill Bainsley's voice carried a hopeful note. After thirty-plus hours of firefighting, a dozen mutual-aid departments had managed to contain most of the north county fire. The three new fires that had started yesterday were under control, as well.

"Are you still angry about being on TV?" Mom asked. She was leafing through a stack of annual reports, giving the newscast half her attention. Mr. Poe was perched on her shoulder, keeping an eye on the turning pages.

"Yeah, I'm mad. If it hadn't been for that, I wouldn't be sitting here worrying that some ecoterrorist was going to burn my house down."

Mom looked up and furrowed her brow.

"I don't think it's a good idea for you to advertise in the Yellow Pages."

"I have to make a living. Investigators can't live on references alone. Not this one, anyway." She gave me a look that said she didn't buy that excuse. "I'll be fine, Mom. Don't worry."

It occurred to me that it was going to be a long and probably sleepless night.

"Oh," Mom said, "I forgot to tell you that Sequoia called again. Wanted to remind you about your appointment tomorrow."

My shoulders sagged just thinking about it. I knew he wouldn't accept a mere excuse like "my house was under siege and I couldn't sleep."

"I don't know why he always calls you here," she said.

"Because he always knows where to find me. Ever noticed that?"

A thoughtful look crossed Mom's face and she started

to comment when Nero jumped up from the floor and started to bark.

"Coyotes, probably," Mom said.

"I'll check."

I got up and walked out the sliding door to the back terrace. The night had definitely cooled down. The change in weather would help the firefighters more than anything. I looked out over the darkened valley. It was always quiet here in Rancho Santa Fe, where lots were large and cars were few. Tonight it was quieter than ever. I thought of Sequoia.

A wise person can hear a lot in the silence.

That's when I heard the sound. Toward the west side of the house, down by the toolshed, Mom's garden depot. I wondered if it might be the coyote Mom had suggested, or perhaps a raccoon. As I walked across the terrace the sound became more distinct. It was a crackling noise.

A fire.

In a flash I remembered that tools weren't the only things in that shed. There was a propane tank down there.

CHAPTER 42

I rushed back just long enough to scream through the family-room door.

"Mom! Call 911—there's a fire out here!"

I sprinted across the terrace and careened down the path to the little garden house. As I approached I could see the fire creeping up one wall. As yet the flames were small. The wood was thick and weather-treated. It would take several minutes for fire to engulf the structure. If I acted quickly it was possible I could put it out. If I didn't, the shed would burn and ignite the propane tank inside.

Propane-tank explosion. A brief memory of the ruins of the Fielding estate went through my head. The charred black dishwasher and melted lump of glass inside it. *I have to put this fire out,* I thought, *I can't let that happen here.*

I stopped at the edge of the embankment and pulled out my gun. A full moon was rising in the east, illuminating the landscape in a silvery glow. Excellent visibility, a boon to me. I stepped forward, keeping my eyes on the shadows. The flames were growing larger.

Water. I need water.

There was a hose attached to a faucet on this side of the

house, but I knew it would never reach all the way down the embankment.

A bucket of water.

By the time I got back here with a bucket, the fire would cover half the structure. It was already too large to be extinguished by a bucket of water, anyway.

Think.

There were tools in the garden depot. I could grab a shovel and throw dirt on the fire.

Gun drawn, I skidded down the embankment. Giving the flames a wide berth, I walked around and kicked open the door. The shed was empty. I tracked the interior with my gun. The propane tank sat in the corner like a time bomb waiting for its moment.

I looked around, keeping my eyes and ears open. I reached inside the door to grab the shovel, but it was gone.

Damn.

Why are things always missing when you really need them? I could hear the flames crackling on the other side of the shed. There were other tools here. A hoe. A rake. Something, anything. I grabbed the long handle of an axe and backed out the door.

It felt as if I banged the back of my head against a metal wall. Before I could turn around, everything went black.

I came to with my face in the dirt. I was disoriented but suspected that not much time had passed. I closed my eyes again. If I kept my eyes closed, she might think I was dead.

I could feel her standing there, above me. Could sense her watching me.

Should I roll sideways, try to make an escape?

I *felt* something come at me this time and opened my eyes just in time to see the shovel come down again.

I was standing in an open field. Wind was hissing through the cheatgrass. The bright light of midday filled my eyes and the scent of sage filled my nostrils. Ten yards in front of me sat a hay bale, draped with a bull's-eye target.

"Go ahead." I turned at the sound of the familiar voice. Sequoia was standing next to me, arms crossed over his chest. He nodded toward the hay bale. "Hit the target."

But I when I looked down, my hands were empty. "I can't. I don't have anything to hit it with."

Sequoia smiled. "What you must do is hit the target."

I felt exasperated. "I can't." I turned up my palms. "I'm empty-handed. I can't."

"What you must do," he repeated, "is hit the target."

I waved my empty hands in his face, imploring him to acknowledge my predicament.

"What do you want me to do, hit it with my bare hands?" I felt a surge of anger. I had the impulse to run forward and pummel the target with my fists. But I was lying on the ground now, and couldn't move.

"I can't." I started to cry. "I'm powerless." I could feel hot tears rolling down my cheeks.

I looked around for Sequoia but from my position on the ground could only see the wind blowing through the cheatgrass.

Then I heard his voice. Not in a dream. For real.

"Use the power around you."

The sound of Sequoia's voice brought me around and my eyes popped open. Lying facedown, I couldn't move. My legs and arms were tied. The smell of gas was strong in my nose and I realized it was coming from the rags that had been stuffed in my mouth and tied around my head.

No way could I get out of this alone. What power around me? Silently, I called for help.

Mom, please come.

Something wet and warm trickled down my back. The feeling alarmed me enough that I managed to roll over. I looked up to see Abby pouring gasoline on me. She wore the same cynical expression she'd always worn.

"I told you this place is hell," she said. She let out a laugh.

Mom, hurry.

"You fucked things up for me, now I fuck them up for you."

I'd fallen—or been dragged—nearer to the side of the shed that housed the propane tank. The blaze on the opposite corner had grown since I'd lost consciousness but apparently it wasn't burning fast enough for Abby. She reached into her pocket and pulled out a book of matches.

"You know what happens to witches, don't you?"

I heard Mr. Poe's voice in my head. *How cliché.*

Abby wasn't as cool as she was trying to sound. Her fingers were shaking as she lit the first match. It sputtered and went out.

"You up on your Salem history?" she asked.

I heard a sound, a soft *thwap.* Abby's eyes went wide, and her face froze in a startled expression. I heard the same sound again.

Thwap.

She jerked and twisted her torso. In the silvery moonlight I could see the feathered ends of two arrows sticking out of her back.

The third time I heard a whooshing sound and another solid *thwap.* Abby gasped for air as her body crumpled and collapsed into a heap next to me.

CHAPTER 43

I stared at the three stiff arrows protruding from the crumpled form beside me. Was she dead? Just as the question crossed my mind, I heard a grunt. Abby rolled onto her side, facing me. She struggled to lift her torso and cried out in pain. She dropped back on her side and gasped for air, making an anguished sucking sound.

The spot where the shovel had connected to the back of my head was throbbing, but my mind was beginning to clear. Mom must have come out and seen Abby tying me up. Not owning a gun, my mother must have used the only weapon at her disposal: the bow and arrows I'd brought over, my gift from Sequoia. I wondered where Mom was now.

I craned my head to look behind me. The garden depot was burning faster. Flames had consumed the far wall and were creeping along the roof. The sound of my involuntary scream was muffled by my gag. I struggled to loosen the bindings on my wrists and ankles but they held tight. Fighting panic, I rolled away from the toolshed and rubbed my head against the ground, trying to work off the rags Abby had wrapped around my head to keep my gag in place.

"How does it feel?"

It was more of a hiss than a voice. With a gag in my mouth, I could only answer Abby with my eyes.

"Sucks to have your home destroyed, doesn't it?" Making another attempt to get up, Abby winced.

I turned back to the fire. How hot would the toolshed have to be before the propane tank inside caught fire? The thought made my skin break out in a cold sweat. I rolled some more, but about ten feet from the shed the ground began to slope upward, making it impossible to put more distance between myself and the flames. With a growing terror, I realized that ten feet wouldn't be far enough to escape the explosion. My heart pounded in my ears.

I looked up toward the house. Something silvery flickered in my vision. I thought it was those stars you sometimes see before you pass out, but as my eyes focused I realized that the silvery flickering was an arc of water coming from the top of the embankment. Shimmering in the moonlight, the stream pummeled the roof of the toolshed. Droplets bounced off the eaves and splashed to the ground. Had the fire department arrived? I hadn't heard a siren. As the flames went out a thick, whitish smoke clouded the night air. Still, the water kept spraying.

My heart lifted. Mom must have found an extension for the garden hose. I wanted to call out to her, but with an oily rag in my mouth, I couldn't. The taste had become unbearable. I rubbed my head against the earth again, harder this time, and felt the knotted fabric begin to slip from my scalp. Shaking my head, I flung off the rags and spit out the gag.

"Way to go, Mom!" I called.

I turned back to Abby. Her face was ghostly white in the moonlight. From this distance I could see only the hollows of her eyes.

"Why did you kill the Fieldings? What did they ever do to you?" I didn't really expect an answer. I wasn't even sure she was still conscious.

"He killed my dad."

"He what?"

"Wireless pollution . . . filled my dad's brain with cancer. It's killing people." She strained to speak; her words were weak and halting. "The land used to be so . . . beautiful. Nothing but cars and cement now."

"You mean Starcom," I said.

"Killed my dad. Destroyed my home."

"Your home, meaning the Mira Mesa Apartments, or your home meaning San Diego County?"

She didn't respond but I knew that the answer was both. For Abby, Frank Fielding and the Starcom executives had become the ultimate scapegoats, the people she could blame for all her despair over the loss of her father as well as the loss of San Diego's shrinking open space. If her father's death had brought her to the brink, the company's plan to expand and tear down her old apartment building must have pushed her into the abyss.

"But so many homes and lives were destroyed by the fires you set."

"For a good cause," she said.

Abby didn't view her arson as criminal, she viewed it as an act of war.

"Why did you take Matthew?"

No reply. From what I'd seen, the arrows had penetrated deeply into her back. Whether her wounds were fatal or not, I couldn't tell. I was beginning to think she'd lost consciousness when she answered.

"I was going to burn down their house that day. The kid saw me. Didn't expect that. Didn't know what to do, so I just took him."

I was aware of footsteps now, hurrying down the embankment. Abby didn't seem to hear them.

"It's so quiet out here. Peaceful. Like it used to be."

As if to mock her, the rising scream of a siren came from the direction of the driveway. At the same time, Mom burst into view. She gave Abby a sideways glance as she rushed to my side.

"Are you all right?"

"Fine, thanks to you. Just hog-tied."

"Thank God. I thought she'd killed you."

As Mom worked to unbind my ankles, I watched Abby. Still lying on her side, she appeared to have frozen where she'd fallen. I had the sense she could no longer hear us. Mom wasn't making much headway untying me.

"I think she used that twine in the toolshed," I said. "You have a knife or anything?"

Mom got up and disappeared into the garden depot, its charred roof still dripping with water. She returned with a pair of pruning shears. I rolled onto my side so that she could cut the twine at my wrists.

"Hold still," she said, "these blades are sharp."

As Mom cut me free I looked toward the house. At the top of the embankment, the silhouetted form of a helmeted firefighter appeared.

"Where's the fire?"

I thought I recognized the voice. "That you, Carolyn?" I called.

"Elizabeth?"

"Yeah. The fire's out but we need an ambulance." I looked again at Abby's motionless form. *Or a hearse,* I thought.

CHAPTER 44

It was nine o'clock on the dot the next morning when I parked on the bluff across from Miracles Café. I'd chosen Miracles as a meeting place for three reasons: great ocean view, low-key atmosphere, and the promise of healing suggested by the name. I needed the healing; it had been a rough week. I was walking up the front steps and heading inside when I heard a voice call out.

"Elizabeth. Over here."

I turned to see a man in a straw hat waving from the porch. Wearing shorts, T-shirt, sandals, and sunglasses, Randy Twain was occupying a table in the sun.

"I didn't recognize you," I said as I approached the table. "You look so—"

"Slovenly?"

I laughed and took a seat. "Not at all. It's Saturday, for crying out loud." I picked up my menu, but before opening it, I looked him in the eye. "I owe you an apology."

"You do?"

"Yeah, I do. I was wrong about you. I wasn't sure that you weren't the arsonist, but I thought you were kind of a jerk."

He chuckled and motioned for the waitress. "That's

okay. I was wrong about you, too. I thought you were kind of a nut. What changed your mind about me?"

"The way you reported last night's events. I can't thank you enough."

Word had spread quickly after Mom's call to 911. Carolyn Arnold of the Rancho Santa Fe Fire Department had been the first to respond. Loebman, Wong, and Blades hadn't been far behind. They mobilized quickly from my house in Escondido, with Twain and his news photographer right on their tail. The scenario had allowed Twain every opportunity to tape and broadcast the entire sordid scene, including the ugly parts. My mom's tormented crying as her shock wore off. The arrows in Abby's back. But none of that had aired on the late-night news.

Twain gave a modest shrug. "We covered the basics."

What had aired wasn't the least bit sensational. Close-up footage of the burned toolshed and the propane tank that might have exploded. Tail-end video of Abby being loaded into the ambulance, no unsightly arrows in view. A voice-over stating the barest of facts:

> Police believe they have found the arsonist responsible for at least some of the fires that have plagued the county over the past week. The suspect, Abby Landon, died at Scripps Hospital tonight from complications related to injuries she sustained during a fire at the home of Dr. Albert Chase of Rancho Santa Fe. Landon is also a suspect in the kidnapping of Matthew Fielding, whose parents died in an arson fire last Sunday. Earlier this afternoon Elizabeth Chase, an investigator on the kidnapping case, found four-year-old Matthew Fielding in a Clairemont house formerly owned by Landon's father. Police speculate that Landon set fire to the Chase home in retaliation for Chase's discovery. An investigation is continuing.

" 'Died of complications related to injuries she sustained during the fire,' " I quoted. "That's pretty basic, all right. You left Mom out of the story entirely. For which I can't thank you enough."

"We reported the truth."

The partial truth, and Twain knew it. He'd seen the arrows in Abby's back as the paramedics started an IV drip and loaded Abby into the ambulance. He'd heard the police talking. The whole truth was that Abby had been shot in the back and sustained massive internal hemorrhaging and lung damage. She'd gone into cardiac arrest on the way to the hospital and attempts to revive her had failed.

A waitress came to refill Twain's coffee, saying she'd be back to take our order. Twain waited until she stepped away before he spoke again.

"It's not necessarily over. The other stations might dig up the rest of the story. Me, I'm done with it. Is your mom okay?"

"Yeah, under the circumstances. Her momma-bear instinct seems to be winning out over guilt and remorse."

Rick Wong had taken Mom's statement in private, with her attorney present, while Bruce Loebman had taken mine. We repeated our performances for the FBI and SDPD. Our stories must have checked out. A follow-up investigation was under way but no charges had been filed. Mom had acted in self-defense. No one was going to dispute that.

The waitress came back with coffee for me and a notepad to take our requests. I avoided the South of the Border Omelet ("Hot!") and went with yogurt and fresh fruit. Twain splurged on blueberry waffles with whipped cream.

"One thing I don't get," he said, "is how Abby Landon knew to find you at your parents' house."

"Maybe she never realized I lived in Escondido. Remember that newscast showing me getting into my truck at the bottom of the Fieldings' driveway? Remember your station reporting that my father was a neighbor of the Fieldings? Once Abby saw that, all she had to do was look up 'Chase' in the Rancho Santa Fe phonebook. My folks are listed." I took a sip from my cup and made a face. "Does this coffee taste funny to you?"

"No. Why?"

"Guess it's in my head. Feels like I'm never going to get rid of the smell of gasoline." I took a deep breath, inhaling warm sea air. The soothing blues of ocean and cloudless sky were working color magic on my nerves. I felt relaxed for the first time in a week. I looked over at Twain, who was staring back at me. "So my finding Matthew changed your mind about me being a nut, huh?"

"No, I changed my mind before that." Twain reached into the rear pocket of his shorts and took out some papers, dropping a folded sheet onto the tabletop.

"What's that?"

"Read it."

I unfolded the paper. It was the note I'd written to him about my encounter with the ghost in his house, the one I'd sealed and dropped into the mail: *While using the bathroom I saw an apparition: a man's body in the bathtub.*

"Now read this." He dropped another folded paper on the table.

I opened a photocopied article. The printing was muddy and blurred, as if this had been copied from a very old newspaper. I glanced at the dateline. June 29, 1949. It was an article about the murder of Rudy Valente, a gangster living near Balboa Park in San Diego. Rival mobsters had gotten to him via a prostitute who'd insinuated herself into his home and shot him in the bathtub.

"The title search on my house turned up eight previous owners. I did death-certificate searches on each name. I learned that Rudy Valente had died of gunshot wounds, and dug deeper. When I read that article"—he nodded to the photocopy in my hands—"I decided maybe you weren't so nutty after all. I'm putting the house up for sale."

"Excellent idea."

"When I find a new place, will you come over and check to make sure it's not haunted?"

How could I say no to those dimples? "Sure. Why not?"

Twain sat back in his chair and looked out at the Pacific. "Let's drive up to San Clemente after breakfast and catch a boat to Catalina."

"Tempting," I said with a smile, "but I can't."

"Oh, come on. Look at this sparkling sea. Feel this warm coastal air. How can you refuse?"

"Got an important meeting later this afternoon."

"Meeting. May I remind you that—and I quote—it's Saturday, for crying out loud? You've earned a break."

"Not a business meeting. More like a meeting of minds. It's important to me."

"Okay, I understand." He frowned at his mug before picking it up and emptying the last swallows of coffee. I could see the disappointment in his face.

After all the fire and isolation I'd endured recently, the idea of an ocean voyage delighted me. I leaned across the table and put my lips close to his ear.

"You wouldn't happen to be free to go next weekend, would you?"

The dimple in his cheek reappeared as he glanced sideways with a smile.

"I am now."

CHAPTER 45

Sequoia had directed me to drive about fifteen miles past the casino and "look for the big flat rock." Although the reservation wasn't entirely unfamiliar to me, I worried that his instructions were too vague. I wondered if finding him was perhaps part of my training today. As I passed the casino I punched my odometer to zero. Minutes later, when the meter told me that fourteen miles had gone by, I began searching.

The big flat rock was impossible to miss. At least twelve feet long and nearly half as wide, the boulder was the only landmark in sight. Certainly it was the only rock with a big dark ponytailed guy sitting on it. I pulled over and parked my car on the side of the road.

"Hi," I called as I got out.

Sequoia held up his palm. "How," he said, mocking the Indian greeting of 1950s TV westerns. "Did you know there's a new Coen brothers movie out?"

"Yeah," I said as I grabbed for purchase and hoisted myself onto the boulder. "I saw that." When I reached the top, I sat down and crossed my legs. The sun had heated the surface of the stone but it wasn't unbearably hot.

"I thought you might not make it this morning," he said.

"What with all the excitement last night and everything."

We spent the next several minutes discussing the case. I told Sequoia about the images I'd seen in my mind's eye that led me to Matthew. I also thought he'd be interested to hear how at the last minute I'd grabbed the bow and arrows he'd given me. He nodded when I got to the part about how Mom had used them to defend our lives.

"You come from a long line of woman warriors." He said it straight-faced, without the slightest touch of irony.

"The police took the bow and arrows into evidence," I said. "I don't expect to get them back. Sorry."

Sequoia shrugged. "No big deal. There's nothing important about that particular bow or those particular arrows. What's important is that you listened when your guidance told you to bring them along."

A car went by along the road. We sat quietly as the sound of its hissing tires receded into the distance. The afternoon sun lit up the surrounding fields with a warm, golden glow. Something about the grass triggered a troubling memory.

"So what else is bothering you?" he asked.

Coincidence, I wondered, *or has Sequoia just read my mind?*

"Come on," he said. "Out with it."

"After Abby hit me with that shovel, I had a dream. I was down in the grass and couldn't move. You were around but you wouldn't help me."

Sequoia nodded, chewing slowly on a piece of ryegrass clenched between his teeth. "Uh-huh. How'd the dream end?"

"Something about . . . you told me to use the power around me, but it didn't make sense because I couldn't even move. And then I woke up and realized why I'd been dreaming that. My hands and feet were tied. I really was powerless."

"Congratulations."

"On what?"

"On using the power around you. You did a good job."

"I did?"

"You're here, aren't you?"

"Yeah, but I'm only here because Mom came and bailed me out, not because I used any powers of my own. I mean, if a powerful medicine man like you had been in that position, I'm sure you would've turned into a snake and slithered out of the wrist restraints or something."

"You think?" Sequoia laughed and tossed the blade of grass over the side of the rock.

"Or manifested a coiled rattlesnake that would bite your enemy before he could hurt you."

"Manifested a snake, that's a good one." Sequoia snapped his fingers. "Just like that, huh?"

"Okay, most likely you'd have been wise enough not to get into that predicament in the first place. My point is, the only reason I got out of it is because I got lucky."

He looked at me, all joking aside.

"You chose that predicament. You set it up to learn the lesson of using the power around you. And by the way, you aced the lesson."

"Aced it? I made a pitiful cry for help."

"Thereby calling on the power around you. Not relying on your own power. Relying on power beyond yourself."

I couldn't repress a groan. "Not to be difficult, but that sounds so . . . simple-minded."

"More like simple. I don't know where your people came up with this notion that the world's made up of beings and objects completely independent of your own consciousness. It's not the Indian way of seeing things. It's also in conflict with quantum mechanics."

"Calling on the power around me," I repeated.

"Yeah," he said with a smile. "Think of it as Shamanism 101."

He stared into the distance, leaving me to gaze at his stony profile. Again I got the sense that he was communicating with someone or something I couldn't see. I wondered what he was doing and worked up the nerve to ask him. Before I could open my mouth, he spoke.

"Be still."

"I just have one more ques—"

"Still," he said through clenched teeth, and I saw why.

A thick gray snake was traveling across the outer edge of the wide rock on which we sat. Its liquid motion was soundless. I saw the bumpy rattle on the snake's tail as it slithered past. It was a big rattler, four or five feet at least. Inch by inch, it disappeared into a crack at the bottom of the rock.

When it was gone, I breathed. "Sequoia, did you . . . do that?"

He got to his feet and shook the stiffness out of his legs.

"We'll cover that in Shamanism 102." Smiling his imperfect smile, he extended a hand to help me up. "Class dismissed. I've got a movie to catch."

ACKNOWLEDGMENTS

As author G. M. Ford once said about our work as novelists, "We make this stuff up." There is no Channel Three News in San Diego. Nor is there a Sapphire Heights. There is a La Jolla Playhouse, but the rock opera *Tommy* hasn't played there since 1992. This is a work of fiction, but it wouldn't have been possible without the assistance of many knowledgeable people.

For technical information, thanks to fire expert Jo-san Arnold, glass expert Gerry Pleysier, and San Diego Metro Arson Strike Team members Fred Herrera and Jeff Sferra.

For investigation and legal details, thanks to kidnap experts Dona and Logan Clarke of Clark International Investigations, Detective Howard LaBore of the San Diego Police Department, Michael Neumann of the Encinitas Sheriff's Department, and Michael Ellano of the San Diego Medical Examiner's Office.

For fun facts about television, thanks to broadcasting veterans Michael Peak and Rebecca Huston.

For making the book possible, thanks to Gina Maccoby, Hope Dellon, the entire team at St. Martin's Minotaur, and all the booksellers who put the final product into the hands of readers.

Finally, thanks to Linda Connelly, whose observation "Living in L.A. is like having ringside seats to the Apocalypse" inspired this book. While Linda was talking specifically about Los Angeles, the same can be said for most of this great but crazy state. Long live California.